ATTACK OF THE FOOD ZOMBIES

Dennis Meredith

Glyphus

For information about this title or to order other books and/or electronic media, contact the publisher:
Glyphus, L.L.C.
2947 Mesa Grove Rd., Fallbrook, CA 92028
www.glyphus.com
editor@glyphus.com

ISBNs:
    Print: 978-0-9818848-0-6
    Kindle: 978-1-939118-26-4

Cover: Ryan Meredith

EXPLORE THESE OTHER BOOKS BY DENNIS MEREDITH

Science Thrillers

Angelians (Angelians.com)
Mythicals (MythicalsNovel.com)
The Neuromorphs (TheNeuromorphs.com)
Solomon's Freedom (SolomonsFreedom.com)
The Cerulean's Secret (CeruleansSecret.com)
The Czar Bomb (CzarBomb.com)
The Happy Chip (TheHappyChip.com)
The Rainbow Virus (RainbowVirus.com)
Wormholes: A Novel (WormholesANovel.com)

Non-fiction

Explaining Research: How to Reach Key Audiences to Advance Your Work (ExplainingResearch.com)
The Climate Pandemic: How Climate Disruption Threatens Human Survival (ClimatePandemic.com)
Earthbound: Why Humans Will Never Conquer Space (EarthboundTheBook.com)

To Buddy M.
and
Buddy M.
Two fun guys!

Contents

Chapter 1

Jenna Louise Bushnell grunted as she hauled her 317-pound body up from the chair at Bob's Belly-Buster Buffet (which *Vegas Reviews* had dubbed "The most repugnant food-like sludge imaginable."). She had already made two trips to the steam tables, and was ready for her third. She had her attack thoroughly planned out, since she knew the buffet layout well from her many previous trips.

She yanked at the back of her elastic-banded pants to make sure the fabric had not wedged in her butt crack. That was embarrassing when it happened. She always wore the stretchy pants to give room for her meal.

She picked up a plate and began to run the first steam table behind a rail-thin, whiskered man in a stained cowboy hat and worn jeans. She took generous globs of the unnaturally yellow, gelatinous mac & cheese; and the congealed, brown beef-like stew. She decided to save for the next trip the pale, rubbery hot dogs, and the slimy, beige shrimp. This trip would involve the first of several desserts. She chose a rectangle of desiccated cake with its slather of gummy frosting.

She was about to return to her table when the counterman brought to the salad bar a new tray heaped with potato salad. She liked potato salad. She made some room on her plate and doubled back. She reached out a pudgy, pasty hand and used the large spoon to plop some onto the plate. The whiskered cowboy showed up and did the same.

Settling in at her table, she took a bite of the mac & cheese, then the stew. Then she tried the potato salad. A look of absolute bliss rose on her fleshy face. Her beady eyes widened. *Food Nirvana!* The potato salad was wondrously delicious! Its taste suffused her very soul with its luscious, delectable savoriness. Uttering a guttural "mmmm," she stuffed gob after gob into her mouth, each one bringing a transporting gustatory bliss even greater than the last. She would remember this moment for the rest of her life!

She had to have more! She hefted herself from her chair as quickly as her poundage would allow. She fast-waddled to the steam table, grabbing a plate and moving to the potato salad. She shoved aside a portly, balding man in a jogging suit and grabbed the spoon, plunging it into the yellow-beige mass to haul out a large mound of the enticing—nay *addictive*—potato salad.

She felt herself grabbed from behind and heaved out of the way, as the whiskered man in the stained cowboy hat and worn jeans shoved forward, snatching up the spoon. A low furious growl rose in her throat, and she plunged forward, grabbing him by his belt and flinging him backward, sending him flying over a table, knocking over a pudgy, elderly lady wearing a jet-black wig, which flew from her head.

Two other Bob's Belly-Buster Buffet diners had also surged forward, their eyes glazed, riveted on the potato salad. But Jenna Louise Bushnell was optimally positioned, and she ducked under the plastic spit shield and plunged her face deep into its gooey, yellow mass.

The nearest counterman stood transfixed, as she gobbled her way into its depths with a loud snuffling. She grabbed the metal tray for leverage, hauling it off the table. The counterman bolted for the kitchen, calling out the skinny manager, whose name happened to be Robert, but was definitely not the Bob of the Belly-Buster Buffet. Nevertheless, he considered himself a Bob-like authority figure. He wore a skinny tie and a short-sleeved white shirt with black pants, which he thought gave him an air of authority. But in his first attempt at asserting authority, he was less than articulate.

"You! What do you. . . hey. . . quit that!" He exclaimed in a quavering, high voice.

He rounded the counter to timorously approach the gobbling Jenna.

She ignored his approach, continuing her determined feed, her flabby jowls quivering with each bite.

The Bob-like manager shouted at the security guard stationed at the buffet entrance. He was supposed to watch for any disturbance. But he was bent over his smartphone playing video poker, as customers walked freely past.

The manager shouted again, and the guard tore his gaze from the game, staring blankly at the growing tumult. The manager gestured wildly for the guard to help, and the guard hefted himself off his stool, watching the melee, still uncomprehending that anybody would fight over food at the buffet.

The manager, expecting little help from the guard, considered whether to stop the madly feeding woman. But before he could, a big-bellied man in a Hawaiian shirt, tore the tray from her sausage-like fingers. He plunged his large hand into its mass, drawing out a fistful of beige, lumpy potato salad and cramming it into his mouth, uttering a loud, satisfied grunt.

Other assorted denizens of the buffet also began shoving forward, shouting variously *"Give it!," "I want that!" "Hey. . . you fat bastard!"* and other exclamations indicating that they wanted in on the largess.

The shoving then exploded into an out-of-control melee, with wrestling, punching, grabbing, and even kicking—all with the objective of getting at the shrinking treasure of potato salad.

Observing the growing food-related violence, the guard concluded that he wasn't being paid to handle such a hazardous event. Seeking help from more well-paid casino security guards, he trundled away into the adjacent Bob's Big Casino (which *Gamblers Monthly* dubbed "A rather seedy backwater joint in the low-rent environs of Vegas.").

Back at the buffet, the cowboy, being the spryest, leaped onto the steam table, landing one boot in the meat-like stew and the other in a beige casserole of indeterminate ingredients. He clambered onto the floor and headed for the kitchen. Several other diners realized his strategy of going to the source and followed him, slamming the Bob-like manager back against the wall, and overpowering the counterman, who cowered beside a rack of day-old bread.

The breaching of the first counter triggered the breaching of all, as the mob stormed the buffet tables. They had quickly discovered that all the cold salads were maddeningly delectable, stuffing globs of coleslaw, tuna, chicken, and other salads into their mouths with abandon. They found almost every fistful addictively delicious, which only whetted their appetites for more.

A phalanx of muscular, blue-blazered casino security guards burst into the dining room, followed at a safe distance by the buffet guard. They bellowed deep, authoritative commands, which rose above the clamor of shouting patrons who had not reached the food, and the gluttonous grunting of those who had.

Four guards shoved their way through the crowd, attempting to determine its epicenter. They finally arrived at the feeding Hawaiian-shirted man. Deciding to start with him, the senior guard wrenched the tray from his hands, leaving him with only a glassy-eyed stare and an open, potato-salad-encrusted mouth. He recovered himself enough to grunt "Gimme it back! Gimme!"

"What the hell?" exclaimed the guard. "What the hell are you doing?"

"'S amazin'!" exclaimed the Hawaiian-shirted man. "You won't believe! Gimme it back. Gimme!"

The guard started to put down the tray, then reconsidered. He'd tried the buffet once when he first took the casino job and could not fathom any of its offerings being remotely edible. He scooped a fingerful of potato salad and poked it into his mouth. A look of pure bliss rose on his face. He wrapped his arms around the tray, and like a football running back penetrating a defensive line, burst through the crowd and ran for the exit.

The Bob-like manager decided even more drastic measures were required. He took out his phone, and amid the tumult, dialed 911.

***

"Chef, he want to see you," announced Daoud Abadi in his Iranian accent. He loomed in the doorway to the dish-washing station at the acclaimed Johanna's restaurant. The assistant executive chef, Abadi was an imposing human with the muscular girth of a wrestler, which he had once been. His shaved head protruded like a battering ram from the black scarf he wore with his blindingly white chef's smock. In fact, he had employed that head as a battering ram when he had wrestled. The beefy Iranian was physically imposing enough, but his growl made him even more fearsome.

The young man in the black apron flinched, nearly dropping the China dish he was stacking. "Chef Nonny? Me? Why?" he asked in his Spanish accent.

"Chef Nonny want to see you," repeated Abadi. He scowled at the young man's impertinence. He turned and marched off. The skinny, dark-haired dish washer pulled off his apron and put down the dish, his trembling hand making it clatter as it nestled among the others. He started to follow, but Abadi stopped, blocking his way.

"Bring you backpack," he commanded.

The young man's eyes widened. He slowly picked up the tattered black backpack and followed. He wondered if he could quickly unzip it to dispose of the evidence of his crime without the burly chef seeing him. But Abadi would have noticed.

So, they walked across the sprawling kitchen of the restaurant, where the night crew had set to work cleaning and polishing the stainless-steel counters and shelves to prepare for the next day's opening.

Abadi abruptly stopped and stared pointedly at one of the black, enameled Molteni stoves, causing the trailing young man to almost collide with him.

"Burner," muttered Abadi, and one of the cleaners hurried over to inspect the stove burner, nodding his head in understanding. It was to be thoroughly disassembled and cleaned.

Abadi continued, flipping his hand in a gesture for the young man to come up beside him, as they exited the kitchen into the dining room.

"You are not to address Chef Nonny unless he ask you question," he instructed as they walked through the dining room, with its Baccarat crystal chandeliers casting their soft glow onto the custom upholstered Perigold dining chairs, Persian tapestries, and pristine, white, linen-covered tables.

"*Si*, I understand," said the young man, ducking his head.

"Do not stare at him. He does not like being stared at."

"*Si*, I understand," repeated the young man.

"And under no circumstances seek to shake his hand or touch him in any way."

"*Si*, I understand. But why—"

"And do not ask questions."

They reached the wide staircase leading to the second floor and mounted it, reaching a dark oak door. Abadi pushed through it into a hallway, to another door at the end. Abadi started to knock, but before he could, a slim, young woman dressed in the gray uniform of a line cook burst out, sobbing, and dashed away down the hall. She clutched a toque to her chest, as if the starched, white chef's hat would fly away if she released it.

The young man backed against the wall. He was trying to decide whether to face Chef Nonny or flee.

But Abadi had already poked his head through the open door asking a question in a low voice. When a voice inside mumbled an answer, he backed away and scowling, gestured at the young man to enter.

The young man found Chef Nonny. . . the famous Chef Nonny . . . the renowned culinary genius Giovanni Pasquale Ciotti . . . sitting behind a massive mahogany desk. The young man had never before been in Chef Nonny's presence, so it made him even more frightened at the prospect of being found out. The room was lined with bookshelves full of neatly arranged cookbooks and reference works. Overcoming his fear for a moment, the young man noted that the walls held none of Chef Nonny's myriads of awards that had distinguished him as one of the world's foremost chefs.

But the center of his attention was Chef Nonny. He had the curly jet-black hair, fine features, and a richly tanned face that the young man had seen on the covers of so many culinary magazines. His dark eyes and even darker eyelashes and eyebrows gave his gaze an intensity that those photos could not possibly have captured. But that gaze was not directed at the two visitors, but down at his folded hands, as if in prayer.

Standing beside Chef Nonny was the pastry chef Jacques-Désiré Bisset, whom the young man had seen only in passing. He was a tall, slim man with an easy slouch and a narrow face with a beak of a nose. Like Chef Nonny's, his expression was stern.

"What is your name?" Bisset asked in a fluid French accent.

"Joaquin," answered the dish washer.

"What is your name?" Bisset asked again, more emphatically.

"Joaquin," answered the dish washer again, his voice lowering.

"*Give me your name, boy!*" demanded Bisset.

The young man began to breathe heavily. "Arturo," he answered, his voice breaking.

"You are not Joaquin Rodriguez, are you?"

"No sir."

"You are using his green card, aren't you? You are impersonating him."

"*Si*. . .Yes, sir, but I—"

"Where are you from, Arturo?"

"Guatemala."

"How did you get here?"

"I walked."

"Thousands of miles?"

"Yes, sir."

"Why did you come to this restaurant?"

"To work for Chef Nonny . . . And for you, sir."

Throughout the exchange, Nonny remained silent, his head down.

"Open your backpack," commanded Bisset.

Arturo lifted his tattered backpack and zipped it open. Abadi snatched it from him and set it on the desk. He plunged his hand into its depths and hauled out a plastic zip bag of white powder. Arturo spread his hands in a pleading gesture, but his voice failed him. He managed only a whimper.

Nonny unclasped his hands and reached for the bag, zipping it open. He fetched a small spoon from his desk, dipping it into the powder, and bringing out a sample. Moistening his finger, he touched it to the powder and tasted it. He remained expressionless.

"This is my flour," he said quietly.

"Why did you steal this flour?" asked Bisset.

"Oh, sir, I did not steal," said Arturo. "I did not. It is cake flour left on the counter surface after the rolls were made. I just scraped it off. It would have been thrown away."

"Then why did you *take* the flour?" demanded Abadi.

Hesitating for a long moment, Arturo reached into his bag and tentatively brought out a plastic container. "I was trying recipes for this *Tres Leches* cake I have created. I only have flour from the *mercado*. But I want to see if cake flour from here make it better."

His gaze downward, Nonny reached out his hand, and with trembling hand Arturo gave him the container. Fetching a fork,

Nonny opened the container, dug the fork into the fluffy, moist cake and tasted it. Without looking at Bisset, he extended the container to him, along with a second fork. Bisset tasted it.

Arturo continued to chatter away about the cake, his tone a mix of desperation and eagerness. "I marble the cake with Abuelita chocolate batter and top with *dulce de leche*, which I make myself. I think maybe cake flour make the batter . . ."

His voice trailed off and his eyes widened in fright when he saw Nonny glance only briefly at Bisset and give the slightest nod.

Bisset flipped his hand at Arturo, gesturing him to leave, following him out the door and down the hall to his own smaller office. He sat down in an armchair, motioning for Arturo to close the door.

"What will happen?" asked Arturo tremulously. "Will I be arrested?"

"You will no longer be a dish washer here," said Bisset.

Arturo braced himself against the door, tears welling in his eyes. "Please! Please, let me—" he began, but Bisset interrupted him.

"Chef Nonny has decided . . . and I have decided . . . You will become an assistant pastry chef."

His eyes wide, Arturo stared wildly around the room, trying to process what he had just heard. "*¡Oh Jesús! ¡Oh, Dios mío en el cielo!*" he exclaimed, an amazed grin dawning on his face.

Bisset also smiled, raising his hands for the young man to calm himself. "You will work here under me. To begin formal training, you will attend The Pastry Academy here in Las Vegas. We will pay for it. And—"

"Oh, thank you! *Gracias!* So much!" exclaimed Arturo.

Again, Bisset raised his hands for calm. He handed Arturo a business card. "This is an immigration lawyer whom we use. He will get you a green card. You will work to become a citizen."

Arturo had trouble standing, so Bisset directed him to a chair. He sat down, still grinning. His grin faded slightly. "The girl who left. Why was she crying? Was she fired?"

"She was happy," said Bisset. "Chef gave her his toque. It is his ultimate sign of recognition for her achievement. She will now become a sous chef. Now, let's talk about that cake of yours."

Back in Nonny's office, the chef still sat with his hands folded on the desk. "Was that good?" he asked Abadi.

"Yes, Chef, that was good. He was happy."

"My mother would have approved?"

"Very much, Chef."

Abadi's cell phone buzzed, and he answered it, raising his hand in apology to Nonny for the interruption. "Where?" he asked into the phone. "And it was certain it was a drug?" He listened for a minute longer, then ended the call.

"Our friend at police department say there has been some kind of riot at cheap buffet off the strip. Some kind of drug was added to food."

Nonny scowled, his hands gripping the desk, now glaring directly at Abadi. His thoughts turned to his other restaurant, the famed Emperor's Feast buffet in the ultra-luxury Grand Forum Casino and Hotel

"The Emperor's Feast, contact security there! Tell them what happened! This cannot happen there!"

***

Jenna Louise Bushnell had required a string of linked plastic handcuffs to bind her hands behind her huge body. The two cops wrestling with her also found cuffing her difficult because she continued to struggle to get at the buffet—even though her first love, the potato salad, was long gone. As she was hauled from the buffet, her only request was that the back of her pants be removed from its embedment in the crevice of her derriere, which a female cop accomplished.

The other members of the gluttonous mob had also resigned themselves to the arrests by the fourteen Las Vegas police who had waded into the riot at Bob's Belly-Buster Buffet.

The manager was glad of the distraction, as he had retreated to his office to frantically search for a hiding place for the six metal cans he had retrieved from the small refrigerator in his office. He decided that his bowling bag was the best place, but had not yet figured out where to put the bowling ball that now had no storage place. So, when the police sergeant entered his office, he was standing before his desk holding a blue-marbled bowling ball. The sergeant wrinkled his brow in consternation, but decided that the bowling ball was the least important element in this weird-ass situation he and his men had encountered.

"Do you know what the hell went on here?" he asked, cocking his head at the profusely sweating little man in the skinny tie and white shirt.

The manager set the bowling ball on his desk, wedging it in place using two take-out bags from a nearby delicatessen. "Uh. . . well. . . they. . . uh. . . just started going crazy."

"Okay, this wasn't just some food fight. They seemed to be on some drug or something. Did you see any drugs?"

The manager sat on his desk and clamped his hands on the edge to keep them from trembling. "No. . . no. . . no drugs. . . no drugs at all."

The sergeant took out his notebook. "Your name?"

"Robert. . . Robert Silver."

"Yeah, well Robert, we ain't seen anything like this before. . . except maybe at concerts where the crowd just decides to go nuts."

Silver brightened. He had an out! "Well, y'know, we've had a ton of people in here. The place was crowded. Maybe it was like that. . . they went nuts."

"But they weren't fighting. They were going after the food. No offense, but *this* food? I know about this place, and it's not. . . well. . . "

Silver decided a little offense was the best defense. He declared emphatically, "We offer a budget buffet for the bargain-minded diner. Maybe these folks just wanted to make sure they got in on the bargain."

"Bargain," the sergeant muttered doubtfully. "Well, we're charging them with disorderly conduct, destruction of property, and a couple of cases of assault and battery. Your security guy gave us your footage, so the judge will have good evidence."

"Footage?" squeaked Silver, with inadvertent alarm. Then he recovered himself. "Look, we won't press charges. It was just some people got too eager. We won't press charges on destruction of property. We want customers not to be mad at us."

"Yeah, well, even so, there are other charges that aren't your call." The sergeant took another suspicious look at the bowling ball, turned, and left.

Silver yanked out his cell phone and started to call a number, then stopped himself. He'd forgotten not to use his phone! He reached into his desk and pulled out the untraceable burner phone. He punched in a number, got it wrong, took a deep breath, and punched it in again.

"Don't get mad," he said to the person who answered. "I kind of messed up. Oh, you saw on TV? Yeah, I messed up. I know you said just add sprinkles to the vats. But I thought, well, if I put in more, business would be better. But I put in too much. . . yeah. . . lots. Now there's cops here. I need to get rid of the stuff. I'll just pour it down the drain. Oh, you don't have much more? *Hell no, I can't bring it to you!* I could be followed. Let's meet. Way out *there?* Really? Well, shit, okay. Yes, yes, I'm going to keep them cold!"

Silver ended the call and stared at the bowling bag. It was too conspicuous to take anywhere but a bowling alley. He pulled out his battered brown briefcase, transferred the cans. He pulled four ice packs out of the freezer in his refrigerator and stuffed them in. Only on the second try did he manage to get the briefcase's worn latches to hold.

***

"I don't like this oyster," declared Chef Nonny, standing on the kitchen side of the serving table of the Gourffet. He scowled down at the glistening, fresh shellfish that had just been deftly shucked and meticulously placed onto the thick bed of crystal-clear ice.

He ignored the other sumptuous seafood being served fresh to diners in the seafood kitchen of the Emperor's Feast gourmet buffet —the tantalizing tangle of crab legs; the deliciously plump, boiled shrimp; the luscious, pink poached salmon; the flaky sea bass. It was famously named the "Gourffet" (which *Vegas Reviews* had dubbed "A delectable pinnacle of both creative cuisine and superb quality in buffets. A worthy partner to Chef Nonny's elegant Johanna's").

Nonny ignored the rest of the buffet tables in the 25,000-square-foot luxuriously paneled Gourffet. And, he ignored the admiring— often libidinous—stares of the young women mesmerized by his classic good looks, fame, and alluring mystery.

The seafood counterman panicked at Chef Nonny's scrutiny. He stood perfectly still, wide-eyed, and mute—like a prey animal trying desperately to become invisible as a predator prowled nearby.

"I don't like this oyster!" Chef Nonny repeated more emphatically, glaring down at the offending shellfish.

The counterman remembered what the other staff had told him. Don't talk to Chef. Watch the eyebrows. No other feature in Chef's famously deadpan expression would convey his mood. If the brows were up, all was fine. If they were halfway down, it was a caution. If they were all the way down, *disaster!* Chef Nonny's eyebrows were fully lowered!

The counterman shrugged and said nothing, still wide-eyed.

"Give me the oyster," commanded Nonny.

His hand trembling, the counterman used tongs to carefully retrieve the offending oyster and place it in a small bowl. He handed it to the chef, who turned and carried it back into the seafood kitchen.

Garbed in his perfectly starched, white smock, he walked through the prep area, where a dozen workers were steaming, boiling, slicing, and otherwise custom-preparing the fresh seafood to serve the eager diners. Several noticed the tall chef's determined stride. They froze until he passed, worried that they were the targets of one of his compulsions.

But they weren't. His gaze riveted on the dish containing the oyster, he sought one particular quarry.

He found Daoud Abadi in the room-sized cooler with a trainee chef, going over an inventory of newly delivered trout.

"I don't like this oyster," Chef Nonny announced to Abadi, vapor curling from his lips.

The squat Abadi turned from the trainee, and smiled warmly up at the glaring Nonny.

"And, Chef, what do you not like about this oyster?" he asked in his lilting Iranian accent.

"Look at the shell. Look at its bowl. It has no flutes. This is a Kumamoto. This is not a Sweetwater."

"No, Chef, it is not Sweetwater."

"I offer Sweetwaters to my diners. I *only* offer Sweetwaters. I do not offer Kumamotos."

"Taste it," said Abadi.

Nonny repeated himself verbatim. "I offer Sweetwaters to my diners. I only offer Sweetwaters. I do not offer Kumamotos."

"Taste it," also repeated Abadi. He knew how to deal with Chef Nonny.

Nonny looked down at the oyster. "Why is this a Kumamoto?"

"Because our purveyor had no Sweetwaters today. He had Kumamotos. I try one. I find it to be actually very excellent batch. Fully equal to Sweetwaters. So, I substitute them."

14

Eyebrows fully lowered, Nonny asked incredulously, "You substituted them? You substituted Kumamotos for Sweetwaters?"

Still smiling, Abadi said, "Yes, I did, Chef."

"Without my permission?"

"At the time, you were tasting the salsas. For an hour. You do not allow interruptions when you are tasting. The seafood purveyor was about to sell them to another restaurant."

The trainee backed away, trying to hide behind boxes of fresh sea bass.

"You're fired!" exclaimed Nonny.

"Try the oyster," repeated Abadi. Then to the trainee's utter puzzlement, he began counting: "One Mississippi, two Mississippi, three Mississippi. . ."

Nonny still glared down at the oyster. It was his tendency not to make eye contact with other people. But scrutinizing food was another matter.

Abadi had reached "Twelve Mississippi," when Nonny abruptly tipped the oyster into his mouth, closing his lips, and staring at the ceiling. For an extended, tense moment, he swirled the oyster around, shifting his gaze contemplatively to different parts of the ceiling.

He swallowed the oyster and looked in the general direction of Abadi. "Get back to work," he said tersely and turned and left.

The trainee emerged from his hiding place. "Why were you counting?" he asked.

Abadi shrugged and grinned. "I want to see how long I will be fired this time. The long record is three hours. The short record is six seconds. This time Chef took twenty-seven seconds. Nowhere near the short record."

"You've been fired before?"

"Know this about Chef Nonny. He is the most obsessive perfectionist you will ever, *ever* meet. He is absolutely passionate and dedicated about food. But people mistake his perfection for cruelty.

He is actually very kind man. Some day you may benefit from that kindness."

"Um. . . uh. . .," stammered the intern, trying to figure out how to phrase the next statement. "I read somewhere that he does not connect with people because he is. . . uh—"

"Do not say what you are about to say," warned Abadi. "Do not pass on rumors. Just do your job."

Appearing at the cooler door was an athletic, middle-aged man wearing a dark gray suit, black silk shirt, and burgundy tie. He nodded at Abadi. Telling the trainee to continue his work, Abadi followed the Grand Forum security director out into the kitchen.

"I have the security footage from the cheap buffet," he told Abadi. "It shows the manager adding something to the food. Our friend at Vegas PD says they are looking to question him."

"Nevertheless, we will do our own investigation," said Abadi, shrugging and cocking his shaved head. "You know Chef Nonny. He would never be satisfied with anybody else looking into this. You remember the other times."

The security director smiled wryly. "Like when he demanded we trace the honey shipment back to the hives. Yes, I know Chef Nonny. And I'll admit he was right then. It was fake. I'll put you in touch with an investigator we use."

***

I should have worn sneakers, Robert Silver scolded himself, as he clambered along the precarious trail in Red Rock Canyon in his dress shoes. The skinny tie and white shirt also didn't do much to help him blend in with the other hikers. He hauled himself onto a boulder, balancing himself by holding out the briefcase. *Why the hell?* he asked himself. *Why the hell would he want to meet out here?* He answered his own question, in the pretend-voice of the person he was to meet. *We need somewhere isolated, y'know? We can't be seen anywhere with people.*

Well, this trail is sure as hell isolated, he thought. He stopped and scanned ahead, sweating profusely, although the desert sun had not

16

yet risen very high. Even the relatively cool July morning in the desert was warm. But the damned cannisters had to be kept cool!

He thought he recognized their meet point ahead—the funny-looking pointy rock in the photo he'd received. He checked his cell phone. The picture matched.

He was concentrating on the cell phone when he took one small step forward, and his dress shoe slipped on the boulder. He went flailing down into a sandy wash, landing on his butt. The briefcase flew away to burst open, launching the cans rolling away and the ice packs spilling out.

"JESUS SHIT DAMN!" he exclaimed, scrambling to his feet and toward the briefcase. Four of the cans had landed sealed, but two had leaked as they rolled, dribbling both their liquids together across the desert floor. He was pretty sure they were the two he had used on the buffet. Obviously, in his haste, he screwed on their lids crookedly.

"Shit! Damn!" Silver cursed to himself, crouching beside the leaking cans. They had emptied their contents into the sand, but nothing that couldn't be cleaned up. Silver picked up one empty can, and began to carefully scoop up the cool wet sand with his hand and try to pack it into the can. A little sand shouldn't be a problem. The guy who made the stuff was a scientist. He knew how to separate stuff. He could easily separate the liquid from the sand. Maybe even separate the two components again. Silver wouldn't really be in too much trouble.

He'd managed to cram a lot of the wet sand back into the can, but there was still some left. He might need to use the second can. He paused to estimate what was left to collect. He absent-mindedly touched his sand-covered hand to his mouth.

He stopped. His eyes grew glassy. He grunted and began to pant with the alluring taste rising within him like a gnawing, demanding demon. *Hunger for this wonderful, delicious sand!*

He emptied a handful from the can and crammed it into his mouth. He began to choke. Undeterred, he continued his compulsive devouring.

***

"Hiring him is the only way to find out what went on," declared Abadi emphatically to Nonny. "I can't go there. . . to that disgusting buffet. I'm known around town. And you *sure* as hell can't go there. God, imagine the famous Chef Nonny Ciotti going to a disgusting buffet! Somebody would see you, and they'd post it on the web instantly."

"But *him*? You want to use *him*?" Chef Nonny crossed his arms and glared at the floor. He didn't like being away from his kitchens during the day. And he didn't like being in this shabby off-the-Strip motel room. And he didn't like the person they were there to meet.

"This Albert Langer detective has a reputation for being discreet," said Abadi. "And he investigates anything for anybody. So, he knows this town. And he never tells."

"Maybe until now," said Nonny.

A knock at the door brought Abadi to answer it. Standing in the door, squinting at the sun was a medium-height, medium-build, bland, balding man in a blue blazer with worn elbows and a stain on the left lapel. He stepped in and stood silently, peering around the room.

He asked, "Anybody follow you?"

"Not that we know of," said Abadi.

Nonny regarded the man coldly. "You are surprisingly nondescript. . . rather shabby," he said. "I would have expected someone with more style. . . a private investigator."

The man chuckled.

"Chef never minces words," Abadi explained.

"It's okay," said Langer. "I pride myself on being nondescript. . . even shabby. And I know Chef Nonny's reputation for bluntness." He held out his hand. "Chef, I'm Albert Langer."

18

Nonny simply stared at the hand, so Langer withdrew it, with no apparent annoyance. Nonny asked, "You heard about the riot at the buffet?"

"I saw something about some people getting out of hand at this Bob's Buffet place. Seemed like only the usual Vegas shenanigans."

"Did you see the footage?"

"No, I work nights. I don't watch the news much."

"I did," said Nonny. "I study people. I know how people react to good food. I've learned to read body language. Those people were having extreme reactions to the food. Ravenous. Addictive."

"Seriously, you can read that into their actions?" asked Langer.

"I study people," said Nonny.

"Well, what do you want me to do?"

"Find out what happened."

"Likely, they were drunk, and they were hungry, and they were in Vegas, and they got carried away," said Langer.

"No, no, it was more than that," said Nonny, shaking his head emphatically. "I study people."

"Okay, I *get* that you study people. Again, what specifically do you want me to do?"

"Find out as much as you can about what went on."

"Okay, that's vague."

"You want specifics?" asked Nonny. "Bring me samples of the foods."

"Samples? Well, going in there and getting intel is one thing. I wouldn't have any legal problems just asking questions. But stealing material. . . that could be prosecutable."

Abadi smiled wryly. He knew what was coming next. "Fine," he said. "Then what will it cost to carry out this 'prosecutable' mission?"

"Ten thousand," said Langer.

"You're not serious," said Nonny.

"You study people, right? Do I look serious? Besides, you drive a Maserati, you ride in limos. It's chump change for you."

"I need to get back to my kitchens," said Nonny flatly. He opened the door and walked out into the blistering desert sun.

"He doesn't like to negotiate," said Abadi. "It's too hard on him. . . the give and take."

"This isn't a negotiation," said Langer.

Abadi reached into his pocket and took out an envelope, handing it to Langer. "Here's two thousand. Eight more when you bring verified, labeled samples of the food from the buffet."

Langer took the envelope. "Okay, but you should know I have insurance." He took out his smartphone and poked the screen several times. "I recorded our conversation, and I just emailed it to my office. A private account, but one that automatically forwards its messages to the police, should I not be around to reset the code."

Abadi laughed derisively. "You think we would do you harm?"

"I've had more famous people than you try to."

Chapter 2

"**Y**ou found his body exactly like that?" asked Rochelle "Leafy" Chun. The petite FBI Special Agent, her long, dark hair held in a precise bun, pursed her fine lips in puzzlement. She took off her aviator-style sunglasses so as to better extract information from the hikers who had found the body. She had discovered that using her penetrating, dark-eyed stare on interviewees rattled them, yielding clues to their veracity. Those almond eyes were set in an oval face with delicate features that gave interviewees the very false impression that she was only an attractive, easily dismissed woman.

She was quizzing the hikers who had found the body sprawled some thirty feet away in the sandy arroyo. Despite the searing desert heat of July, she was dressed in a dark pantsuit and white cotton blouse, wearing low-heeled shoes.

The hikers sat on a boulder beside the park ranger who had called in the body. One of them nodded grimly and said, "We thought he'd slipped or something. I asked him if he was okay. He didn't answer, so I just rolled him over. And then I saw. . ." the hiker made a gesture around his mouth.

"The dirt on his face?"

"Yeah, the dirt. I guess somebody shoved his face in the dirt."

Returning to the corpse, Chun shook her head decisively. She knew better. She spoke to her partner, Rydell Tate, who was examining a wallet he had just extracted from the corpse's clothing, along with a cell phone.

"Look at the face,' she said. "Perfectly intact; no bruising or bloody nose from being shoved face-down in the sand. This doesn't look like an accident."

"Guy's name is Robert Silver," said Tate, handing Chun the wallet and the driver's license he had extracted from it. He stood fidgeting as Chun examined the wallet. His wiry-muscular body showed a coiled-spring tension at being outdoors. He was a creature of night clubs and casinos, not these sprawling desert mountains. His eyes hidden behind framed, Gucci sunglasses, beads of sweat glistened on his shaved head, visible against skin the color of dark caramel. He poked at the cell phone screen, then scratched at the black stubble on his thin jaw.

"Phone's got an access code," he said. "I'll turn it over to the techs. So, you think foul play? Really? It's just so weird."

"If not an accident, then it was foul play." Chun made a call to her office, to bring the Evidence Response Team, then walked back to the hikers.

"And you didn't make the marks in the sand?" She pointed to the deep scratch marks in the desert floor that radiated away from the body.

"No, they were there," said the hiker. "We walked on some. But we had to."

"And the briefcase is his?" She gestured to the battered, open briefcase near the body. It was empty, and beside it lay two melted freezer packs.

"Yeah, of course," said the hiker. "We don't carry briefcases."

She returned to the body. "He wasn't out here hiking, that's for sure. Look at the dress shoes, the tie. You're right, Rydell. It's weird."

"Gets weirder," said Tate. He frowned down at his own shoes—seven-hundred-dollar black Maison Margiela sneakers. He wore a dark blue pullover shirt and khaki dress pants. He paused to raise one foot, brushing away sand, then did the same with the other. "Take a look." He reached down and with his gloved fingers pried open Silver's jaw, made difficult because rigor mortis had firmly set in. The mouth was stuffed with sand. "Somebody forced him to eat the dirt."

"Yeah, but again, no marks on his face like somebody would have shoved it in. Call the helicopter, tell them we need an aerial search. After the ERT's done, get him out of here. And since it's on federal land, it's an FBI case. Shut down the park. Video everybody leaving. And get ID on everybody on this trail."

"Got it," said Tate, walking away as he punched numbers into his phone.

Chun called after him. "And notify the public affairs people to make an announcement about the body. Somebody might have seen something." She managed to suppress a wry smile. "Wow, I'd heard the saying, but I never thought I'd actually see it. He really *did* eat dirt and die."

***

"*Shit, shit, shit!*" Edwin Kane breathed to himself, as he peered anxiously through the blinds at the tile-roofed, stucco house across the street. The house was one of dozens of such cookie-cutter houses along the streets of the Las Vegas subdivision.

Riveting his attention were the law-enforcement people coming and going at Robert Silver's house. They had arrived thirty minutes earlier, speeding up to the house, leaping from two police cars, two black sedans, and a white van. The last people wore white isolation suits and respirators, leading Kane to his panicked exclamations. The suits signaled that the searchers believed Silver might have kept some gustatene other than the supply Kane had given him! As the cops stood outside, the people in isolation suits entered and left, periodically emerging with boxes, bags, and a laptop computer. But no bottles or other containers. Maybe he was okay.

But maybe not! Now, the cops were fanning out up and down the other side of the street. They would eventually cross over to his side and come to his house! Of course, they would! His neighbor and accomplice Robert Silver was dead under suspicious, even weird

23

circumstances. They would want to know if somebody in Silver's neighborhood could give clues to that death.

Sure as hell, Silver's neighbor across the street—him—would be questioned for clues to that death. In fact, that neighbor had the six cans of the chemical that caused Silver to cram his mouth with dirt until he choked to death. They were the cans that Kane had ever-so-carefully retrieved from around the sand-choked dead man so as not to spill the chemicals on himself.

Even he, as gustatene's inventor, would not be immune from its gluttonous effects. Fortunately, the chemical was preserved. The cans were still cold when he had arrived, stuffing them along with ice packs into his backpack.

Why couldn't he have done a regular clinical trial! Why couldn't he have recruited volunteers to try foods treated with gustatene, instead of persuading that idiot Silver to sprinkle its two interacting components on the buffet?

He comforted himself by rationalizing his decision. He couldn't do a trial because he'd been fired from his job at GloboChem, ending his research there. That bastard Carson Hayworth had charged him with faking results. Okay, so he did change a few numbers years ago, when his work had hit a snag.

So, because of the idiot Silver's overdosing of the food, the first field trial was, well, suboptimal. He could just lay low and let things blow over. But no, his work demanded that he do his own field trial and do it right; not like some careless buffet manager.

He brought himself back to the predicament at hand. He picked at his scraggly beard, as was his habit when his nerves were jangled. He licked his lips and scrunched them around in thought. The cops would knock on his door very soon! *And, if he seemed suspicious, they might even search the house! And he'd stupidly brought the cans here, not to the lab!*

And, true, he was an inherently suspicious-looking person, he admitted to himself, with his nervous tics and beady, staring eyes. Other people noticed the oddities, like that tipsy girl who called him

24

freaky and rejected him in a bar in his one rare excursion into society. He'd discovered his type was known as an "incel," involuntarily celibate, when he did an internet search. The category included a pretty nasty bunch of young males, and when he'd learned of his classification, he immediately quit surfing the sites.

Cops just crossed the street to his side! He needed to hide the cans! He darted from the window, snatching up the backpack, and only then tried to think of a hiding place. When cops tossed a place, they were incredibly thorough! He should have already built a hiding place for material he brought from the lab! He started up the stairs, then came back down. He started for the kitchen, then returned. He started for the garage, then returned.

So, he was standing in the middle of the living room holding the backpack, when the doorbell rang. He shoved the backpack into the hall closet. He went to the door, realized he didn't want to appear too eager, and stood there taking deep breaths.

Assuming what he hoped was a totally innocent expression, he opened the door to see a tall, burly cop in sunglasses and a crisp blue uniform with a very large gold badge.

He attempted a smile and greeted the officer, clutching the door with white knuckles that he hoped the cop didn't notice. What followed were ten minutes of questions.

The cop asked his name.

He managed to remember it.

Did he know Robert Silver?

Only slightly.

Had he seen anything suspicious?

No, not at all. Nothing at all.

When the questions ended, the cop offered his card, which Kane took. He declared, perhaps too emphatically, that he would certainly contact the officer if anything occurred to him.

After the interview, Kane tried not to slam the door, which would have given the cop reason to think he was freaked by the questions—

which he was. He stood behind the door and tried to tamp down his trembling. The questions had been innocuous enough, but he knew the cop was sizing him up the whole time. And even if his body language didn't get him in trouble, his answers could.

He cursed himself for telling the cop he only knew Silver casually. What if other neighbors told the cops they'd seen them together many times?

And he cursed himself again for saying he hadn't seen anything suspicious around Silver's house. But the neighbors could say that Kane had *himself* been suspicious around Silver's house. The old lady two doors down had seen him when he stupidly went over earlier that day and peered into Silver's windows, to check whether there was any obvious evidence that he had been there.

Putting the stupid answers behind him, he managed to calm himself enough to start thinking strategically. He had an escape plan. He had his camper van parked outside his laboratory. He'd bought the battered vehicle with cash and managed to register it under the same fake identity he had used to rent the warehouse for his laboratory. He made a mental note to make sure it was stocked with food and other stuff he would need.

But more important—far more important—were his plans for the next step in his research.

He had four full cans of gustatene solution, another empty and another full of soaked sand, where Silver had attempted to retrieve the spill. But he'd only need two for another major field test. He had to move quickly. He had to assume the cops would be onto him soon. He needed to prove his research at least one more time. If he had more unequivocal evidence of gustatene's power, he would not be seen as just some crank neuropharmacologist, but a misunderstood genius.

He decided he needed an upscale buffet as a test site this time— one that used no taste-affecting additives to pump up flavor. He needed a large, busy buffet where he might not be detected, as he administered the gustatene and gathered observational data.

He knew just the place.

***

The private detective Albert Langer's shabby blue blazer served him well when he asked to see the manager of Bob's Belly-Buster Buffet. The jacket marked him as the mid-level bureaucrat that he pretended to be.

"Southern Nevada Health District," he announced to the assistant manager. "Just getting some ducks in a row, here." He chuckled at the subtly ironic joke he had made. Bob's Buffet would likely never have served anything resembling duck.

The assistant manager, a dumpling of a man with a belly that hung over his belt and a shock of jet-black hair attempting to escape his white cap, looked nervous. He'd had enough problems without dealing with a health inspector.

"Certainly, whatever we can do. What do you need?" he asked, scrubbing his hands on his apron.

Langer scanned the staff going about the business of setting large trays of undefinable food onto the steam tables. "Well, after all the hullabaloo on the news, my supervisor asked me to come on down here and check to make sure everything was okeydokey. That the food wasn't contaminated, or whatever. Don't want us to have problems. Because if *we* have problems, *you* have problems, righteo, sport?" He grinned his best mid-level-bureaucrat grin.

"Sure, sure," declared the assistant manager.

"So, is your boss around?"

"Well, uh no. He didn't come in today. Don't know when he'll be back. Can't reach him."

"Strange, eh?"

"Yeah, he's been strange for a while."

"What do you mean?"

"Well, like, a couple of weeks ago, he made a rule. He said that he was worried about too much. . . product. . . being eaten by staff. Kind of weird, I thought. Most of us either bring from home or go out to the food court. Not here, for sure. Anyway, he said nobody is ever, ever, *ever* to taste any of the food we put out. He said three 'evers' just like that."

"Three, huh. That's a lot."

"We were all really curious. We figured it had something to do with his inspections."

"Food inspections? That's not unusual. He is the manager."

"Yeah, well, it was weird the way he did it. He'd tell us all to check the steam tables out front, or take inventory in the back. But then, he'd stay alone with the food trays, the cold foods, the salads and such. He carried these two cans with him. A blue and a red. One of the cooks said she thought he was sprinkling the food with them, but we couldn't be sure."

Langer worried that his questions might raise suspicions in the assistant manager, so he decided to switch gears away from his snooping mode.

"Well, whatever. Let's get this done. You go collect the ID cards from the staff on this shift, and photocopy them. Then you can get the others done when they come on shift, I'll come back later to snag them."

The assistant manager turned to go, but swiveled back. "Look, about the health violation. We've fixed those, okay?"

Langer pretended he knew what the man was talking about. "Okay, well I hope so."

"Yeah, yeah, I know it was my job to check the food temperature."

"Yeah, well—"

"And I know we kind of let the cold stuff get too warm. But we fixed it. Switched the circuit breaker on the cooler back on. It was only a week that it was off."

"The staff cards?" Langer reminded the assistant manager. "Can you go ahead and get them?"

"Yeah, right, right, for sure." The man bustled off to get the chore done. He left Langer standing in the sprawling kitchen with its battered stainless-steel trays and pots that had once held the questionable fare of Bob's Buffet. All were empty, clean. Langer felt an ache in his wallet. If he didn't get samples, there would be no eight grand! He had to think fast. He knew these low-rent places were not likely to discard leftovers the way the fancy buffets did. He took a chance and ducked into the room-sized cooler, to see plastic-covered trays of green beans, hot dogs, potato salad, and other tired-looking foodstuffs on metal shelves.

Jackpot!

He whipped out a fistful of zippered plastic baggies from one jacket pocket, and fetched plastic spoons from another. He began to scoop a healthy glob of each food into each bag, zipping it shut. He was careful to discard a spoon after sampling each dish. He didn't want to be accused of cross-contamination if one of the trays held the mysterious—probably mythical—stuff that caused the people to go nuts.

He had just gotten to a half-filled tray of gooey baked beans, when the assistant manager's voice behind him declared,

"What are you doing in here?"

***

Clutching their food trays, crowds of eager diners roamed the glittering expanse of the Emperor's Feast Gourffet. Witnessing their quest for its wealth of delectables were the marble statues of nymphs and gods arrayed in the walnut-paneled serving hall. At the entrance, long lines snaked out of the hall into the Grand Forum casino, as diners chattered in anticipation at entering a realm of cuisine they would boast about to their envious friends.

The diners who had gained entry eagerly sought the dishes because this was the brainchild of the renowned Chef Nonny. He allowed no foods laid out on steam tables to age unappetizingly. Rather the counters were festooned with luscious photos and vivid descriptions of each dish—glistening imported sausages, flaky white fish, iced crab legs, lobster, oysters, shrimp, steaming stews, tender dumplings, crunchy tacos, fresh-from-the-oven pies, moist layer cakes, crisp salads, oven-warm breads, and tender, flaky croissants.

Each dish was served across the counters or delivered to tables only at a diner's request. Oysters were freshly shucked. Fresh pies and cakes were sliced. Soufflés were popped in the oven. Wagyu beef prime rib was drawn sizzling from the broiler and carved. Delicate sushi was sliced from fresh-from-the-ocean Bluefin otoro tuna. Ice cream was scooped directly from the ice cream maker.

Always vigilant to maintain this quality, Chef Nonny entered the kitchen to make his nightly prowl through the thirty-thousand-square feet of copious haute cuisine. As he strode its gleaming expanse, the diners who spied him greeted him with praise, heartfelt thanks, even applause. Intent on the food, he did not acknowledge them; certainly did not stop to sign autographs.

That is, until one lucky diner, a well-dressed elderly matron, happened to ask him about the recipe for his "amazing seafood chowder." Nonny stopped at the soup station, seriously regarding the large crock of fragrant, steaming chowder.

He launched into a recitation, intoning, "Ingredients are Wild Cherrywood-smoked bacon, Bianca Di Maggio onions, Yukon Gold potatoes, Devon butter, Hawaiian Red Alaea sea salt, Victoria Taylor parsley, Madras curry powder, Nakazawa milk, and flown-in sea scallops, lobster, shrimp, cod, and haddock."

He continued with a detailed explanation of how they were blended into the chowder. Finishing his explanation, he moved on, leaving the matron wide-eyed and open-mouthed.

Watching him intently throughout his patrol was the legion of white-garbed chefs behind the counters. They took care not to stop their work. They continued to move smoothly among the gleaming stainless-steel serving counters, fulfilling the diners' requests. They knew theirs was a culinary ballet, and they saw Nonny as the dance master. He would detect any false move, any slip-up in perfect purveying of the dishes.

Another observer also watched Nonny with an intense stare. Edwin Kane was now disguised, freshly shaven and bespectacled, wearing a large coat and dark blue baseball cap. His ponytail jutted out of the back of the cap. He sat at a small table in an inconspicuous corner of the dining room.

"Max-min-max," he incanted to himself over and over. "Max-min-max." It was his shorthand for the mantra he had developed for this field test: *Maximum* chaos, *minimum* time, *maximum* data.

Maximum chaos would be required to hide his escape. *Minimum* time should be taken because the staff and security would be alerted quickly. *Maximum* data would have to be gathered on the effects on people of the prototype binary gustatene.

The huge Emperor's Feast Gourffet was the perfect place for Kane's next, and likely final, field test. For one thing, each diner had their own plates of food, so he could dose them individually. He needed to know how different doses affected people. There were many other research questions, and he ticked them off in his mind:

How were different people affected—young, old, male, female, varied ethnicities?

Would the drug lure people to one food over another?

Were the rat tests accurate about the sensitivity of the combined components? They showed that the chemical mixture was acutely temperature-sensitive, so only cold foods could be treated.

Were some foods less effective carriers of the drug because of their acidity, or sugar content, or some other property?

Would the drug cause a general obsessive hunger for all foods, even those not dosed?

His rat tests had helped answer some. But rats weren't people. Now he could try to find out the effects definitively in humans.

Chef Nonny had disappeared back into the kitchen, so that source of interference was gone.

Kane stood up and adjusted his camera glasses, which served both to record data and as part of his disguise. He pulled from his left sleeve the control button for the drug-dosing system and placed his thumb on it. And he pulled from his right sleeve a pair of plastic tubes. He clipped their nozzles to the sleeve, making sure they aimed directly outward. He shifted the insulated bag containing the bags of chemical and ice packs under his coat. He still felt the cold, so the chemicals were still active.

Wandering casually over to the meat counter with a tray, he perused the images and read the descriptions to give himself the cover of an ordinary diner. It wouldn't be hard to go unnoticed. The other diners were so intent on the food, they paid little mind to the strange little man in the too-large coat wandering among them.

He began the experiments.

His first subject: An ample, middle-aged lady in blue pants and a white blouse was requesting a helping of the exquisite Culatello di Zibello Italian ham. She was a perfect subject because her tray was already full of a variety of dishes. As the chef sliced, the woman's gaze strayed in the direction of the bakery counter.

Kane took advantage of the distraction. He brought his sleeve near her plate and pressed the button to mist her food with each component of the ten-percent gustatene mixes. She left the line, and he thought it best to request a slice of Kobe prime rib, to avoid notice. He found a vantage point where he could video her reaction, aiming his gaze and thereby the glasses' camera lens.

The woman sat down with her husband and what appeared to be grandchildren. She took a bite of salad. After a moment, she sat up straight, a look of wide-eyed wonder dawning on her round face. She plunged the fork into the salad, cramming a large chunk into her mouth. But along with the salad came a bit of macaroni and cheese. She looked confused, glancing from one to the other. She shoveled a golden morsel of the truffle-infused macaroni and cheese into her mouth.

"*Ith all tho good!*" she lisped, through the mouthful. "*Wow!*"

She began to work her way through her plate, stuffing salad, vegetables, meat into her mouth. "Mmmm!" she declared continuously as she gorged. Then, her plate empty, she stared longingly at her grandchildren's plates for a moment.

"Lemme just try this," she said, reaching over and grabbing a granddaughter's plate, shoveling its contents into her mouth.

"Joyce!" her husband exclaimed, standing up and reaching for the plate. But Joyce would not give it up, bolting upright, sending her chair careening backward. She grabbed the grandson's plate and backed toward the corner, setting both plates on a neighboring table and grabbing handfuls of their contents and cramming it into her mouth.

Aha! thought Kane. The drug appears to affect *all* foods, and even has a remnant effect on un-dosed foods!

The dosing system had worked! Now, he had to act fast, to get many subjects, to get more data.

He moved as quickly as he could without raising suspicion, dosing diners throughout the length and breadth of the vast complex of dining areas. He dosed an elderly man, a teen girl, a young boy, an Asian man, a Hispanic woman. All happened to look away from their plates at an opportune time. And all had a spray of the gustatene mixture directed at their plates.

The reactions began. People launched into gobbling their own food, grabbing for their partners', even bolting back to the serving tables to demand more of what they believed to be the best dish ever!

Kane moved as quickly as he could among the drugged diners, aiming his camera glasses at each one to try to catch their reaction. Later he would go through the video, frame by frame, to try to tease out the scientific data.

Now, the tumult had reached a zenith, with the undrugged diners staring in shock at their drugged fellows, as they madly devoured food, scuffled with one another, and begged the staff for more. Unfortunately, it looked as if he had overdosed the diners, even with the small amount he had used. But that might have been an advantage. After all, he was looking for overt, easily observed reactions. Later, maybe, he could do experiments with lower doses, seeking to observe more subtle effects.

"WHAT IS THIS? WHAT IS GOING ON?" bellowed a husky, bald man in a chef's white smock. He had emerged from the depths of one of the kitchens, beside him Chef Nonny.

"I know precisely what is going on!" exclaimed Chef Nonny. "The creature is here!"

Kane ducked quickly behind a pillar, backing away toward the entrance. He reached the door and bolted out; he hoped unseen. Behind him echoed a cacophony of shouts, grunts, and a few screams.

***

"This guy wasn't murdered," declared the Clark County coroner, his brow furrowed as he peered down at the corpse of Robert Silver. Its splayed-open chest showed pale, dry internal organs. "This is just weird," declared the coroner. A slim, balding man in his fifties, the coroner took up a metal probe and peeled back the flesh of Silver's esophagus, to reveal a packed cylinder of sand.

"Wait, you mean somebody didn't stuff that down his gullet?" asked Chun, whose short stature meant she didn't have to bend over to examine the body closely. She carefully clasped the jacket of her black pants suit to prevent it from touching the body, and looked closely at the chunk of sand. "I mean, come on, who would do that to himself? What was in his stomach?"

"Yeah, check his stomach contents," called Tate from outside the examining room. He pointedly avoided looking at the body.

The coroner shook his head in puzzlement and turned to lift a jar containing scummy brown liquid, and a settled layer of sand on the bottom. "Sure, his stomach was full of dirt. But here's the kicker." The coroner held up the victim's fingers, whose shredded tips showed spots of clotted blood. "These abrasions mean he dug all those furrows in the ground that I saw in the crime scene photos. And he didn't get them struggling with an attacker. We looked for tissue or fibers under his fingernails that would mean a struggle. But there was only that dirt."

"So, he was drugged?" asked Chun.

"Well, not that we could find. We ran the drug panel on his blood. None of the usual suspects."

Declared Tate from the hallway, "Okay, you've raised all these damned questions. You got any possible solutions?"

"Maybe a drug we couldn't detect," said the coroner. "Maybe he suffered some weird version of Prader-Willi syndrome."

"Prader-Whatty?" asked Tate, as his cell phone played a tune signaling a call.

"It's an inherited syndrome where the person is compelled to eat food. But it couldn't be that because they are hugely obese and have short stature. This guy wasn't either."

"So a drug maybe that made him suicidally compulsive?" asked Chun.

"Yeah, well, there are appetite enhancers around. But nothing that would make somebody kill themselves eating dirt."

"But still it could be a drug. And nothing you could find?" asked Chun.

"Yup, this poor guy could've gotten hold of some seriously weird stuff."

"Well keep doing whatever you can," said Chun, shaking her head. "We need more analytical firepower, more expertise. Pack up blood and tissue samples. I'll tell you where to send them. I'm bringing in the FDA."

Tate ended his call and said, "You better get the FDA here pretty quick. There's been another attack. At a buffet."

"Now, it looks like terrorism," said Chun quietly. "Now, it's *really* an FBI case."

***

"They coming down from poison," declared Abadi, settling his heft into a chair in the Emperor's Feast dining room, peering at the aftermath of the attack. The recovering diners were being tended to by casino security staff, Las Vegas police, and emergency medical technicians. The shouting, even growling of the drugged diners had subsided, as they were restrained in handcuffs and the mysterious drug was wearing off. Some shook their heads in puzzlement at being transformed into ravening creatures craving food. Others whimpered.

"*Samples!*" exclaimed Chef Nonny once more—a declaration he had made over and over to his chefs. "Take samples of the food. Do not taste it. Put it into a bag, then wash your hands." Nonny himself had just thrust a chunk of dry aged beef into a bag and sealed it shut, carrying it off to the kitchen.

Abadi checked his fingers for bite wounds. He had tackled a burly teenager who had cleaned his own drug-infused plate, then snatched a roll from another diner. The teenager had jammed the roll into his mouth, making it all but lost to analysis. But Abadi had lunged forward, grabbing the young man in a practiced wrestler's hammerlock with one muscled arm, and forcing his mouth open with the other. Abadi had suffered a bite, but not before thrusting a thick finger down the teen's throat producing a gag reflect that yielded not only the half-chewed roll, but everything else the young man had eaten during that dinner. However, that regurgitated bounty was spread across the floor, so Abadi had dragged the young man away, shouting an order to preserve the brownish puddle at all costs. The staff had obediently collected it all for analysis.

Nonny returned from the kitchen, his hands newly scrubbed, and the casino security chief approached him. "What the hell happened here?" he demanded.

"A monster happened here," declared Nonny, eyebrows fully lowered. "A monster attacked us."

Chapter 3

Even the scenes of people wrestling one another for food were useful data, concluded Kane. Absentmindedly stroking his clean-shaven face where his beard had once sprouted, he perched on a stool and scanned through the video from the buffet on his laptop. True, it was a little disconcerting when some of the diners began battling for the food, but it still told him something about gustatene's effects. It showed the effects of a higher dose. And one objective of the field trial was to observe the effects of a range of doses.

He couldn't do a detailed analysis now. He had to abandon the secret laboratory that had been the scene of his still-unrecognized scientific triumph. He slapped the laptop shut, feeling a knot of frustration in his stomach. He could achieve so much more with his work. The gustatene he'd tested at the buffets was only a prototype. It activated both the taste buds and the brain's taste-sensing system. But it was suboptimal, requiring two components and degrading quickly. And it didn't affect the brain's appetite center.

He absolutely knew that with time and resources he could create a stable molecule that could trigger in the brain not only a sense of deliciousness, but also hunger. But then he sighed in resignation, admitting to himself that his work had outgrown this modest personal lab. He needed to go back to the company.

So now, agonizingly, he had to obliterate his lab. He could leave not a shred of evidence that he had developed his revolutionary theory of human taste here; and that he had created the ultimate taste-enhancing compound. He had to; the cops might find the lab because of some overlooked clue to the lab he'd left at his house, even though he had scoured it. He'd destroyed receipts, photos, notes, even takeout menus from places near the lab.

He picked up a hammer, his jaw set. He would have to smash the glistening labyrinth of interconnected glass reaction chambers and flasks on the chemical bench. There, he had created test compounds—all failures until gustatene became his crowning success.

He would have to trash the computer station whose wall-sized screen swirled with the complex molecular geometry of the gustatene molecule. That computer had enabled him to construct the mathematical models of the human gustatory system that led him to gustatene. Then, he'd have to set fire to the place, to obliterate any trace of gustatene or its components.

But then he rejected the idea of destroying his lab. He shook his head decisively, pitching the hammer against the wall, sending it clanging off the metal. By all rights, this room should be preserved like the laboratories of Edison or Pasteur. He muttered a determined curse under his breath. He *would* preserve the lab! But it would mean flushing every bit of glassware with acid to destroy any remnant chemical.

And he would have to shred all the files on his lab computer. He would certainly scrub the videos of his animal testing, as well as the only test on himself. He had put into a can of spinach the most infinitesimal bit of gustatene, and then found himself devouring the heavenly-tasting vegetable that he'd hated only minutes before. That had been the only self-test. It was bad science, and he shouldn't have succumbed to the temptation.

Of course, all that erasing would come after uploading all his data to his cloud account. He'd also change the login and password to make sure only his mind would hold the key to his scientific revolution. Now he would triumphantly go back to his old boss Carson Hayworth holding all the cards! He could write his own ticket at GloboChem, get back his lab, his budget, and his reputation.

And he would leave for posterity a perfectly preserved laboratory for future generations to turn into a museum. Or, maybe even a reconstruction at the Smithsonian!

He would also have to make sure to erase all traces that he had secretly used the high-tech analytical instruments at DesertTech.

He had lied his way into a job as a night janitor under his fake identity, giving him access to a million-dollar collection of chemical instruments. He could not possibly have afforded them, given that he was supporting his lab on his meager janitor's salary, his dwindling savings, and the inheritance from his grandmother.

On his first night alone in the lab at three in the morning, he had plugged keyloggers—small innocuous-looking plastic cubes— between the keyboards and computers at the lab. They had harvested a wealth of login names and passwords, so he could analyze his samples under the users' identities. If he was afraid of being discovered, he could simply vanish. Nobody would even notice the absence of a night janitor who worked for a cleaning contractor.

Now for his last foray to the lab, he donned the gray janitor's overalls and gathered vials containing samples that he would analyze using the mass spectrometer and other machines.

He started to leave, but stopped himself. He realized that he needed to erase all traces of his animal experiments. He would have to take with him the empty plastic animal bins that had held the rats. He stacked them up, including the ones that still showed blood smears. He would pitch them in the dumpster at the lab, where they could not be connected to him. He would hate for future historians to document his tragic discovery with the rats about gustatene's unfortunate effects on the animals.

True, the rats in those bins had shown him he was on the right track, when they began heartily gobbling rat chow laced with bitter quinine. They had shown him his prototype gustatene had worked brilliantly.

But then that one accident, that one slip of his hand, had revealed a shocking truth—that he had also created a drug that could be used as a horrific weapon of mass murder.

***

"That's the monster! Take off your hat, monster!" Nonny exclaimed, as if the figure on the large screen in the casino conference room could hear him and be intimidated. He glared at the screen with all the smoldering rage of one whose most cherished principles had been violated.

But on the screen, the wiry man in the dark blue baseball cap kept the hat on. The security video showed him weaving among the diners at the crowded Gourffet, pausing at counters where one or another diner was obtaining their food. At each spot, he would wait until a diner was distracted, perhaps reaching for a proffered dish. He would lift his right hand, and bring it near the diner's plate.

The casino security chief stopped the video and leaned against the wall beside the screen. "We've analyzed the footage, and each of the people he was near later went nuts over the food." He smiled at the significance of the finding, nodding his head in triumph at Nonny, Abadi, and Langer the detective.

"Where is video of his face?" demanded Nonny.

"Couldn't see his face. Believe me, we have enough cameras that if he'd taken off that cap, we would have gotten him."

"Can't you find other footage that shows his face?"

"Unfortunately no, even though we tracked him all the way to the tram outside the casino. After that, he may have changed clothes because none of the other cameras around the area showed him dressed like that."

"So, what now? We do have food samples from the other place, the cheap buffet," said Abadi.

"Yeah, I got a bunch," said Langer. With that he hauled a cardboard box full of plastic bags onto the conference room table.

"And, we have our own samples," said Abadi, gesturing at the roller case he had brought. "Chef, we need to take this evidence to the authorities."

"*We* will find the creature," said Nonny in a monotone, almost as a chanted declaration. "*We* will find this creature ourselves."

Abadi shook his head emphatically. "Seriously, Chef? We do not have the resources to equal US federal government with all its scientists and laboratories." To himself, Abadi began his count of *One Mississippi, two Mississippi. . . .* He anticipated a very long count. Often it had taken days to get Chef Nonny to change his mind about one of his obsessions. The short record was five minutes.

Nonny stood glaring at the screen, ignoring Abadi, who had begun haggling with Langer over the additional fee. He then assigned Langer to try to trace the movements beyond the casino of the mysterious gaunt, baseball-capped man. Langer answered that this new assignment would require him calling in favors with the Vegas police—for an extra fee, of course.

Abadi had just agreed, when Nonny abruptly declared, "Very well. We will take this evidence to the authorities. Who?"

"FBI probably. I'll find out," said Abadi. It had been a full seven minutes for Chef's mind-changing. The short record would stand.

***

"Ponytail, is the guy," declared Agent Rochelle Chun quietly. She touched a key on the keyboard to pause the park's security video, peering intently at the frozen image. "It's the guy in the cap with the ponytail."

The wiry man in the video image wore a dark blue baseball cap, so the camera in the Red Rock Canyon visitor center parking lot didn't capture his face. Just the ponytail that brushed back and forth as the man strode through the camera's field of view, wearing a backpack. But Chun had enough points of identification. She recited them to her partner, Rydell Tate.

"Blue backpack, hiking boots, jeans, walks fast. He's nervous, looking around. He's guilty of something."

"Yeah, well, Leafy, there were lots of other guys coming off the trails during that time," said Tate, leaning back and stretching. Two hours watching videos was enough for him.

Chun pushed back. "Well, he looks like a hiker who's been on the trail before. Whoever met Silver out there chose the place because there were no cameras to catch the meeting. And this guy walks guilty."

"Walks guilty? That's a new indicator."

"I just made it up."

"I'll call Quantico. They'll want to add walking guilty to their profiling." He grinned, showing white teeth against his dusky skin.

Chun gave Tate a mischievous sideways glance. "Rydell, just start looking for his car, okay? Check the other cameras."

Tate sighed deeply and slid his chair over to his desk in the large, busy main office of the Las Vegas FBI Division. As agents and staff came and went about their business, he frowned and began scanning laboriously through the videos from the four cameras monitoring the visitor center parking lot.

Chun began to sift through video from the now-notorious food riot at Bob's Belly-Buster Buffet. The coincidence really nagged at her—that the guy in charge of that buffet-gone-wild had turned up dead from an eating-related murder. Even though the ingested material was sand not food.

After an hour, both of them had come up dead-empty.

"He must have parked his car down the road from the parking lot," said Tate. "Did you see anybody who walked guilty at the buffet?"

"Everybody walked innocent. And no ponytails. And most everybody at that buffet was fat, not skinny like the perp."

"It's late. I'm going to consider this finding over a glass of wine. Want to come?"

"You mean a bottle. And that expensive stuff you like. Yeah, but first I'm calling somebody I know at the FDA. This is looking like a food crime."

"Food crime? Is that a new category?"

"Just made it up."

"Another thing to tell Quantico to add to their training. Who's this FDA person?"

"They call her Doctor Balmy. I worked with her on a case where a Chinese company was selling adulterated food to Vegas restaurants. She really knows food chemistry."

"Doctor Balmy? Why's she called that?"

"Just wait. You'll find out."

***

"You've synthesized the compound?" asked Carson Hayworth. "*You've actually made the compound. . . here?*" The GloboChem scientific supervisor glanced disdainfully around at the shabby warehouse with its stained concrete floors and cobbled-together wooden lab benches. The aroma within was a funky combination of chemicals and a vague animal odor. Hayworth started to touch one of the surfaces, but thought better of it and withdrew his hand.

"Yes, here. I made gram quantities," replied Kane coldly.

"And it worked?" asked the rumpled, middle-aged Hayworth. His face bore the effects of half a century of gravity, with sagging jowls and substantial bags under rheumy eyes. The jowls were decorated with salt-and-pepper stubble, which had been shaped into a precisely defined landscape that covered his jaw and chin. The effect was of a well-groomed dapper sea captain.

"Yes, I've tested it."

"On rats?"

"And on human subjects. My compound gustatene works on humans."

"Gustatene? So that's what you named it?"

"And making it was no shot in the dark. It was based on my model of the gustatory system."

"Which means—"

"That I have the theoretical basis to improve the molecule, to develop it into a product. . . a revolutionary product."

"Well, if what you say is true, I can talk to McAndrews. We can try—"

"It is true. I have data."

"Okay, but any tests on humans would be unethical, even illegal."

"I was careful."

"Whatever the case, GloboChem would have to be insulated."

"It would be. I've taken precautions. It was a blind test with the subjects. They didn't know they were subjects. And nobody can trace gustatene since the molecule and its binary components degrade quickly."

Again Hayworth's brow wrinkled. "Okay, here's what will happen. You give me your field data, the model computer file, the gustatene structure, and we'll—"

"*Oh hell no!* I'll give you enough data to convince McAndrews and anybody else at GloboChem. But I want back into the company. I want my lab, my budget. . . everything. And I want GloboChem's lawyers to get me off, if the cops arrest me. And I know you've got other. . . people. . . operatives. . . who can use other means to make things go away if there are complications."

"Okay, okay, we can do that. I'll take whatever data you want to give. I'll get you a very advantageous deal. Big bucks, Ed. And a big lab."

"You're sure singing a different song, now, Carson. Not like when you told me to get the hell out of the company."

Hayworth spread his hands in apology. "Ed, I am so sorry about that whole episode. You know I had no choice. You put bad data in the reports. When management found out, dismissal was automatic. In hindsight, I should have been more supportive—"

"You should have had faith in my theory. You knew it was basically sound."

Hayworth considered excusing himself and trying to send a text message giving their address, but thought better of it. Kane would be suspicious. Thankfully, at least he'd get some data, as Kane nodded and handed him a thumb drive.

"Great!" exclaimed Hayworth, waving the small piece of plastic happily. "We'll just confirm the data and get back to you with a contract. Once that's signed, we can get the full dataset."

Kane chuckled sarcastically. "By the way, in case you thought about getting somebody to come search the lab, the data's not here. It's in my cloud account. And the username and password are up here." Kane tapped his head, glaring at Hayworth.

"Oh. . . well. . . as long as it's safe. Look, can we at least have a sample of. . . what's the name? Gustatene?"

"No samples," said Kane, walking pointedly to the door. "Once I'm sure we've got a deal in place, papers signed, and so forth, I'll come in and begin setting up my lab again. There's lots more to do."

"Look, we're always worried about security. We want to make sure you're safe," said Hayworth, pulling out a cell phone. "Keep your data safe. Here's a company phone. Use this to contact us. It's a secure phone."

Taking the phone, Kane opened the door, letting the blinding desert sun stream into the lab.

Hayworth left, striding away through the withering heat to his car, passing between a parked blue Toyota Prius and a small grime-covered RV. Once inside his sunbaked car, as the air conditioning began to alleviate the blistering temperature, he took out his own phone, punching in a number.

"I left him the phone you sent. You can track his location? It's his lab. . . but he won't be there long. Look, I'm doing what you told me, but I need . . . sure, I'll keep doing it, try to make a deal, but tell me who you are My boss said . . . yeah, need-to-know basis, okay."

Hayworth ended the call shaking his head. Was he being sucked into something bad? The guy on the phone sounded downright sinister.

***

"Yeah, it's the same guy as in the park," declared Chun emphatically, viewing the video of the food-poisoning at the Gourffet. She and Tate had been contacted by Abadi, who brought in the video. He sat beside an eyebrows-down Chef Nonny in the FBI conference room around the walnut table, peering at the wall screen. "Look how he walks. He walks—"

"Thanks so much for bringing this to our attention," interrupted Tate. He was not particularly keen on anybody else hearing Chun's assessment that the man was "walking guilty."

"We *will* help catch him," declared Nonny. "This drug, or whatever it is, is an affront to cuisine. It's criminal! It's obscene."

"We understand your concern," said Tate. "But we'll take it from here. Now, I'm just going to take you to an interview room, so you can make a full statement. And I understand you have samples from your restaurant."

"Do you know who this is?" demanded Abadi, gesturing at Nonny like a magician's assistant. "This is Chef Nonny! You've seen him in magazines, newspapers. He has an award-winning restaurant. And he invented the Gourffet!"

"The *what*?" asked Tate.

"The gourmet buffet. A total re-imagining of the traditional buffet as a gourmet experience. No assembly-line food. Every dish is a gourmet dish, made with care from the best ingredients. He can help catch this criminal—"

"This monster," interrupted Nonny.

Another voice interceded, declaring emphatically, "We don't need y'all. This is a federal case. Just let us take care of it." The voice was from a young woman who had entered the room moments earlier. She wore tattered jeans, a faded t-shirt and scuffed boots.

"You are?" asked Abadi.

"Lou Baumgartner, FDA. I'm here to work with the FBI," she said in a mellow, mint-julep-on-the-mansion-porch southern drawl. She fished crumpled cards out of her jeans pocket and handed them around, vigorously shaking hands as she went. They read "Mary Louette Baumgartner, Special Agent, Office of Criminal Investigation, Food and Drug Administration." She nodded to Chun, who nodded seriously back. She plopped down on the chair at the head of the table, crossing her feet at the ankles.

Abadi and Nonny both scowled at the slim, early-thirties woman with a pale face framed by thick brown hair. It was parted down the middle and barely constrained in a loose pony tail. Her features were conventional, with a small straight nose, and a mouth that turned up at the corners. But they were distinguished by steel-gray eyes that gazed directly, even disconcertingly, at them.

"Do you live in Las Vegas?" asked Abadi, his tone accusing.

"Nope, LA."

"Do you know the food scene? Do you know everybody involved in the restaurants and buffets in this city?"

"No, sir, I do not."

"Well, Chef Nonny does. And I do. And we can get them to tell things they won't tell you. You cannot do without us."

"Tell y'all what. I'll give it a shot without y'all. And I think I'll get by knowing food chemistry and with the full resources of the FDA to trace this. . . whatever it is. And Special Agent Chun knows the area right well. So, we'll need those samples and your information."

Abadi glanced at Nonny, frowning back at Baumgartner. "The samples are in our possession and will stay that way until you let us in on this case. Same with our information."

"We'll just see about that," said Baumgartner. "We can subpoena what we need. Now, if y'all don't mind, we got to get to the victim's house."

With that, she rose lithely herself to her feet, and she and Chun strode out of the room and away down the aisle of the large array of cubicles of the FBI offices.

"You boys should better consider your position," said Tate, as they watched Baumgartner's departure. "Those are two tough-ass women." He started off toward one of the interview rooms around the perimeter of the offices. "C'mon, now. Let's see what you know."

"As a matter of fact, nothing," retorted Abadi. "Now, we leave."

He and Nonny made their departure, marching out of the offices and through the lobby, pushing through the glass doors of the building and into the sun.

"What you think of that one?" Abadi asked Nonny, as they both watched Baumgartner climb into a bureau car with Chun and speed away. Abadi noted that Nonny had been intently watching Baumgartner's departure.

"She will be difficult. And she is sexually active."

Once they were in Nonny's limousine, Abadi sat back and grinned at him with undisguised amusement. "Seriously? Where the hell did that come from, 'She is sexually active'?"

"I study people's movement, body language. You know I have trouble reading people."

"Yeah, sure I know that, but. . . *sexually active*?"

"I read a scientific paper years ago. The *Journal of Sexual Medicine*, I believe."

"You read the *Journal of Sexual Medicine*? That's no cookbook."

"I read journals that help me understand people. The article found that it was possible to distinguish women who are more likely to have had considerable sex. They walk with more freedom, more energy, less muscle tightness."

"And did you actually test this? I hope not!"

Nonny shrugged and stared straight ahead, saying nothing.

"Oh, Allah, you *did* confirm it!" exclaimed Abadi, his eyes widening, shaking his bald head.

"I asked women about how active they were after I watched them walk."

"Just women on the street? I'll bet you got quite a few slaps. And given who you are, probably some bed partners."

"A few. I made observations on them."

"Observations? You mean on the women you've dated?"

"Yes. After we were intimate, I asked them to walk for me. I could tell a difference between those who were less active and those who were more."

Abadi chuckled. "Okay, now I understand yet another reason why these pretty ladies date you for a while, then vanish."

"Well, some did think it was strange."

"I'll bet." Abadi's amused contemplation was interrupted by a text message. He read it and reported. "Langer thinks he's traced our guy."

Within fifteen minutes, the limousine had glided to a stop in front of the strip-mall office of Albert Langer. The small storefront was nestled between a pizza take-out place and a shoe-repair shop. Nonny started to get out, but Abadi stopped him. "Chef, you shouldn't be seen here," he cautioned. "Won't you ever remember you're famous?"

Nonny settled back, and Abadi phoned Langer to bid him to join them. Shortly, Langer climbed into the limousine hauling his battered satchel and was anonymously hidden behind the tinted windows.

"Well?" asked Abadi.

Langer stared at him expectantly until Abadi sighed in annoyance and produced a check. Langer examined the amount and stuck it into his satchel. "Your guy's name is Edwin Kane. He's a scientist."

"How did you find out?" asked Nonny.

Langer dug into his satchel and pulled out a smudged iPad, swiping its screen to bring up a series of grainy, black-and-white images. They showed sequential views from different cameras of the thin man in the baseball cap exiting Bob's Casino, coming into the frame down the road, and disappearing around the corner at a pawn shop. Next, there were images from a camera outside the pawn shop showing a dark blue Toyota Prius, which quickly sped away.

"That's not much," said Nonny.

"I don't need much. Buddy of mine traced dark blue Priuses. Here's the owner of one." He tapped the screen to bring up a driver's license photo of a thin-faced man in his thirties with a scraggly unkempt beard and mustache and a wayward mop of dark hair. The man stared at the camera with a tense deer-in-the-headlights expression.

"That's the monster?" asked Nonny.

"Yes, in fact, there's more. There was a death."

"At the buffet?" asked Abadi.

"No, in the desert. There's a police report that the buffet's manager was found dead. He appeared to have choked on sand."

"Sand? What do you mean?"

"Well, I got the coroner's report from a source. It looks like he ingested some of the drug that had spilled. And it drove him to eat sand."

"We must find this monster before more people die!" exclaimed Nonny. "Where is he?"

"Well, I checked the address on his license. Nobody home. I couldn't break in. I've got scruples. Besides, I wasn't paid for that. In any case, it would be better for you to go see his former supervisor."

"Former?"

"Yeah, he used to work at a place called GloboChem. But I found a record of him being fired for faking results. I'd bet the guy who fired him, Carson Hayworth, could tell you more about him and his work. . . and maybe where he is."

Abadi waved his hands in caution. "Chef, we should tell the FBI about this. . . the woman from the food administration."

"Remember, they didn't need our help," said Nonny coldly. "We go after him ourselves."

***

50

"This is useless," grumped Lou Baumgartner, as they surveyed the living room of Robert Silver's tract house, with its cheap furniture and movie posters tacked to the walls. "I'm sure the lab boys would have found something."

"Well, we do need to be thorough. We follow procedure," said Chun.

"Procedure," Lou repeated robotically. "You mean you don't follow your gut sometimes?"

"The procedures were developed for a reason. Following them means you've been thorough."

"Yeah, well, it also means you might neglect an inspiration that could be important."

"Perspiration trumps inspiration in my book."

"If you don't mind me sayin', you are kind of a tight ass." Lou began to roam through the house, opening drawers, peering under a bed, and poking her head into the refrigerator.

"Well, that may be. In fact, I checked you out. You know they call you Doctor Balmy?"

"Helps to be a little crazy in this business. Like when you have to spend a day in an abattoir monitoring slaughter practices."

"And you have a reputation for being a loose cannon."

Lou shrugged. "Yeah, well, I own that. Loose cannons sometimes hit an unexpected target. Okay, maybe I call you TA, you call me LC."

Chun chuckled wryly. "Yeah, well, let's see how we work out."

"Say, speaking of nicknames, why do they call you Leafy? Going into the hallway, Lou pulled up a chair, mounted it, poked open the plywood cover to the attic crawl space and hoisted herself up to peer inside.

"'Leafy' came from a drug bust I was involved in."

"Big one?"

"Yeah, and the nickname refers to how it came about. I was fresh out of the academy at my first assignment. One day, I was making a

51

Chinese dish that used an herb called Kaffir lime leaves. I was chopping up the leaves when I saw that they just didn't look right. It turned out that coca leaves had gotten mixed into a batch that was sold as Kaffir. I told my supervisor, and asked to be lead on the case, since I was well known at the market. He said yes. Well, over a period of months, I traced the leaves to a company that turned out to be an importer not just of leaves, but cocaine. We ended up making a big bust . . . three tons."

Chun's cell phone issued a melodious tone, and she answered the call. A grin spread over her face.

"Yeah, as a matter of fact, we're pretty close," she told the caller, ending the call. Then to Lou, "The tail we put on the two cooks paid off. Seems they met with a detective named Langer. An agent questioned Langer. He said as long as we agreed we owed him a big favor, he'd tell us what he found. Seems he identified the guy we're looking for. . . a scientist named Edwin Kane. Langer had checked his house, but he's gone."

"Well, shoot, let's get over there and check it out!" exclaimed Lou, heading for the door.

Chun shrugged, still smiling. "Actually, we don't even have to get back in the car. He lives across the street."

Chapter 4

Daoud Abadi directed a steady, demanding stare at Carson Hayworth, while Nonny's gaze wandered around the cramped office. The office in the vast GloboChem Las Vegas research complex held bookcases crammed with scientific journals, and floors piled with printouts of research papers.

"Why do you want to know about Ed Kane?" asked Hayworth, leaning back in his creaking chair, scratching the salt-and-pepper stubble on his sagging, middle-aged face.

"He's a monster," blurted out Nonny; and Abadi gave him an annoyed "you-could-have-been-more-diplomatic" look.

"Okay, then what did he do?" asked Hayworth.

Abadi leaned forward, poking a finger toward Hayworth. "I tell you what. You tell us what *you* know, and only then we tell you what *we* know."

"Sorry, his problem was an internal personnel matter, and I'm not—"

"Yeah, well, we found out about it. Now it is *external*. You want to know what we know? You talk."

Hayworth regarded them sourly, then sighed. "Well, okay. He was just one part of an ongoing research project here at GloboChem. We are exploring the gustatory system, and—"

"The what?" asked Abadi.

"The body system that controls how the taste of food is perceived. Taste buds are the sensing part of that machinery. The six tastes—"

"There are only five," interrupted Nonny.

"Ah, supposedly only five," said Hayworth. "But now we know that besides sweet, sour, bitter, salt, and savory, called umami, there is also likely a *fat* taste. . . called oleagustus."

"Aha! I knew it!" Nonny transferred his gaze to the ceiling, his eyebrows up.

Hayworth continued. "Okay, well, each taste is triggered when a chemical that activates it plugs into a sensory receptor on taste buds on the tongue. That signal transmits to the brain. For example, sugars are sensed by the sweet receptors on the taste buds, and the sweet signal is interpreted by the brain as the perception of sweet."

"But taste can be fooled," said Nonny.

"Yes, by artificial sweeteners, for example. Like saccharin. And it's hundreds of times sweeter than sugar."

Nonny gave a sarcastic humph signifying his disdain for the molecule.

"And interestingly enough, we've found out that the same taste receptors are in the stomach, intestines and other places," said Hayworth.

Nonny nodded his head emphatically, a dawning smile signaling that this scientist had entered his realm of expertise. "So taste is a symphony for the whole body."

"Exactly," said Hayworth. "Somehow, the brain integrates different tastes into a single sensation. The chemical equivalent of musical chords."

"And what does this have to do with the monster?" asked Nonny.

"Well, before Dr. Kane's . . . uh . . . departure, besides helping with the project to understand the gustatory system, he was part of a large team figuring out how to create not only simple chords, but the equivalent of a Bach concerto on the taste buds. We were trying to create a chemical or mixture that could enhance all tastes. But also, we are working to develop drugs to control appetite. As you well know, obesity is a serious disease in the world, and we want to contribute to fighting it. That's why our team was creating a very sophisticated mathematical model of the whole gustatory machinery, all the way from the taste buds on the tongue to the brain's primary gustatory cortex and hypothalamus."

"So the object was. . .?" asked Abadi.

"To develop compounds that did two things. First, to play the taste buds like a concert pianist, causing any food to have a highly alluring taste. Such a compound would affect the taste buds and the brain's gustatory cortex. And second, to trigger the appetite center, the hypothalamus. It would mimic the hormone that triggers hunger. . . called ghrelin."

"So, he sought to create drugs to drive people to devour any food that contained it?" asked Nonny. "Well, he did it! And he used his drug to poison many, many people!"

Abadi sighed in frustration. Nonny had given away their only informational bargaining chip. But perhaps Hayworth would not get the connection to the particular events of the past week. Abadi was wrong.

"*The riots at the buffets on the news? Those were his work?*" exclaimed Hayworth. He frowned, a look of realization dawning on his face.

"He drugged my diners with just such poisons," said Nonny.

"More than that, he was responsible for a death," said Abadi. "He indirectly caused the death of one man, the manager at the cheap buffet. In the desert, the man ate dirt until he died."

Hayworth sat for a long moment staring at them. Then, he shook his head sadly. "I saw the news about the death. Well, I wish I could help. But we lost track of him after he was let go. He could be anywhere."

"Well, we must stop him," said Nonny. "You need to help."

"I'll make some inquiries. Maybe somebody here at the company has kept track of him. He didn't have any real friends that I know of, though." Hayworth stood, indicating that the interview was over.

He escorted them out of the building, standing outside the door to make sure they had entered their limousine and left. Then he returned to his office, took out his cell phone, and pressed a contact. After a long moment, there was an answer. It was the sinister voice of the person he contacted before.

"I just had a visit from some guys looking for Kane," he said. "We need to settle this one way . . . or another."

***

"*Duck waddle!* Nothin' so far," exclaimed Lou Baumgartner. Her slim body was shrouded in a baggy, white isolation suit, her hands latex-gloved. A paper cap barely contained her mop of hair, and the mask over her face muffled her speech. She carefully pulled items from the refrigerator of Kane's house and placed them in plastic bags—canned sodas, a container of brown lunch meat, and a pizza box with desiccated, curled up pizza.

"What did you say?" asked Chun, who had come in from the living room. She wore the same protective suit, having spent an hour minutely examining the other rooms.

"I'm trying out new cuss words. My boss got on me for my potty-mouth language at the office. *Succotash!*"

"What's with bagging the refrigerator stuff?" Asked Chun. "Seriously?"

Lou began to explore the cupboards, pulling out boxes and cans. "Even common household items could leave clues. Maybe the guy had grabbed a soda when he'd just come back from the lab and still had some drug on his fingers."

"Well, so far we've found nothing that links him to the attacks," said Chun.

"Yeah, we've got to find his lab," said Lou, who put the bags on the floor and exited out the back door. She shifted her attention to the plastic garbage bin there. She tipped it over, unleashing a cascade of sodden garbage that included food waste, crumpled packaging, and soaked magazines. The cascade caused Chun, who had followed her, to deem it prudent to retreat to a remote corner of the sandy, sun-blasted yard.

"Looks like a . . . rich . . . source of evidence," said Chun, wrinkling her nose.

Lou crouched down and began to paw through the trash, pulling out semi-liquid food waste, bottles, cans, plastic bags and other detritus. "Yeah, I'm sure Kane went through all this before he took it out, to get rid of papers and such. But they always leave something." With that, she took off her helmet and leaned down close to the pile.

"Jeez, Lou, what the hell are you doing?"

"I got an educated nose. I used to do analyses in organic chem by just smelling the test tube. I . . . wait a second!" She paused, breathing deeply of the aroma. "Okay, I got the usual stink, but there's somethin' else. He spilled a chemical and cleaned it up with a . . ." She paused, and after a moment, picked up a wadded-up paper towel, sniffing it. "It's a chemical he must have brought home from the lab. Yeah, yeah. It's a complex amine, probably with a couple of benzene rings, some aliphatic side chains. Probably related to aminoquinoline. They're used as precursors in pharmaceuticals. It would be an unusual chemical. We get this to the lab folks and let them ID exactly what it is, I bet we can find out where it was ordered and trace it back to his lab."

"Impressive," said Chun. "We'll go see his old boss at the company. I asked Rydell to set it up." Retreating out of range of any chemicals that Lou might spread, Chun stripped off her gloves and isolation suit and pulled out her phone, calling her partner.

"We're on our way," she said. "Is the guy available?" She paused, listening to the reply. "Well, shit!" she exclaimed.

"What?"

"The cooks were already there!"

"Okay, now those ol' boys are officially impeding an investigation," declared Lou. "They got to be dealt with!"

***

Carson Hayworth hurried into the executive conference room fresh off the flight from Las Vegas to Philadelphia and to GloboChem headquarters. He knew to respond instantly to a summon from Vice President Gabriel McAndrews.

The thickly carpeted room held a vast rosewood table that would seat twenty people, its walnut-paneled walls lined with paintings of dignified middle-aged male executives.

But where was McAndrews? Hayworth shot a puzzled look at the slim man in a tailored tan suit and a brush cut, seated at the table, his hands folded in front of him. The man wore circular glasses that emphasized dark eyes and sat erect at the table, as if he might suddenly spring from it. A cell phone rested before him on the table. The man gave Hayworth a steady, appraising look that a snake might give its prey. He did not offer to shake hands or invite Hayworth to sit. So Hayworth remained standing across the table from the man, shifting from one foot to the other.

"Um. . . I thought Mr. McAndrews might be here," said Hayworth timorously. "The call said I was to meet him."

"The call said you were to meet in the executive vice president's suite," said the man quietly. "I am Joseph, his representative."

"What's going on? All I know is that after Kane contacted me, my boss told me that somebody would give me instructions on what to do. Then some guy called me and told me I was to try to persuade Kane to give his data. And I tried. Then after some people came looking for him. I called the guy back and told him. I tried."

"Not very successfully. I'm to lay out more clearly what your mission is."

"Mission? Who exactly are you? What do you mean by you're Mr. McAndrews' 'representative'?"

The man ignored the question. "We're looking for a binary outcome. All or nothing."

"Binary?"

"This drug Kane developed could ruin GloboChem. Or it could make the company the most powerful in the food industry."

"How could it ruin GloboChem?"

Joseph gave Hayworth a disgusted look. "What if there were a compound that made our whole business moot. . . that made any food irresistible?"

"Oh, right, I see. Our food products business would disappear. So, what do you mean by binary?"

"You are to work with the operative who contacted you."

"I should meet him, right? I should know who he is, right? And again, what is *binary*?"

The man ignored the first questions. "You are to either obtain the formula and mathematical model exclusively. Or, you are to make sure nobody else has it. . . ever."

"You mean. . . ?" Hayworth stopped himself, eyes widening.

"Neutralizing the source."

Now Hayworth sat down in one of the leather chairs and leaned forward, returning the man's stare.

"That's it! I'm done! I've done what was asked until now, but I'm not going to have some go-between. . . " He paused, took a breath and spat out, ". . . some *lackey* giving me instructions. If I don't get my marching orders from the top, I walk."

The man glanced down at his cell phone, then leaned back in the chair. They waited in an ominous silence for several minutes.

Then from behind Hayworth came a resonant voice. "Ah, Mr. Hayworth, I understand you have reservations about our planned course of action."

Hayworth swiveled the chair to see the well-known face of Gabriel McAndrews, executive vice president in charge of GloboChem's Engineered Food Product Division. He exemplified an executive, with his vested, pin-striped suit, coiffed steel-gray head of hair, and tanned, smooth face.

Hayworth bolted up from the chair, but McAndrews smiled warmly and motioned him to sit back down. He took a seat across from Hayworth, beside Joseph.

"Sir, what you want me to do. . . it's just that I'm not sure that this course of action is, well. . . legal or ethical. . . or whatever," said Hayworth.

"Coffee, please," McAndrews said, seemingly to no one. "You'll have coffee?" he asked Hayworth, who after a long moment nodded, as did Joseph. "Ah, coffee for three, please. And some of those very nice cookies. Now, Mr. Hayworth, you are a loyal and valued employee of GloboChem, and I'm sure you have the company's interests at heart."

"Of course, certainly."

A young woman appeared at the door, carrying a tray with a silver coffee service, China cups, and a plate of cookies. She served them as McAndrews sat silently, still smiling. She left, and McAndrews continued, standing and serving all of them coffee and cookies as he talked.

"I've followed the fine work of your research group, and I'm aware of this person Kane's activities. We are a multi-billion-dollar company, and our job is to sell food product. I like to say that it's food when it's in a restaurant, or on a dinner table. But it's product to us. A product to sell. Our sauce products enhance foods' appeal. Our additives mimic or enhance flavor. Our objective is *not* to nourish. Our objective is to make consumers *consume*. We've done very well with our strategy. We engineer our products to entice people to consume more and more . . ."

Now McAndrews sat down and leaned forward conspiratorially. ". . . and when they consume, and they get a bit overweight, our diet product division sells them the dream of becoming slim again. We don't give people what they need. We give them what we *want* them to need."

"But how does—" Hayworth began, but McAndrews waved him to be silent.

"You, sir, will play an invaluable role ensuring the continued success of our company. Imagine if we can successfully bring out a taste enhancer such as the one that Doctor Kane has developed. Adding just a tiny amount. . . not even a detectable amount. . . to our products could do wonders for our sales, and for our bottom line. We would be most grateful for your participation in bringing us that technology."

"But I can't. . . I couldn't. . . "

"Our contractor will handle the process of obtaining the technology . . . or ensuring no one else does. You just have to create the opportunity."

"And if I can't?"

McAndrews took a cookie, rose smoothly, and left.

After he was gone, Joseph said quietly, "Then you are no longer useful. And you are in possession of knowledge that should not be disseminated. Do I make myself clear?"

***

"How did you find me?" asked Nonny, standing at the open door to his mansion in the mountains, the glow of Las Vegas' lights in the distance. A faint, dry desert breeze had begun to relieve the blistering heat of the day.

"You live here alone?" asked Lou. "Hell of a big joint for one person." She stood back and took in the stark glass-and-stone structure, an assemblage of square forms with a two-story portico. The landscape lighting cast the structure in a soft glow and reflected off the glimmering pond in front of the house.

"How did you find me?" Nonny repeated, not moving from the open doorway.

"Invite me in," said Lou. "That's the polite thing to do."

Nonny backed away from the door to allow her entrance, and she strolled into the spacious living room populated simply with a stark array of minimalist furniture.

"What do you want?" asked Nonny.

"I want you to tell me where your guy is. His name's Abadi, right? And where are the samples? And I'll have a glass of red wine."

"I won't tell you because I don't trust you. You're a government agent. You don't care like I do. You won't let us help you, so we won't help you. What kind of wine?"

"A cabernet would be nice. We got a winery in Savannah. . . Butterducks Winery. . . that makes the tastiest cab. Haven't had the equal of it."

"I have Marchesi Antinori Cabernet Franc." Nonny headed for the kitchen, and Lou followed. He disappeared into a room-sized wine closet and appeared with a bottle, proceeding to open it. But rather than uncorking it, he heated a circular iron over the stove, placed it over the wine bottle neck, doused the heated neck with water, and neatly severed the neck from the rest of the bottle.

"You don't know how to use a corkscrew?" asked Lou.

"Avoids disturbing the wine." He decanted the wine into a crystal flask. "It needs to breathe."

"It can breathe in my glass. Pour it."

Nonny's eyebrows lowered to half mast, but he proceeded to pour the wine into a stemmed glass, hesitated, and then poured himself a glass.

Lou returned to the living room and nestled herself on the simple, square-backed couch. "Look, Chef Nonny, I need those samples. We need to find out what the guy Kane dosed everybody with."

"No. I don't trust you. You don't have a commitment to catching this monster who is poisoning food. Your agency doesn't fight for pure food."

"*I* do. I hate additives as much as you do. Like, I loathe sodium nitrite! *Horrible* preservative!"

Nonny contemplated his wine glass for a long moment, then took a sip. He quietly declared, "Potassium bromate is worse. Damages kidneys, nervous system. . . causes cancer. I do not allow it in any baked goods."

Lou smiled and held up her glass in agreement. "I bet you ban propyl paraben, too."

Nonny shook his head emphatically, eyebrows lowering. "Yes, absolutely. And butylated hydroxy anisole. Devastating to the brain."

"Yeah, and then there's butylated hydroxytoluene. God, I hate butylated hydroxytoluene!"

The two of them then launched into a back-and-forth recitation of loathed additives.

"Propyl gallate," he said, as if it were a curse.

"Red dye number forty," she countered with disgust.

"Blue dye number two," he said, shaking his head.

"Diacetyl," she said coldly.

"So, you hate food additives," said Nonny, refilling her glass. "But are you truly committed to purity of cuisine? I've dedicated my life to bringing the best to the table. . . the best tastes. I can't believe that you, as a government agent, would be."

"Yeah, well, this is how committed I am!" Lou shifted on the couch to turn away from him and lifted her t-shirt to reveal a bare back. On that smooth, slim back were tattooed an array of molecular structures.

"Molecules? What do they mean?" asked Nonny.

"The purity of tastes," she said smiling over her shoulder. "Each molecule represents the purest example of a taste."

"And they are. . .?" asked Nonny.

She reached behind her back to point out each molecule:

"Left clavicle. . . tripalmitin. . . The fatty taste oleagustus."

Nonny said, "Yes, I've learned about that."

She went on: "Upper spine. . . acetic acid from vinegar. . . sour.

"Right clavicle. . . theobromine from dark chocolate. . . bitter.

"Left rib cage. . . sodium chloride. . . salty.

"Lower spine, glutamate. . . savory umami.

"Right rib cage. . . fructose. . . sweet taste."

Nonny's expression grew dark. "*Sugar.*" He uttered the word as if it were a curse. "Addictive, poisonous. Causes obesity, diabetes, liver disease."

Lou lowered her shirt and turned back toward him, nodding emphatically. "You said a mouthful! It is terrible stuff, and the food industry laces everything with it. A cheap additive. They disguise it with dozens of different names, and—"

Nonny interrupted, launching into a chanted litany. "Fructose, sucrose, dextrose, galactose, maltose, beet sugar, castor sugar, coconut sugar. The worst is corn syrup. Then there's date sugar, panela sugar, turbinado sugar—"

Now Lou interrupted, realizing that Nonny would most likely name all fifty or so sugars. "Yeah, yeah, you know your sugars, babe. I went off sugar and other bad stuff long ago. In fact. . . " she lifted the front of her shirt to just below her breasts, pointing to a tattoo just under her left breast of an outline of a heart. The top of the heart formed a green V, and one arm of the V sprouted a leaf.

"Vegan symbol," he said, scrutinizing the tattoo.

"I hate additives, *and* I'm a vegan. I just wanted you to know where my head *and* my heart are." She lowered her t-shirt. "That's all the show for now," she said, grinning slyly. "You trust me now, right? You know I'll be as dedicated as you to finding this. . . 'monster'"

Nonny reached over to the coffee table and picked up his cell phone. "Daoud is at the Cosmopolitan hotel," he said. "I'll call him. I'll tell him to go with you; to give you what you want."

***

"Give us the fu—" began Lou, but interrupted herself. "Give us the *faxxing* samples!" She sat across the metal table from Daoud

64

Abadi, who glowered back at her, his muscular arms folded. The interrogation room in the Las Vegas FBI field office was institutionally bland, its walls a flat gray, its furniture basic—a stark contrast to the fiery confrontations that had taken place within it. "Your boss told you to give them to us, right? And to cooperate?"

"Yes, he tell me to give you and FBI agent samples."

"Then, why don't y'all hand them over?" Lou gave Rochelle Chun, standing beside her, a frustrated, eye-rolling look.

"Chef Nonny is sometimes too easy to persuade. He does not like to disagree with people. I do not have that problem."

Chun joined the argument. "You know, we can charge you. . . and him as well. . . with obstructing a federal investigation. And there goes his rep."

"He is not obstructing. He tells me to give you samples. I am obstructing. It is all on me."

Lou softened her expression to one of amiability. "C'mon, what could you do with the samples? We got expertise. We can analyze them far more effectively than you ever could."

"And would you share the findings? Will you let us in on the investigation? That is what Chef wants. That is what I want."

"You know we can't do that," said Chun.

"Hmph," declared Abadi. "Chef, he would be invaluable. Then I go to jail."

"Son, why are you so faithful to this guy?" asked Lou, "He's just your employer."

"*Just employer?*" asked Abadi, his tone sarcastic. He frowned at the two interrogators. "He save my life."

"Yeah, right. A cook saved your life," said Lou.

"Yes, he save my life!" Abadi leaned forward, placing his beefy hands on the table. He shook his bald head at the memory. "I have restaurant in Khuzestan in Iran. I make incredible dishes. . . delicious Iranian Ghalieh Mahi and Ghalieh Meygu and ashe-mohshala! Chef Nonny, he is visiting Iran to learn more about Persian cuisine, get new

65

recipes. He comes to my restaurant. He loves my dishes. While he is there, the morality police raid my restaurant. They find drugs that one of my cooks had hidden. The cook, he gets away, but I don't. They find out I'm a Sunni. They hate Sunnis. They say I am enemy of God. . . corrupt. They say I have committed a beheading offense. They are about to take me. Chef Nonny, he pays one of the police to look the other way for just a little bit of time, while Chef gets me to his car. We barely make it. Police chase us. He could be imprisoned, even executed, but he takes me anyway, and we get to airport, to his jet. We take off. Iranian air force is scrambled to come after us. But my city is near Iraq border, and we make it across. And Chef Nonny knows state department people, so he persuade them to give me political asylum."

Lou leaned back, stretched out her blue-jeaned legs, and crossed her arms. "Dang, I guess that does qualify as saving your life!" she exclaimed admiringly. She turned to Chun and shook her head resignedly. "This boy ain't gonna budge." She raised her eyebrows expectantly at Chun, in an unspoken question.

Chun frowned. "You want to involve civilians in an FBI investigation? This is not policy."

"So, you're not willing to bend a little bit for the sake of the investigation. . . *TA?*" Lou pronounced the tight-ass acronym with smiling sarcasm.

After a long moment, Chun made a humph and glared at Lou, then Abadi. "Hell . . . okay . . . we let you in as consultants. The instant you get in the way and cease to be useful, you're out."

"Oh, we will be useful," declared Abadi, grinning. "Chef, he will never stop until monster is caught."

***

"I saw it myself!" exclaimed drug dealer Leno Beppo to his boss, fidgeting excitedly, as if he were on cocaine, which he probably was. "The people at that fancy buffet in the Grand Forum went nuts over the food! Fighting over it! Security came in! And five-oh came in! And they could barely control them!"

66

The scrawny dealer flipped his long, greasy mane out of his face and stared at Oskar Joachim Dunst expectantly. He grinned, showing a mouthful of yellow teeth with an incisor missing.

Dunst considered that he might have to discipline his dealer for using too much of the product. Dunst seldom allowed dealers into his presence, preferring to work through chain of command. But Beppo's lieutenant had convinced Dunst that the dealer's information was worth an audience.

"And why are you telling me this?" asked Dunst in a mellifluous Austrian accent. He was dressed for the evening in a handmade charcoal suit and black silk shirt. He stood at the floor-to-ceiling glass wall of his penthouse condominium, behind him the swirling kaleidoscope of lights that marked the Las Vegas strip.

The penthouse condo sat high in one of the famously leaning Sheer towers, so he could look straight down at the ant-like stream of tourists below. All had brought money. Many looking for drugs. And his organization readily provided them.

"Boss, I think somebody put a drug in their food," said Beppo, his hands flapping like startled birds. "A drug like I never seen before. I think it's a new opportunity."

"How so?" Dunst already knew the answer. He hadn't survived for two decades in the drug trade without being savvy about new opportunities. But he always listened to his underlings.

"Well, it looks like people go nuts for whatever food it's on. The restaurants and the food companies. . . they would pay big money for a supply!"

Dunst's smooth, angular face, assumed a warm smile, but not directed at Beppo. Diana Vodkonen had appeared. Her model-slim figure was sheathed in a sky-blue, silk Armani Privé evening gown, with a pearl-encrusted bodice. The dress's thigh-high slit gave tantalizing glimpses of her long legs as she glided into the room, tall and willowy.

She smoothed back her long dark hair from her perfect features with full lips, a delicately upturned nose, and depthless azure eyes. She moved gracefully to kiss Dunst. She stood beside him—the two of them a matched image of graceful elegance—and regarded Beppo with an amused smile.

Said Dunst, "My dear, Leno here has come to us with interesting information. Perhaps a new product we might procure the ability to produce. Tell me, Leno, how do you suggest we proceed?"

Beppo almost danced with the excitement at the prospect of being in on a deal with his big boss. "Well, it was in Chef Nonny's buffet that I saw the drugging. I was outside supplying a client when the shit all started, so I hung out and watched. After it was all over, I saw his people take samples of the food. I saw his second guy, a bald guy, take them away. They know something, I'm sure."

"Thank you, Leno. We will consider your information."

"Sure, sure, okay… but, sir, can I be in on it? After all, I—" Leno stopped himself abruptly, glancing nervously over at a hulking man in a ponytail who had appeared from the hall leading to the door.

Dunst's bodyguard, Mutante, had arms and chest that were massively muscled out of all proportion to his slim hips and squat bow legs. His freakishly top-heavy physique had earned him the nickname Mutante—"Mutant" in Spanish—during his days on the lucha libre Mexican wrestling circuit. Below his large broken nose hung a bushy black mustache that hid his upper lip and cascaded down his cheeks. Above that nose shone two snake-dead eyes overhung by thick eyebrows that sprouted wildly from the prominent outcropping of his forehead. His thick, black hair formed a luxuriant mop on his head.

He scowled and raised his thigh-thick right arm, with its tattoo of an anaconda encircling it. He fixed his stare on the drug dealer and flicked his hand.

Beppo knew Mutante's gesture was the signal that he was to leave—that the foyer of the condominium was deserted so he would not be seen. He was well aware that others who had disobeyed the

Mutant were not seen again. He slipped past the hulking man, nodding obsequiously. Mutante watched him steadily until he was out the door.

"We will be a while yet," Dunst told his bodyguard. "Postpone our reservation for half an hour." Then, he relayed Beppo's information to Diana, finally asking, "What do you think, dear?"

"A possibility," she replied, delicately lifting the hem of the gown and sitting down at the glass-topped dining table. She opened a laptop and began typing, her finely featured face scrunched up in concentration.

Dunst popped open a bottle of champagne and poured them both a glass. He silently set her glass beside the laptop. He knew better than to interrupt her concentration. She hadn't graduated Wellesley, and gotten a Stanford Ph.D. and an MIT research fellowship, without the ability to concentrate utterly on a problem.

After twenty minutes, she sat back and raised her fine eyebrows and pursed her lips in an expression indicating that Beppo's information was of interest. She picked up the champagne, and held it up in a toast. They clinked glasses.

"So?" he asked expectantly, taking a sip.

"The incident at Chef Nonny's was the second in which people were apparently driven to obsession over food at a buffet," she said, taking a sip herself. "There was a death. . . the manager of the first buffet. The coroner's report indicated it was a clogged airway, from consuming dirt. Maybe drug-induced."

"Fascinating. Your recommendation?" asked Dunst.

"Wire thirty thousand dollars to Tate's account. Tell our money-hungry FBI agent we want full details on the FBI investigation. And, put the word out that we want to find whoever made the compound... certainly he's a chemist. Let Beppo take the lead. If the situation goes sideways, he is merely an underling. We can. . ." she did not finish the sentence, shrugging her gowned shoulders dismissively.

"And the chef?" he asked.

"He should be neutralized. But he is too high profile to be eliminated."

"Do we have anything on him we can use?"

Diana typed for another minute, scrutinized the computer screen, then looked up and nodded, smiling faintly. "Enough to ruin him."

***

Lou Baumgartner frowned at her laptop, sitting with her booted foot propped over her blue-jeaned knee in Kane's newly discovered laboratory. Milling around her, white-suited FBI technicians swabbed surfaces and gingerly disassembled Kane's intricate, glass laboratory apparatus to extract samples.

As she had predicted, they had located the laboratory by tracking a shipment of the exotic organic chemical her trained nose had identified on the paper towel from Kane's garbage. But now her pleasure at her success had given way to a new frustration.

"*Nothing from the damned food samples!*" she exclaimed to Rochelle Chun. "No hint at what that drug was. I'm looking at the results from the FDA lab. They analyzed the samples from the buffets. Got nothing on GCMS, HPLC, NMR. . . *Damn!*"

"And I thought the FBI was full of acronyms," wisecracked Chun, who was sorting through bagged evidence on a lab bench.

"Oh. . . sorry," said Lou, closing the laptop. "I was talking about Gas Chromatography-Mass Spectrometry, and High-Performance Liquid Chromatography, and Nuclear Magnetic Resonance spectroscopy. Standard analytical gadgets."

"So no clue what the drug was?"

"Drugs. Plural. Remember, when we zoomed in the video from the buffet attack, it shows him squirting two liquids from two tubes. That means it's a binary system that activates when the chemicals mix. No clue what they were. They could be just about anything . . . proteins . . . carbohydrates . . . some even more complex. And they're masked by all the complex crap that makes up the foods Kane dosed with it."

"And that means?"

"That means even though we know the drugs are in the foods, we can't find them."

"So that means we've got to catch the guy," said Chun.

"Not just catch him, but persuade him to give us the formula," said Lou.

"Well, maybe his lab will tell us something," said Chun, also watching the FBI forensics team go about its business.

Lou stowed her laptop in her backpack and stood, frowning in concentration, scanning the large room. "I know your techs are good. But let me see what I can see here. I've been in a lot of labs in my time."

Carefully avoiding touching anything, she walked slowly through the laboratory, studying the lab benches, the chemical apparatus, and the shelves of chemicals.

"Rats," she muttered after some minutes of scouting.

"Didn't find anything?" asked Chun.

"Yeah, I did. Rats. There were rats here. There's rat turds on this table." She pulled out a baggie and carefully scooped some rat droppings into it. "I'll send this for analysis."

"So, what? It's a warehouse. Warehouses have rats."

"This is a lab. Kane was a meticulous guy. He would've made sure there were no infestations of any kind. They would have totally screwed up his results."

Now Chun enlisted her own powers of observation in addressing the rat question. "Okay, so it wasn't an infestation." She scanned the row of lab benches, then moved her attention to the large separate table where Lou had found the droppings. "I've spent time in drug labs that used animals. These rats were in the plastic bins that hold rats."

"What makes you say that?"

"The droppings were on this table, not on the floor. Rats don't like tables; they like floors." Chun bent down and picked up a wood shaving. "And here's some of the bedding that was in their cages."

"So your conclusion?" asked Lou.

"Our guy was trying to hide the fact that he was using rats."

"Why would he do that?"

Chun didn't answer, having bent down to examine the table closer. "Something happened to these rats. Something not good."

"What do you mean?"

"There are little flecks on the table around where the bins sat. I've seen lots of blood flecks. These are blood flecks. I bet rat blood." She motioned to one of the lab techs, directing him to take samples.

"Well, I know one thing. He had a damned good reason for hiding the rats. He obviously didn't care that we would see everything else in his lab, once we found it. But this still doesn't help us find him."

"I think the chef could be of help here," said Lou. "He knows Vegas. He knows the people."

"Okay, then, I'll get our agents on the search. You see what the chef knows. You already went to his house. You didn't say much about that night. What happened?"

"I got him to trust me." Lou smiled and tossed her head. "And maybe I teased him a little bit."

"So, you won't mind handling him?" asked Chun. "Making sure he stays out of mischief?"

"Handle him? No problem." Lou wriggled her eyebrows up and down, grinning. "I'll stay on top of him."

Chun hmphed. "Funny. Very funny."

***

"Okay, I'm here. So, now what?" Brigham Baltazar, dragged his roller bag past the jangling slot machines in the Las Vegas McCarran Airport baggage claim area. "You really think this thing with the drugged foods is a big deal?"

"It's scary!" said Alex Teo. The small, thin man stretched out his stride to keep up with the much taller Veganite leader, with his gangly, loose-limbed stride. Baltazar had the imperious, looming presence of the leader of the vegan cult—with beady, close-set blue eyes, a hawk nose, and long, coarse salt-and-pepper hair bunched in a ponytail.

"I looked at the video of the buffet before I left Atlanta," said Baltazar, nodding to the black-suited limousine driver standing in the crowd holding the tablet computer displaying Baltazar's name. He passed his bag to the driver, who strode away ahead of them. He turned back to Teo. "Okay, it was a strange scene, I'll grant you that. But scary? Convince me it's worth my while coming out here."

"You know I work in the salad kitchen at the Gourffet, right? I was there. I saw the mad look in the people's eyes! This drug. . . or whatever it is. . . could be a means to the ultimate statement. . . the ultimate—"

"The ultimate what?" demanded Baltazar. "Look, we're committed to whatever revolutionary actions necessary to advance our cause. But you tell me what kind of action would be warranted in this case."

"I . . . I don't know. But we need to at least get our hands on—"

"Shut up!" interrupted Baltazar, as they approached the limousine, with the driver holding its door open. "We'll talk in the meeting. Meantime, we can't be seen together." He left Teo standing in the baggage claim area, as he folded his long frame to get into the limousine.

***

"I found the scientist guy," said the private investigator Langer, pulling out his smudged tablet computer and poking at it to bring up a photo. "One of my hookers saw him. She took pictures." He took care to hold the tablet so that Abadi could not get a clear angle on the photo.

"Your hookers? You employ hookers?" asked Abadi, shaking his head, frowning. He didn't bother to close the door to Chef Nonny's office. It was two in the morning, and the only people about were the crew scrubbing the kitchen.

73

"Hey, I'm not a pimp. They're effective agents," said Langer. "They get around. Their clients tell them everything. Or, they can persuade their clients, if you get my drift. And they have street smarts better than anybody."

"He says a hooker found him," Abadi relayed to Chef Nonny, who had returned from an inspection of the scrubbing crew's work. He still wore his white gloves and carried a magnifier.

"Where is he?" asked Nonny. "Can we get him?"

"First, you owe the hooker five hundred dollars. Then, I show you what I've got," said Langer. "That's the usual reward I give when one of my people does a service."

"It should come out of your fee," retorted Abadi.

Langer held up a single stubby finger. "If I use this finger on the delete button, you've got nothing," he warned.

"Pay him," said Nonny, slipping off the gloves and gesturing for the tablet. Langer smiled and passed it to him, and he flipped through the images, spreading his fingers to magnify some.

"He's in a white camper van," said Langer. "My lady friend said he appears to be living in it. He was in an RV park off the Strip. She was servicing a client there."

"What is that. . . an RV park?" asked Abadi.

"It's a big parking lot where people can camp," said Langer.

"So, how do we know this woman's information is accurate?"

"She positively identified him. Hookers have great memories for faces. She saw him return to the van. And after her session with the client was over, she stayed around to take this picture." Langer reached over and swiped at the tablet screen to bring up a photo of Kane holding a bag of trash.

"Let's go get him," declared Nonny, rising to go.

But Abadi waved his hand in caution. "So, Chef, you are thinking we should capture him ourselves? Shall we take the limo, and bring all our chef knives as weapons?" Abadi chuckled at his own joke. "Or, perhaps shall we drive the Maserati?" His shook his head vigorously, "No, Chef, we must take this to FBI."

"My fee?" reminded Langer. "And my agent's fee? It's now up to you what to do with this information."

Nonny waved his hand impatiently, and Abadi shrugged and went to a scheduling board on the wall. He swung it out to reveal a safe, and punched in the combination. He handed an envelope to Langer, and counted out another five hundred dollars.

"All right," said Nonny resignedly. "Call the FBI agent. And call the FDA woman. She should be there."

Abadi had begun the call, when a white-garbed member of the scrubbing crew appeared at the door, a face mask dangling from his neck.

"There's a man out here wants to see you and Chef," he said to Abadi. He shook his head in caution. "He's squirrelly-looking. Says his name is Beppo."

"What does he want?" asked Nonny.

"He says to tell you he knows about the truck."

"The truck?" asked Abadi, ending the call. "He knows about the truck?" He gave Nonny a worried look. "Chef, I told you something like this would happen! He knows! And the truck will be at the Gourffet soon!" He turned to Langer, saying, "You should go."

"No," said Nonny. His gaze on Abadi. "He should stay. You say he is discreet. You say he will investigate anything. We may need to know what this Beppo person is planning."

Nonny stood and nodded for the visitor to be admitted. A twitchy, gaunt man appeared at the office door. He brushed his long hair back from his face and grinned. His upper right incisor was missing. "Hey, guys," he said. "I am Leno Beppo. I have a message from Oskar Dunst. You know Mr. Dunst?"

"I do not," said Nonny. "And I do not care that—"

"We know Mr. Dunst," interrupted Langer, giving Nonny and Abadi a cautionary shake of the head. "What does Mr. Dunst wish to tell Chef Nonny?"

"That he knows about the truck."

Scowling, Abadi moved menacingly toward Beppo, his large hands flexing, as if preparing to grab him. "What truck? There is no truck. What do you mean?"

Beppo backed away, his grin fading slightly. He looked at his watch. "It oughta be backin' up to the loading dock of your buffet about now. And your people should begin loading stuff. Lots of the very nice food you serve there."

"What do you want?" asked Nonny.

Beppo cocked his head back and forth in a "no-big-deal" gesture and raised his eyebrows. "Just tell me what's the deal with that drug that your customers got. Where is the guy who made it? We know you took samples, and we want them. We bet you kept some from the FBI."

Nonny's eyebrows lowered to a full glare, but he said nothing.

"Go to hell!" exclaimed Abadi. "We will give you nothing!" He reached out for Beppo, who backed away, bringing up his arms. But Nonny laid a hand on Abadi's muscular shoulder.

"Get the samples we kept," he told Abadi coldly. "Give them to him." Then to Langer, he said, "Tell him what you discovered about Edwin Kane's location. Mr. Beppo, Kane is the man's name."

"But we can't—" began Langer.

"We must," interrupted Nonny.

Langer sighed resignedly and told Beppo that Kane had been seen at the RV park. "I'll send you photos if you give me your email," said Langer.

Beppo gave Langer his address, took out his smartphone, and shortly displayed his snaggle-toothed grin at seeing the photos.

"Cool," he said, pocketing the phone and turning to go. "Mr. Dunst will be in touch if he needs anything else."

After the drug dealer had left, Langer asked, "Why did you do that? Are you stealing from your own restaurant? You need to tell me."

Nonny sat heavily in his office chair and stared straight ahead. "We couldn't let anybody find out."

"Why?" asked Langer. "Stealing food. . . that's not a big deal."

Abadi gave his boss a sympathetic look. "Well, it is," he said. "It's illegal what he's doing with it. But he has to, even if he was prosecuted. Lives are at stake."

Langer shook his head in confusion. "Lives at stake over food? I just don't get it."

"You will," said Abadi.

***

"*Okay! Great!*" exclaimed Kane into the phone, crouched in the back of his camper van. He squatted on a cooler full of chemical cannisters amid the clutter of his rapid exit from his home and lab. He held the phone Hayworth had given him tight against his ear, as if the information from Hayworth would leak out, should he allow a gap. "I get the big lab on the third floor, right?"

"Absolutely," said Hayworth. "I've got the memo in front of me. I've also got the contracts giving you what we discussed. . . patent rights, signing bonus, legal representation. . . everything. Look, I just want to go over some details with you, so we can have everything nailed down before we send you a final draft."

"Why don't you just email me the current draft?" asked Kane. "I can go over it and—"

"Ed, we want it to be as perfect as possible before you get it. Let's keep going over it."

Kane shook his head, confused. Why wouldn't Hayworth want to go over stuff on the phone? But he concentrated, as Hayworth launched into a long recitation of lab equipment, budget, fund transfer, and other details.

As Hayworth rattled on, Kane shifted uneasily on the cooler. Something didn't feel right. Hayworth was stalling for time. He got up and began to pace the small interior.

A faint click of the van's side door alerted him, and he gasped, realizing that he'd left it unlocked. He leaped for the door, but was too late. The door slid open to reveal a small man in a baseball cap and windbreaker, pulling a semiautomatic pistol out of a shoulder holster. He held the pistol close against his body, so passersby couldn't see it, his other hand grasping the door. Oddly he was smiling and nodding amiably, again for the benefit of a family passing by. But his words were anything but friendly.

"Sit down on your hands, or I will kill you," he said coldly. He climbed in and slid the door shut behind him, shutting out the sun's glare and the skin-shriveling heat.

Kane obeyed, sitting on the seat across from the door. "Who are you?" he asked. "What do you want?"

"Just a little bit of information that's in your head. Give me that, and we will be just fine."

"What information?"

"The name of the cloud service holding your data, your username, and your password."

Kane stared with shock at the phone he'd just been talking on. "You're from GloboChem! You work for Carson!"

"Just give me the—" the man stopped abruptly, staring out the van's windshield. A skinny young man with an unkempt mane of greasy hair had just appeared, squinting through the van's windshield, shading his eyes against the desert sun. With his other hand, Leno Beppo pulled out a pistol.

"What the hell!" breathed the man in the baseball cap, moving forward to get a better look at the interloper. Kane took advantage of the distraction to pull two plastic tubes from his right sleeve, and a control button from his left, hiding it in his palm. He was thankful that he had been planning to do another field trial of concentrated gustatene at a nearby hamburger joint.

"Let's continue this conversation elsewhere," said the man in the jacket. He retreated into the back of the van, keeping his pistol leveled at Kane. "When I tell you, get into the driver's seat, start the engine, and take off."

"But the van is hooked up to—"

"Do it!" whispered the man. "Otherwise, you get a bullet!" He watched the greasy-haired man move around to the side of the van, then commanded, "Okay, *now!*"

Kane moved forward, slipping himself into the driver's seat and turning the key to start the van. But before he could drop it into gear, the passenger-side door opened, and the skinny young man leaped in. He held his pistol on Kane.

"Hey, dude, I'm Beppo, and I'm here to—" he began, but froze when he felt a gun jammed against the back of his neck.

"We have a little problem here," said the baseball-capped man. "Or rather, you have a little problem."

"Yeah. . . uh. . . listen, dude—" began Beppo, but the baseball-capped man interrupted him.

"Give me the gun. Come in the back."

"Yeah, sure, dude, yeah." Beppo handed over the gun and climbed into the back of the van, as the baseball-capped man kept space between them.

He said, "We'll take a little ride to a quiet place, and—"

But Kane abruptly pivoted in the seat and doused him in the face with spray from the nozzles, quickly swinging his aim around to soak Beppo.

"Hey, man, what the hell!" exclaimed Beppo, sputtering and spitting the liquid from his mouth. But then he stopped, went silent, and smacked his lips, as a glazed look rose on his face. The baseball-capped man had also become frozen, glassy eyed.

Kane flipped a switch on a small box attached to a gas can behind the passenger seat. An indicator light on the box began to blink, as he leaped from the van's driver-side door into the blinding sunlight and sprinted away through the sprawling RV park through its rows of motor homes, travel trailers, and vans.

Behind him in the van rose an animalistic chorus of guttural grunts and moans. The vehicle began to rock back and forth with the gyrations of struggling bodies within.

Kane zigged and zagged wildly among the rows of campers, sprinting through a picnic area and playground to the shocked exclamations of parents of the children there. Running at top speed, he glanced back to see if he was being followed. He ran through the park gates and onto the highway outside.

He was slammed by a speeding RV, his rag-doll-limp body vaulted through the air impacting the asphalt pavement and rolling four times before coming to rest.

***

Two black SUVs carrying Lou, Chun, and four other agents sped up to the stucco gates of the Desert Oasis RV Park. The lead vehicle jerked to a halt in front of Kane's body splayed on the baking asphalt, blood running from his mouth and nose, clotting instantly in the sun. His head was cocked at an unnatural angle, his eyes closed. A crowd had gathered around him. The agents leaped out, moved the crowd back, and Chun bent over Kane's inert form.

"That's him," said Chun. "That's Kane." She bent down on the road and felt his pulse. "He's alive, but barely."

"Jesus, God, I'm so sorry!" declared the portly, balding RV driver slumping against his motor home. "He just ran out in front of me. I couldn't. . ." He waved his hands in frustration, shaking his head in disbelief.

But Chun wasn't listening, calling an ambulance.

"What went on here?" asked Lou of the people.

80

"He was running away from somebody when he came through," said a leathery-skinned, middle-aged woman. "I'm the manager. A couple of guys were at his camper. They're still in there. Something weird is going on. Fighting."

Chun, Lou and two agents left others to tend to Kane, following the manager's directions, running down the asphalt drive past the vehicles. Reaching space B450, they found the white van rocking back and forth, grunts and growls emanating from within. Chun and the agents drew their pistols, and one agent wrenched open the side door.

"*Mother Francis!*" exclaimed Lou.

Two men locked in bloody embrace erupted from the van and rolled onto the pavement, grunting and straining, each trying to bite chunks of the other's flesh while holding off the other. Their expression blank, their eyes wild and glassy, they were oblivious to the blood streaming from their wounds.

"We've got to separate them!" exclaimed Chun to the agents. One raised his hand in refusal and shook his head, and the other did the same, declaring, "Not without gloves and masks. We don't know what the hell's got into them." Meanwhile, people from neighboring vehicles began to gather, and the agents diverted themselves by moving them back.

"Stop it!" commanded Chun. "Hands up!" But the men continued their mad combat.

A gush of water suddenly drenched them, and Lou moved forward holding a hose. She directed the water at their faces, causing them to flinch, sputter, and shake their heads, spitting water from their mouths.

"I think I figured it out," said Lou, who continued to play the stream over the men. "He sprayed them with the stuff, the food additive. Each decided the other one would be tasty because he had the stuff on him. So they started lunchin' on each other."

"Oh, dear God, they went cannibalistic." breathed Chun, watching the drenched men begin to groan and slump away from one another as they came to their senses.

A loud beeping arose from within the van, but Lou didn't notice it, busy hosing down the bleeding men.

"That's not good," declared Chun. "The beeping."

"What do you mean?"

"That's a warning! Help me pull these guys away!" she commanded the two agents. They dragged the struggling men away from the van just as a ball of flame burst from its open door, its furnace-like heat competing with that of the scorching day.

Lou immediately turned the hose on the burning van with little effect on the billowing flames.

"Hope to hell that Kane guy doesn't kick off," she said. "Lord knows what else he's been up to."

Chapter 5

"The stuff's heat labile," said Lou disgustedly, leaning against the wall of the hospital room, regarding the comatose form of Edwin Kane lying in the hospital bed. His skull was swathed in bandages. A clear tube ran from his head to a bag hung beside the bed, reddish liquid flowing inside. His right wrist was connected to an intravenous drip; and a respirator tube was taped to his face. His left wrist was handcuffed to the bed.

"And heat labile means. . . ?" asked Chun. She stood beside Lou, as they watched the monitor trace a steady jagged line across its screen. It had gone flat once already, triggering a rush of doctors and nurses and a jolt of electricity into Kane's chest to revive him.

"Whatever chemical was in the food samples, and the sand from the crime scene, and his spray gadget. . . it all turned to crap. . . uh. . . junk."

"But his spray worked on those guys. There was active chemical in the reservoirs he had on him."

"Yeah, but when he was laying on that hot road, the bags warmed up, degraded. Fu—. . . *fugacious* heat!"

"Fugacious is not a real word. You made it up."

"Naw, that's a real word. I only fake-cuss real words."

The neurosurgeon appeared at the door in his light blue scrubs, his surgical mask dangling around his neck. He paid little attention to the expressionless black-suited FBI agents flanking the door.

"Okay, now," he said with a tired sigh. "The craniotomy went fine. His brain is still swollen of course, but the bone flap we removed will give it room until the edema subsides. And we did a ventriculostomy. That's the tube that's draining cerebrospinal fluid from his skull. And he's on medication to help remove water from the brain."

"When can he talk to us?" asked Chun.

The surgeon shook his head slowly. "Not sure. Maybe soon, maybe never. We do know there was not much brain bleed, so that's good."

"Give us a time," said Lou. "We really need to talk to him. This guy has made some drugs we need to find. We don't know if he's got other drugs out there, or partners, or whatever. One person is already dead, and we've got some bad wounded."

"Days probably, maybe a week," said the neurosurgeon. "Best I can estimate."

"Let's go talk to those two clowns from the van," said Chun. "They've recovered from their bloody tussle."

"Who are they?"

"Couple of lowlifes. One's a street-level drug dealer, a Leno Beppo. The other is some kind of freelance thug, Karl Pratt. They've got lawyers, who just appeared out of nowhere, so we won't get much. And they really didn't commit any kind of crime that we can prove. Maybe assault, but neither said they want to press charges against the other."

The two headed down the hall past a nurse carrying a medication tray and a dietician pushing a meal cart. They passed a slim, balding man in a white coat with a stethoscope slung around his neck. He eyed the two agents warily. Beside him walked an orderly in gray scrubs and a cap covering a mop of black hair. He was a hulking man with a bushy black mustache and one arm encircled with a snake tattoo.

***

"No, no, no," whispered Nonny to himself, as he stood at the stainless-steel counter in the kitchen of Johanna's restaurant. He announced, "The marinade needs a different salt." He took another bite of the duck breast. "Himalayan Pink. Yes, use that."

He was testing a new dish for the restaurant—a concasse of steamed oysters, green and blue lobsters, caviar with smoked sabayon sauce, and spice-marinated duck breast.

"Yes, Chef," responded Abadi, taking notes. Surrounding them were Johanna's other chefs, watching the process intently. Some took notes of their own, thrilled at being able to witness Chef Nonny's legendary culinary inventive process.

"About the caviar," continued Nonny. "Try the Ossetra. That will add an extra note of nuttiness. Tell the purveyor we want caviar harvested in spring. It is butterier. The fish are feeding then from more insect larvae."

"Yes, Chef," said Abadi, taking more notes, smiling and shaking his head in awe. "And the presentation, Chef?"

Nonny regarded the dish intently for a full two minutes. He rearranged the components. "Duck breast in the center. Good. Lobster surrounding the . . ." His voice trailed off as he continued. He took up a ruler, measuring the thickness of the slices of duck breast. "Four millimeters," he said. "Make it seven. That will bring out more flavor note." He used a spoon to scoop a dollop of caviar onto the top of the lobster. "Between fifty-three and sixty-five pearls of caviar," he instructed. Using tweezers, he deposited a tiny bit of gold foil on top of the caviar, adjusting it until it curled delicately up from the surface.

Finally, he took up a small gravy boat, drizzling a precise pattern of velvety ivory sauce onto the white China plate. "Now," he said, the faintest smile of satisfaction appearing on his face. Abadi took a photo of the dish.

Without looking at the surrounding chefs, he intoned "You reach for perfection. But if you think you have achieved it, there is something wrong."

Abadi's phone signaled a call, and he answered. "Chef, the creature has been captured. He is in hospital."

Nonny stood up abruptly, his expression clouding with anger, and the crowd parted to give him room. Without a word, he strode toward the kitchen and the back exit, still wearing his white smock. Abadi followed, snatching up Nonny's sports jacket, to try to get him to change in the limousine.

***

Two medical alarms beeped urgently in syncopation from down the hall of the hospital trauma wing, as Chun and Lou emerged from the elevators. Two crash teams rushed past in rapid succession, hauling their carts, swerving into adjacent rooms.

Chun and Lou sprinted after them, pausing at one door, where a team had just applied defibrillator paddles to the skinny, pale chest of Leno Beppo. He jerked with the electrical jolt, the EKG trace spiking. Then, it settled into a featureless line.

Chun rushed to the next room, where the lead physician was already pronouncing a time of death over the body of Karl Pratt.

"This couldn't be coincidence!" exclaimed Chun. *"Somebody got them!"*

"That means somebody is here!" exclaimed Lou. "They might go after Kane!"

Chun drew her pistol and, holding it aloft, raced down the hall, followed by Lou. Not waiting for the elevator, she bounded up the stairs and onto the floor where Kane's room was. As she ran, she tried to raise the two agents on her radio, but got no answer. Lou followed, and they stopped short to see Abadi standing outside Kane's room. He beckoned urgently to them.

"He has gone after them!" declared Abadi.

"Who?" asked Chun.

"Nonny! We found out the creature Kane was here, but when we got here, nurse says a doctor and an orderly took him to get scan of the CAT. Your agents went, too. So, Nonny follow. I stay here to tell you. But nurse says she never had seen the doctor or orderly before."

The three of them raced back to the stairwell and down to the basement radiology center. There, they found the two agents sprawled on the floor, doctors and nurses bent over them.

"*Are they dead?*" asked Chun.

"Unconscious," answered one of the doctors. "The two men with the patient got them with tasers." He turned back to the two agents, who were beginning to stir, moaning.

"Where's the patient?"

The doctor pointed down the hall to double doors at the end.

Chun, Lou, and Abadi ran down the hall and burst through the doors onto a loading dock to find Nonny standing outside, peering down the road, still wearing his white chef smock.

"They are in an ambulance!" he shouted, as his stretch limousine pulled up. "I am following!" He leaped in, and the others barely had time to follow before the limousine lurched forward, swerving and accelerating ponderously down the hospital drive and onto the main road.

Ahead, they could see an ambulance turn on its flashers and careen into a right turn. Chun took up her phone to call in an alert to the police.

"Faster!" urged Nonny to the driver, a dumpy middle-aged man with a fringe of hair ringing a bald scalp. Chewing a wad of gum nervously, he leaned forward over the wheel, as if trying to urge the massive car to go faster.

"We can't possibly keep up," declared Lou. "They're going to get away."

Fortunately, though, the ambulance was blocked temporarily by a bus lumbering through the intersection ahead. The limousine surged forward to draw abreast of it, as the ambulance surged forward, its siren blaring to life.

"We don't need to keep up," said Chun. She leaned forward and commanded the driver, "Give me your gum."

"Lady, you that nervous?" asked the surprised driver. "I got new gum."

"I need it chewed," said Chun. "Give it to me."

The driver complied, depositing a wad of chewed gum in Chun's outstretched hand.

"Get as close to the ambulance as possible and hold steady," Chun instructed.

As the two vehicles sped side-by-side down the street, Chun lowered the back left window of the limousine and drew her pistol. She extended the pistol and loosed a single shot that shattered the right-hand mirror of the ambulance, which swerved wildly.

"He can't see us now. Steady!" commanded Chun, motioning for Lou to hold her legs as she extended her small body far out the window. Reaching out, she slammed her phone against the side of the ambulance, the gum holding it in place. Lou barely managed to haul her back in as the ambulance lurched to the right, sideswiping the car with a metallic screech.

"Okay," declared Lou. "Let's not do that again. I thought I might be hauling back just your lower bloody half."

Chun shrugged. "Yeah, not exactly a standard tactic. Give me your phone." Lou handed over her phone, and Chun punched in commands and began to scrutinize the screen. After a long moment, she said, "I've installed an app that lets it track my phone. . . . *Got 'em!*" she declared as the ambulance accelerated away into the distance. "They're headed for the Strip." She called in the ambulance's position to the police. "They won't get far."

Nonny, sitting in the front seat, eyebrows lowered, urged the harried driver on, as the car ponderously careened through the streets of Las Vegas, its sidewalks crowded with startled tourists. A group of young men cursed the limousine as it nearly hit them in a crosswalk, leaping back and pitching their beer cups at it.

Chun issued terse directions, finally declaring, "Signal's gone, but I see where. It's at a casino parking garage just off the Strip. On Fauci Boulevard."

She directed the driver to the multi-story garage, as police cars hurtled up to its entrance. The limousine eased into the garage entrance, followed by the police cruisers, as a line of cars and several trucks exited. The limousine and police cruisers, their lights flashing, careened up the garage ramp, floor after floor, until the ambulance came into sight on the third floor.

Chun motioned for the others to stay in the car, as she leaped out, pulling out her badge and displaying it to the police, who had exited their cars, guns drawn. They ringed the ambulance, warily approaching it, but Nonny was already stalking toward it, reaching it before them.

"Damnit, Chef!" scolded Abadi, but Nonny had already thrown open the back doors of the ambulance, glaring inside.

Chun shoved him aside leveling her pistol at the interior.

The ambulance was empty.

***

The white box truck with the sign "Desert Sun Fine Furnishings" on the side backed slowly up to the loading dock of a windowless cinder block warehouse. The anonymous structure was tucked into an isolated desert arroyo along with a few other warehouses far outside the city. An hour before, the same truck had eased out of the casino parking garage and driven with great care to the warehouse, so as not to jostle the precious cargo inside.

Oskar Dunst and Diana Vodkonen waited at the loading dock, their eyes hidden behind sunglasses, their expressions impassive. Despite the blistering heat, he was dressed in a blazer and slacks, and she wore a rose silk pantsuit.

The door of the truck slid up to reveal the massive Mutante still in hospital orderly garb. Beside him, leaning over the hospital bed within, was the slim balding man in a white coat with a stethoscope slung around his neck. The bed held the inert, draped figure of Edwin Kane, a breathing tube down his throat, an intravenous drip attached to the back of his hand.

"Did he make the journey safely, doctor?" asked Dunst quietly.

"Yes," said neurosurgeon Axel Bargman. "His signs are good, although of course, he is still in critical condition."

"I am sure you will do an excellent job of bringing him back to health," said Dunst. "He is an incredibly valuable asset. The first installment of your fee has been deposited, as agreed."

"And the equipment?" asked Bargman.

"All in place. And please let Mutante know of any additional needs."

Two male nurses emerged from the building, and together with Bargman, slowly wheeled the hospital bed inside. Mutante stayed behind, watching them leave.

"You will let us know of his progress," Dunst told him. "And ensure that the doctor attempts no communication that would give away their location. Should there be. . ." He did not finish the sentence. Mutante, his face an impassive mask, nodded his understanding.

Chapter 6

Edwin Kane felt engulfed in a mottled grayness, before he began to slowly emerge into consciousness. The thick cloud began to clear, penetrated by a vague awareness of light, of sound, of a voice. He felt a dull ache in his head, and an unsettling contradictory sensation of constriction in his throat, but of air flushing his lungs.

"You are okay, Edwin," said a gentle female voice through the dissipating fog. "You are safe. You are fine."

Kane kept his eyes closed, trying to focus his thoughts, to remember something . . . anything. He finally opened them to find himself looking up at fluorescent lights. He felt a floating mellowness, and he let it buoy him.

"Edwin, can you hear me?" asked the voice. "Relax. You are fine. Dr. Bargman is going to remove your breathing tube."

Kane gagged and choked as he felt the constriction sliding from his throat. He breathed in and sighed out.

"Good," said a male voice. "You're doing fine, Doctor Kane. Now, let's check your signs." Kane felt a cool stethoscope on his chest.

"Where . . . ?" he managed to choke out hoarsely.

"You're in a private facility we set up for you," said the female voice. "I'm Diana. We're taking good care of you."

He opened his eyes to see two figures—one a smiling, fine-featured woman with long dark hair pulled back in a ponytail; the other a slim man in blue hospital scrubs.

"Where. . . am I?" Now he managed to complete the question.

"What do you remember?" asked the woman. The doctor finished his examination, patted Kane on the arm and left.

"Uh . . . nothing . . . *wait* . . . I was in my van."

"Yes, you were. You were trying to avoid the police. A man came from your company. He tried to kill you. The police wanted to take you into custody." She held up a pair of handcuffs. "They handcuffed you to your hospital bed. We got you out. You are free."

"What happened to me? Why was I in the hospital?"

"You were hit by an RV. You were in bad shape. But we got the best possible care for you, and you will be all right."

Kane lay still and quiet for a long moment, trying to gather his vague thoughts into some semblance of coherence. "Why are you helping me?"

"We believe in you, Edwin. We want you to continue your research. We want to provide everything you need to continue your research. You want that, don't you?"

"The company . . ." He started to say, then paused, trying to remember what the company had promised. "They're going to help me."

"No, they aren't. They sent somebody to get your information. . . or to kill you."

"They did? What happened?"

"He won't be a danger to you anymore. Nobody will." Diana stood, leaned over and lightly kissed his cheek. He could smell the delicious aroma of her perfume. "You just get better," she whispered. "There are nurses here who will take care of you, get anything you want. When you are well enough, you can set up your new laboratory. We will get you any equipment you need. Now you just sleep."

And Kane did, allowing himself to float on the softness of drugs, sinking into slumber.

***

"Well?" asked Dunst, looking up from his tablet computer. He sat in a wing chair that had been placed outside the newly constructed medical enclosure that held Edwin Kane. Arrayed around the walled-off enclosure in the warehouse was an MRI scanner and other assorted medical equipment, as well as a kitchen area with stove, refrigerator, and microwave oven. In the kitchen, the hulking bodyguard Mutante was making a cappuccino using a Victoria Arduino espresso machine brought in for the day.

Diana replied, "He remembered nothing of the events at the campground, as the doctor predicted with head-injury patients. Retrograde amnesia."

"Ah, then we can fill that empty head. And you, dear, are just the one to do that. You are the perfect liar." He took the small cup of cappuccino from Mutante, who assumed a position that gave him an optimal view of the warehouse door.

"I want to wait a few days before introducing you to him," said Diana. "Gain his confidence a bit more. You are rather imposing."

Dunst smiled and ducked his head in mock modesty. "Ah, but I can be charming."

"As in Frankfurt? As I recall there were no survivors."

"No, but until they died they were charmed."

Dr. Bargman appeared from the other side of the medical enclosure, now dressed in a polo shirt and slacks.

"Well, Axel, what's his prognosis?" asked Dunst.

"He's mending. Brain swelling is down. We'll do a scan soon and see how well—"

Dunst interrupted. "Axel, I am more interested in whether this memory loss is permanent, and how quickly he will be fully functional. I want his lab up and running. I want him to give us data to enable manufacture of his potentially very lucrative drug. I want him to improve it."

"Of course, of course. I'll run some tests to see whether his memory loss continues, and how much cognitive function he has retained. I'll bring him along as quickly as possible."

"And when he is out of his bed and ready to work, you will receive the second installment of your fee."

"Certainly, I understand."

"Doctor, in the past, you have always understood very well. Let us hope that continues into the future." Dunst glanced briefly at Mutante, whose subtle return nod signaled that he understood the import of the comment. Dunst then rose from the chair, straightened his jacket and started with Diana across the empty expanse of the warehouse. Preceded by Mutante, they stepped out the door into the glare of the desert sun.

***

"Leafy, that was quite a stunt in the limo," said Lou grinning, as they gathered in the conference room of the FBI division office. "I guess even tight-asses take chances."

"When appropriate," said Chun coolly, peeling the gum off her phone. "But it didn't get us Kane or his kidnappers." She turned to Nonny, who sat at the conference table staring straight ahead. "And it didn't particularly help that you rushed the ambulance. You could have been killed."

Abadi chimed in, standing behind Nonny. "Well, if it weren't for Chef, you would have never even seen the ambulance. I told you we would be useful."

"I'm on the verge of kicking you guys out," said Chun.

Lou raised her hands in a placating gesture. "Now, we kids just hate it when you grownups fight. What do you think they'll do with Kane?"

"Depends on who has him," said Chun. "At this point, we haven't got a clue. He could well be dead, although they would have killed him right in the hospital if that was their aim."

Sitting farther down the table, Tate uttered a triumphant "Ha!" holding up his tablet computer. "We rushed the prints from the ambulance. There were dozens, as you might imagine, but we concentrated on those that were on the medical equipment that keeps

Kane going. One set of prints didn't match any staff!" He slid the tablet down to Chun, who examined it and smiled. "Okay, let's start running them through IAFIS."

"What's that?" asked Abadi.

"Integrated Automated Fingerprint Identification System," answered Chun. She turned to Tate. "You know what? Let's run them through Interpol, as well. You never know. Whoever it was might be an import."

Tate took the tablet computer and sent a message to the FBI lab. He also casually set his phone on the conference room table. The others didn't notice that he had left the line open.

Chapter 7

Kane slumped in the wheelchair, trying to focus on the laptop. But his head still ached dully with any mental exertion, so he gave it up, closing it. One of the male nurses served him the latte he had requested, and he took a sip and looked out over the empty warehouse. It was a fortress of cinderblock, the overhead lights illuminating an expanse of concrete floor, empty but filled with possibility. But at what cost? What would he have to give these people who had saved him? Now, he would find out.

"You look much better, my friend," said Dunst, who had just arrived with Diana.

"Still foggy," he answered wanly.

"I hope not too foggy to talk a bit. Okay?"

"Sure," Kane touched his bandaged head tentatively, as if the act would give him some indication of the status of his bruised brain.

Dunst sat in a chair across from Kane, leaning forward. "Diana, I believe, has raised the issue of our offer?"

"I know who you are," said Kane coldly. "I searched for your name."

"Indeed, I wanted you to do that, which is why I gave you the laptop and internet access. I want us to be honest with one another, yes?"

"You are a drug dealer."

"I am. And you sir, are the creator of one of the most revolutionary drugs ever developed. And for that, you have been persecuted. . . your life threatened. . . arrested."

96

Diana sat down in a chair next to Kane and took his hand. "You have been getting better under our care. Dr. Bargman is one of the world's best neurosurgeons. Our objective, Edwin, is precisely the same as yours. We want to see your work gain great success, and we want to see your drug in wide use."

"You mean you want to sell it to people who want to use it for bad purposes."

"Well, not really," said Diana. "Just to enhance their foods. And isn't that what restaurants and food companies do, anyway? On the other hand, I'm sure you are aware of the good your drug could do . . . curing wasting diseases, giving appetite to cancer patients, advancing veganism. . . since it would render healthy foods far more appetizing. We want to help you develop your drug for those purposes."

Dunst sat back and folded his hands. "And the fact remains, Doctor Kane, that we are your only route to continuing your work. We all have an interest in seeing it advance."

Kane placed his hands on the laptop, as if it would impart some kind of wisdom. "I do want to continue my work. I have ideas."

"We're sure you do," said Dunst. "We know that the current drug is . . . how do you say . . . heat labile? And—"

"I need to improve my gustatory mathematical model," interrupted Kane, his voice stronger with the prospect of continuing his work. He looked over at Diana, smiling, and placing his hand over hers. He took a deep breath and remained silent. Dunst and Diana let the silence settle, the only sounds being the echoes of faint noises from elsewhere in the vast space. Finally, Kane said, "Okay, I will do this. I will make a list of equipment I will need."

"Certainly, as you wish," said Dunst. "Cost will be no object. And, to be clear, we wish you to design your research lab, but also a production facility for your current chemical."

"I will. But it will be complicated. The molecules of the two binary components are not simple."

"Which is why we are so confident that they will not be duplicated by lesser producers. Now, Edwin, I do need assurance that the investment will be worth it."

Kane smiled faintly. "It will. The production of gustatene will be high quality and substantial. And I have improvements in mind. To design a whole new compound. . . gustatene X. I call it GX."

"And what would that be like?" asked Dunst.

"A single component. Very stable. Far more potent," said Kane.

Diana smiled and patted Kane's hand in encouragement.

***

"Dr. Bargman has done a fine job of bringing Doctor Kane along," said Dunst, as they settled back in the limousine for the trip back to Las Vegas. He stared pensively out the tinted window as the flat desert landscape slid smoothly past.

"Yes, he has," said Diana, crossing her long legs and pouring Kona Nigari mineral water into a crystal glass. "He is a very talented physician."

Dunst shook his head, his expression somber. "It is so very unfortunate that we heard through Tate that his fingerprints were on equipment in the ambulance. He really should have worn gloves."

"You have decided?"

"He will die in a car accident in Prague. Probably in a week or so."

"So sad," said Diana, taking a sip of water. "We will send flowers."

With a wry smile, Dunst patted Diana's knee. "My dear, you are a very considerate person . . . for a sociopath."

***

"This is our chance!" exclaimed Brigham Baltazar, stalking back and forth in the hotel suite, his fists punching the air. "This is our chance to strike a blow *for* the planet, to strike a blow *against* the murder of hundreds of thousands. . . of *millions*. . . of defenseless animals!"

The room was filled with the enthusiastic clamor of the ten Veganite activists.

"*We're with you!*" declared a paunchy, professorial type. He wore a jacket and slightly soiled tie and had a neatly trimmed beard and round glasses.

"*Whatever it takes!*" said a gaunt, long-haired man, who wore a white linen suit and sandals.

"*Down with Big Meat!*" muttered a rotund, florid-faced woman with a pug nose and a bowl-haircut, who wore a shapeless print dress.

Baltazar gestured at the video showing the maddened hunger gripping the diners at the Gourffet.

"This will be our weapon! This will be our sword to strike at the very heart of Big Meat! We will use this drug to expose the vicious addiction to animal flesh promoted by an industry that poisons the air, the water, our bodies, and our very souls! It is an industry that is causing the rise in greenhouse gases in the atmosphere that will bring about the end of the human race."

Baltazar waited for the ensuing enthusiastic chatter to subside. He smiled benignly and spoke almost in a whisper, bringing a silence as his acolytes strained to hear the words of their mesmerizing leader.

"Indeed, I have already made contact with an operative who can supply us with this remarkable substance." He turned to his lieutenant, Teo, saying, "Make the call."

Teo punched a number into his phone and texted "Ready for our meeting."

The immediate knock on the door brought surprised laughter, but Baltazar raised his hand, smiling. "I'm sure that's not him. We need sustenance, so I've ordered a buffet brought in."

He opened the door, and waiters wheeled in a line of carts containing an array of vegetables and soups, along with drinks, dishes, and utensils. The waiters left, and the people crowded around, filling their plates.

They were just finishing their meal, when another knock on the door brought Teo to his feet. He opened the door to reveal a husky, leather-jacketed man in a stained beige New Orleans Saints baseball cap. His long hair jutted from beneath the hat, and his whisker-stubbled, round face held a dead-pan expression as he stared at Teo.

"Leno?" asked Teo.

"Nah, I'm Boudreaux."

"Leno was the contact I got from the cook at the restaurant."

"Yeah, well, Leno, he no longer with the organization," said the man with a lilting Cajun accent. "He retired."

"Well, you're not Leno, so I'm not sure—"

"Hell, I don't know you neither. My boss, he just says come here and show you what we got. The food drug thing." He turned to leave, but Teo raised his hands in agreement.

"Yeah, okay, come in."

The drug dealer entered, scanning the room warily. "You tol' my boss you got restaurants? Where? What kind food?"

"In California," said Teo. "This is our CEO, Malcom Baker."

Baltazar stood and shook hands with the thug. "We're modified American cuisine. A mix of popular dishes. We understand you can make them much more popular. These are some of my managers." The group only nodded, not rising from their seats.

Baltazar continued, "We understand your boss is Mr. Dunst."

Boudreaux scowled. "We don't use my boss's name. You don't say his name again, okay?" His scowl quickly disappeared, replaced by a grin. "So, what's your chain? I wanna know not to eat there." Boudreaux laughed, but the others did not. "Hey, jus' jokin'. I see you got food. I could use a meal while we talk." He went to the buffet, his back to them, moving its length and filling a plate. He took some time in the process, returning to sit on one of the empty chairs. "Too bad,

100

you got no gumbo, no étouffée. But the veggies look good, all right," he said as he ate.

"So, Mr. Boudreaux, can you give us what we want?" asked Baltazar.

"Yeah, we got production underway for the whatdyacallit . . . gustatene."

"That's the name? How much can you provide?"

"All you want, for a price."

"We want enough for our very large . . . chain of restaurants," said Baltazar.

"Yeah, we can give you gallons of the stuff. Twenty grand a gallon."

"That's incredibly expensive."

"Yeah, well, you want it, you pay. And you can dilute the hell out of it. You'll make a lot of money 'cause people will buy more food."

The man in the white linen suit stood up, whispered into Baltazar's ear, and moved to the buffet. He put some salad on his plate and moved on to add helpings of other dishes.

"Well, we want to make sure it works first," said Baltazar, nodding at the man in the linen suit.

"Yeah, I gotcha," said Boudreaux. "So, I brought a sample."

"Okay, let's have it."

"Yeah, just wait a second." Boudreaux sat for a long moment, with an occasional glance at the buffet.

The man in the white linen suit still stood at the buffet, not moving. Abruptly, he began making a low grunting noise, bending over and stuffing random globs of the salads, fruits, and vegetables into his mouth.

"I think he gonna need a little help," said Boudreaux, smiling wryly.

Teo and two others leaped up and grabbed the man in the white linen suit, spinning him around. They could barely contain his frantic struggle to get at the food. His front was stained red with the juice of tomatoes and raspberries, his mouth stuffed full, his eyes glassy.

"Jesus, what did you do to him!" demanded Teo from the buffet.

"See? The stuff works real good," said Boudreaux. "Of course, I used it full strength. Like I said, you'd want to dilute hell out of it for your restaurants. But you see it works."

"Indeed, it does," replied Baltazar, who had remained sitting in his chair, a faint smile on his face. "We'll take fifty gallons."

"*C'est bon*," said Boudreaux putting down his plate and pulling out his cell phone. "I give you the number of the account where you can deposit the money. It's two chemicals you mix together and just spray on cold foods. Only cold foods. And you keep the chemicals cold, okay?"

"And him?" asked Baltazar, gesturing at the struggling man.

"He be okay in maybe half an hour. Tie him down till then." Boudreaux left as the man in the white linen suit continued to struggle weakly toward the buffet.

From the couch, the paunchy, professorial type, raised his hand timidly. "He said only cold food. Meat is hot. The drug won't work."

Baltazar smiled conspiratorially. "We don't spray it on the food. As Mr. Teo found out, at a local hospital they brought in two men who had attacked one another. They seem to have been sprayed with some kind of drug that made each. . . well. . . *delicious* to the other."

"Ahh, so," said the paunchy, professorial type, nodding and smiling in understanding.

***

Three black SUVs and one white limousine pulled up to the Gulfstream G650 jet. The gleaming white plane sat inside a hangar of the Las Vegas private airport, with Joseph and another GloboChem security guard flanking its steps.

From two of the SUVs emerged eight men. They were dressed variously in sports jackets, windbreakers, slacks, cargo pants, sneakers, and dress shoes. But all shared the same characteristic bulge at the ribs that told of shoulder holsters. They arrayed themselves at the hangar entrance, half facing outward, half inward. From the third SUV emerged Mutante, dressed in a blazer straining to contain his bulk. He walked to the plane's steps and opened his coat to the security guards to show he had no weapon. He mounted the steps, causing them to dip with his weight. After a moment, he emerged, nodding toward the white limousine.

From that limousine emerged Oskar Dunst and Diana Vodkonen, their eyes hidden behind sunglasses. Dunst wore black slacks and a sky-blue polo shirt; Diana's slim body was sheathed in dark blue pants and a white silk blouse. They entered the shade of the hangar and removed their sunglasses, climbing the steps and into the plane's cabin.

Greeting them was Gabriel McAndrews in a crisp, long-sleeved dress shirt and slacks, and Carson Hayworth in a gray suit.

McAndrews smiled and extended his hand, shaking both Dunst's and Vodkonen's hands. The two did not match his smile, staring at him as if he were an object of mere casual curiosity. When introduced, Hayworth merely ducked his head in deferential greeting. McAndrews offered them wine, which they accepted. They sat down in the cream-colored leather chairs of the jet's lounge.

"I understand we have a mutual acquaintance," said McAndrews.

"Let us dispense with the maneuvering," said Dunst. "We do have Doctor Kane. He is now working for us. He has been made to understand that you tried to kill him—"

"We did no such thing," interrupted McAndrews. "We were only trying to persuade him to share his research."

Now Dunst smiled. "Ah, I did not say it was the truth. I said he was made to understand. We are in a position to define the truth, since as you may know, victims of head injury lose memory of previous events."

Any hint of McAndrews' smile faded, replaced by a sour expression and a set jaw. "Why are we meeting?" he asked curtly.

"I can offer you an opportunity. We have begun making gustatene in considerable quantity. I am sure you will find it useful in your industry."

"We do not peddle drugs."

Dunst laughed derisively, and Diana answered. "Mr. McAndrews, you know very well we are in the same business. We both peddle addictive drugs. The only difference is your product is legal . . . and much more widespread."

"But you are killers. You murdered my operative in the hospital."

Dunst raised his wine glass in a toast. "The operative who was known by the police? The one who would readily give you up for a plea deal? You're welcome."

"Well, he was not a company person. I have deniability." McAndrews glanced coldly over at Hayworth, a silent caution that Hayworth was not to reveal what he had just heard. McAndrews continued. "So, what if I were to tell you I will tell the police what you have done? That you have kidnapped Kane and killed two people?"

"Well, that would be unfortunate. It would cause. . . let's see . . . seven more deaths, I believe."

"What do you mean?"

"You, of course. Your pilot, co-pilot, attendant, Mr. Hayworth who is now looking very frightened, and your two security men. My own pilot is waiting outside in the car. He's also a former British army paratrooper. He would fly your plane containing your bodies west, as if you were going to Los Angeles. He would put it on autopilot and bail out. And it would fly itself far out into the Pacific before running out of fuel and ditching. I believe the range of this aircraft is far enough to make it over the South Pacific."

McAndrews sat back in his chair, gripping its armrests for a long moment, his expression grim. He took a deep breath. "And if I agree not to report you?"

"That is no real guarantee," said Dunst.

Again, a long silence. "Then, I will give you one hundred million dollars for Kane's research data . . . obtained by whatever means you deem effective."

Taking a sip of wine, Diana said, "Ah, Mr. McAndrews, we know you are a businessman like us. You are in business to make a profit. That offer means that you expect to make much more from those data. No, we prefer to keep Doctor Kane with us and to enable his research. And to enable large-scale production of gustatene."

"So, what *is* your proposal?"

Dunst answered, "That we provide you with a sample of the two gustatene components. I suspect you have no idea what their structures are. The samples would enable your scientists under Mr. Hayworth to begin analysis. Perhaps to advance your own work."

Hayworth nodded emphatically at the prospect of having a sample, and at not being murdered.

"And in return?" asked McAndrews.

"You will invest in our enterprise. Twenty million dollars," said Dunst.

"*Bullshit!*" exclaimed McAndrews. "Why would I give you twenty million dollars?"

"Well, it ensures your safety, of course. And you know that Doctor Kane is a scientific genius. And even though the two-component gustatene is not terribly useful as a stable food additive, he is working toward a new compound that is."

McAndrews sat silently glaring at the pair. Then Dunst leaned forward, as if to prepare to leave. "Ah, well, there are other companies besides GloboChem."

"Just wait!" said McAndrews, waving his hands. "Just wait a second." Again, he pondered the two drug dealers in silence. Finally, he said, "Send me your private bank account number."

Diana poured herself another glass of wine and raised it in a toast.

Chapter 8

Kane shuffled gingerly, slowly, along the fifty-foot-long laboratory bench inspecting the intricate network of glass tubes, flasks, reaction vessels, distillation columns, and fractionating columns. The warehouse was suffused with the faint sweetish aroma of amines, esters, and other organic chemicals that were being piped from the many blue plastic barrels arrayed along one wall.

Following him walked one of the male nurses, ready to support him should he falter. Beside him walked one of his new assistants, a rotund, bearded, frizzy-headed young man in a lab coat. He had been brought in blindfolded, along with ten other technicians in SUVs.

"Good, fine, okay," Kane intoned, as he scrutinized one component after another. "Wait, look, this needs to be connected differently, and are you sure the water jacket has ice water, rather than tap?" he asked the assistant.

"Sure, of course, of course," said the assistant, rather obsequiously.

"Sorry, I forgot who you are," said Kane. He had been given the assistant's resume along with the others', and he knew that the assistant was an experienced chemical engineer who had worked in the drug industry. However, a drug conviction had made him unemployable until Dunst had offered him a highly lucrative job working on some mysterious project in the middle of the Nevada desert. All the engineers and scientists were experts whose prospects were tainted by various convictions for offenses ranging from the non-violent to murder.

Kane stopped to support himself against the lab bench. He was still woozy from the injury and the drugs. The male nurse stepped forward, but he waved him off.

"What is production, so far?" he asked the assistant.

The young man consulted his tablet computer. "Three hundred and twenty liters of compound alpha, two hundred and fifty of compound beta. So, this pilot run is getting good yield. We're ready to scale up to industrial production."

"Not with these compounds. I'm developing a more advanced one that I'll want to take to large-scale output."

"Y'know, we really need to know what the purpose of all of these compounds are, if we're to figure out whether any contaminants might impact biological activity," said the assistant.

"No, you don't," snapped Kane. "And there are to *be* no contaminants. You've got the analytical instruments to detect any."

With that, Kane continued across the expanse of the warehouse to his research area, his face registering pain, but his step quickening in anticipation. There, technicians were setting up the computers and analytical instruments he would need to further advance his work. He patted the tan case of the gas chromatography-mass spectrometry machine that was already being used to test the production runs. This was a premier, two-hundred-thousand-dollar instrument, one that he could never afford before. He nodded to the technician who ran it— another Ph.D. with a criminal record, armed robbery.

His energy spent, he motioned for the nurse to help him back to his hospital bed. He was met by Boudreaux, who had been a frequent, pesky visitor over the last week.

"Hey, you doin' okay?" asked Boudreaux in his Cajun accent. "Man, I got *beaucoup* customers for your stuff. *Laissez le bon temps rouler!*" Grinning, he followed Kane into the hospital room at the corner of the warehouse.

"Production is going okay," said Kane, climbing into bed. "You can take the containers in the cooler. You are keeping them refrigerated?"

"Yeah, sure, like you tell me over and *over.*"

"And you're making sure everybody has the dosing instructions?"

"For sure, *mon ami.* I give them the papers you made. They know they just have to use a little bitty bit. Don't want no crazy people like with those buffets."

"That was not my fault. It was when I was just starting field testing," said Kane defensively, laying back his head and closing his eyes.

"Yeah, I know. Now I got to get the supply to my boys. They're already getting steady customers!"

***

The drug runner—a fidgety young man in a dark windbreaker and bright blue sneakers—paced nervously back and forth at the loading dock of the Alta Calabria gourmet restaurant. A rotund chef in a white smock appeared at the door, peering warily around before emerging into the alley.

The runner shoved him against the wall. "Dude, when I say *eleven,* I mean *eleven*! Don't leave me hangin' out here with . . ." He held up the black satchel he was carrying.

"Well, we're in the middle of closing, so—"

"You got the cash?"

The chef pulled out a fat manila envelope and handed it over, in exchange for the satchel. "We'll need another shipment next week," he said.

"Fine, but you're watching the doses, right? My boss says you screw up and overdose, people will find out. . . like cops." The runner shook his head at the words that had just come out of his mouth. It was the first time in his career as a pusher he'd ever been told to warn customers about overdosing.

"Sure, of course, we're careful."

"And you're *only* mixin' and usin' it on cold stuff, right? You know it don't work on hot."

"Sure, sure, just get us another batch."

"You got it, dude." With that, the drug dealer faded into the darkness of the alley, heading for his car and the next delivery.

***

The line chefs at the exclusive Roche Noire bistro regarded the sous chef with puzzlement. He was still insisting on the rather suspicious practice of hovering over the plates, as they fashioned the restaurant's elegant, sculptured gourmet creations of poultry, beef, and seafood. He had been doing his hover for the past week.

As in previous nights, he insisted emphatically that each plate be drizzled, swooshed, splashed, or dotted with two of the many cold sauces and purees produced by the restaurant's saucier. Every plate had to be decorated with the bistro's special adaptations of Béchamel, Velouté, Espagnole, Bordelaise, Béarnaise, and Hollandaise—even some that did not warrant such addition.

When the sous chef had begun his eccentric practice, the restaurant's expeditor had objected. The sous chef was thwarting the expeditor's mission to speed the dishes as quickly as possible from the back of the house to the front. During the first nights, he had scolded the sous chef that he was slowing the progress of the plates to the diners.

But as the habit continued, the expeditor noticed that the diners were especially animated in praising the dishes. The cordial buzz in the richly paneled dining room seemed to become more animated.

And the wait staff was returning from clearing dishes with far more compliments to the chef.

And the diners exiting the restaurant were crowding around the front hostess podium clamoring for new reservations. It might not have been the added decorations of the sauces. But the expeditor decided not to question the success.

***

The dining couple chatted quietly about their planned yacht trip to the French Riviera, as they began their first course at Le Chic restaurant. The young woman, wearing a slinky, black Vince Camuto jumpsuit, smiled warmly at her husband, a slim middle-aged man with a gray pompadour. Showing perfect teeth, she delicately lifted the silver spoon containing the first sip of the cold vichyssoise to her lips. She tasted it.

Her almond eyes widened, and after a long lip-smacking, she uttered an un-epicurean, almost animalistic, grunt. She immediately gulped another spoonful, then another.

"*God, this is good!*" she blurted loudly through a full mouthful.

"Really?" asked her husband, his tone registering mild surprise at her unseemly emotion. He had ordered the cold gazpacho, and he took a spoonful. He, too, widened his eyes in surprise. "*Wow! This, too!*" He gulped spoonful after spoonful, spilling some on his burgundy silk shirt—the stain being relatively invisible given the matching colors of soup and fabric.

All over the restaurant arose similar exclamations, as the diners tasted the various cold soups and salads served that evening. Some diners requested follow-up bowls of the cold soups, all of which were new to the menu. Several, in fact, lifted the bowls to their lips, abandoning spoons in favor of direct gulping.

However, those who managed to wait until the main courses were similarly captivated by the cuisine. The barramundi fish, the Kobe beef, the squab—all with plates decorated with cold sauces—proved preternaturally delectable, drawing raves. A dowager who had been patronizing Le Chic for years insisted on being helped to the kitchen to hug the executive chef.

And the restaurant critic for the Western Dining website, who happened to be eating there that night, wrote a review declaring that Le Chic had entered "the absolute pinnacle of cuisine!"

***

Brigham Baltazar's hand trembled slightly as he ever-so-carefully poured the syrupy yellowish liquid from a quart-sized plastic bottle into the graduated cylinder. He wore a respirator, thick yellow gloves and a protective rubber apron. Then, just as carefully, he poured the measured liquid into a pint-sized bottle and handed it to Alex Teo, who was garbed the same. They were working in the bathroom of his hotel suite, crowded with the coolers full of bottles.

"Goddamnit, I wish the guy had let us know before he brought it how potent this stuff is," he grumped.

"Well, he's a drug dealer not a chemist. I wouldn't have trusted him, anyway." Teo filled the rest of the bottle with water, capped it, and shoved it with six other containers into the ice in a cooler. "Only seven to go," he told Baltazar.

Baltazar saw that his quart bottle was just about empty, so he refilled it from one of the gallon-sized containers embedded in ice in the bathtub. All had been delivered by Boudreaux, who had exited quickly after learning that the two Veganites planned to handle the two gustatene components in the hotel bathroom. He had declared, "Yeah, I know that guy killed himself eating dirt with that shit on it, so you guys have fun without me."

For the next hour, the two filled separate bottles with the two chemical components. Then, they packed them into insulated foam shipping boxes, along with ice packs.

Finally, shed of his protective gear, Baltazar opened his laptop to display a map of the United States showing fourteen blue dots in major cities. "I'm emailing everybody to tell them the packages are coming," he told Teo, who was attaching address labels to the fourteen boxes. "I'm telling them the action will take place noon our time on the 13th."

"Yeah, that'll give them time to suss out their targets . . . to figure out maximum impact time and ingress and egress." Teo smiled as he attached the last label. "Boy, it'll be quite a shit-show!"

Chapter 9

Chun handcuffed Nonny to the chair in the FBI conference room, just to be safe. "We wouldn't want our miner's canary to fly the coop if he got an overdose," she joked.

"More like a guinea pig," grumped Abadi, who had objected strenuously to the testing.

Nonny did not smile, concentrating on the thirty plastic food containers in the iced coolers on the table in front of him. But the others in the room—Chun, Lou, Tate, and Abadi—were concentrating just as intently on the renowned chef with "supertaster" taste buds and an encyclopedic knowledge of foods.

Nonny had volunteered, indeed insisted, that he test the food samples surreptitiously gathered from restaurants suspected of dosing their food with the gustatene compounds. For the past week, Abadi had been quizzing his fellow restaurateurs for information over drinks at various bars, coming home very drunk, but with scribbled lists of restaurants whose food had been attracting more praise than usual.

"I just don't understand," he complained. "Why don't you just raid these places? How is having Chef taste the foods help?"

But Nonny answered. "Proof is needed. I can tell when the ingredients don't justify the allure of the taste. Have faith, Daoud."

With that, he pulled the first container from the cooler, peeled off its top, and took up one of a box of plastic spoons. He dug into the fillet of Wagyu beef stuffed with peppercorn sauce, took a bite, and chewed thoughtfully.

"Beef was aged properly, sauce contains ten-year-old brandy . . ." his voice trailed off as he considered the complex mélange of flavors. Finally, he declared, "Not poisoned."

He proceeded through five more gourmet dishes, rinsing his mouth between each bite, declaring each "not poisoned."

Then, he came to a broiled fillet of halibut with truffled oysters and wild boar sausage. It was covered with a white sauce. He chewed reflectively. "Halibut was frozen. Truffles are old. Oysters were not fresh shucked. Sausage was second-rate. Taste is too good. *Poisoned!*" He exclaimed.

Chun checked the label for the restaurant name. "Alta Calabria. Bingo!" she exclaimed.

Over the next hour, Nonny continued his tasting, declaring five more restaurants—including Roche Noire and Le Chic—as "poisoned."

Then, he slumped over, whispering "Tired." He took a drink of water and slowly set the glass on the table.

"That's enough!" declared Abadi, moving to Nonny's side. "We are out of here." With that, he yanked impatiently on the handcuffs, signaling Chun to free Nonny, which she did.

"I understand," she said. "We've got enough places to search. And I think his declaration is enough to get us a warrant for the dealer Beppo's place." With that she instructed Tate to begin obtaining warrants and prepared to escort Abadi and Nonny out of the building.

But before she left, Lou took Chun aside. Throughout the testing, she had been scribbling chemical structures on a yellow pad, amassing a pile of loose pages. "Leafy, I think I know what chemical components would have to be used in making the stuff. I'll bet I can trace shipments, if you give me access to your system."

"Done," declared Chun as she left.

Tate walked toward his office, watching warily as Chun departed. When he was sure he was alone, he took out a burner cell phone, punching in a number. "You have some problems," he announced to Oskar Dunst.

***

Nonny sat silently staring into space as the limousine carrying Abadi and him inched along the traffic-choked Las Vegas Boulevard.

Abadi watched him with concern, wanting to pat him on the shoulder in reassurance, but knowing that Chef did not like to be touched. Soon, they would reach his house nestled against the mountains outside Las Vegas. There, Abadi could leave him to rest and prepare to oversee dinner at Johanna's. Actually, Abadi knew Chef would not rest. He would probably throw himself into developing one recipe or another for the restaurant or the Gourffet.

"They poisoned the food," Nonny finally said somberly. "They poisoned people."

"They will catch them . . . the FBI agents and the food agency person. They are very good." Then, Abadi smiled to himself. "The woman Lou, she is very nice, isn't she?"

Nonny paused for a full minute before replying. "She is a capable person. She knows the chemistry of foods."

"Actually, Chef, I am not talking about her knowledge. She is also quite attractive, is she not?"

"Yes," said Nonny simply.

"You have not dated since the model."

"No. She didn't eat food."

"Do you find the chemist attractive?"

"Yes."

"Do you think you might date her?"

Nonny was silent. Abadi knew that meant he was still deciding.

They pulled into his driveway and Abadi climbed out of his side of the limousine. At first, he failed to notice the black SUV that had eased slowly up behind them. He heard the limousine's other passenger door open and a loud grunt from Nonny's side of the car.

Peering through the car, he saw two men dragging a struggling Nonny away, shrouding his head in a hood.

"SONS OF BITCHES!" he bellowed hurdling the trunk of the car, slamming into one of the attackers, ripping him away from Nonny. Their driver had also leaped out, grabbing the other abductor, who punched him hard in the face, sending him slamming to the concrete, blood streaming from his nose. Abadi felt a massive arm encircle his neck from behind in a vice-like choke hold. Abadi could see that the arm had a snake tattoo, as he tore at the arm and slammed his elbows over and over into the rock-solid stomach muscle of his attacker. But then his consciousness faded.

***

"*Shi—*" Lou caught herself and started over. "*Shitake mushrooms!* I cannot *shucking* believe they would be that *shucking* stupid!" Grinning in triumph, she stood up from the computer in the FBI offices and thrust her fist in the air. She sat back down, punching in Chun's cell number and putting her on speaker.

Chun answered. "Hey. Nothing here. Beppo's apartment was scrubbed."

"Well, I've got something, for sure," chortled Lou. "They were dumb enough to order all their chemicals from a local distributor."

"Excellent work. Can you trace their destination?"

"Not directly." Lou scrolled through a list of chemical orders on the screen. "The invoices say they were all picked up by the customer. But I'll bet there are cameras at the company warehouse. I'll bet we can ID the truck and follow it with traffic cams."

"I'll get Tate on it." She paused, then uttered a curse that would have been off-limits for Lou. "I just got a text from Vegas PD. They had a report of a disturbance from a homeowner up in the hills. What's the chef's address?"

Lou recited it to her.

Again, Chun spat the curse. "The tip from a neighbor said that some people in an SUV just abducted two men from that address."

"They took them!" exclaimed Lou. *"The sons-of-bitches took them!"*

***

Before the smothering hood had been ripped from his head, Nonny had heard the dull sound of fists punching flesh, and the sounds of grunts that he believed were coming from Abadi. Then the breathy groan of air being expelled from lungs. The hood came off, and he found himself in a bare room, sitting in a metal armchair to which his wrists had been zip-tied. Standing in front of him was a hulking ratty-haired man in a t-shirt with a Hellrockers heavy metal band logo on it. The man was wiping blood from his scarred hands on a paper towel.

Nonny managed to twist his head around to see Abadi slumped on the floor, his eyes shut, his face bloodied, his hands zip-tied behind his back.

"Your man did not cooperate," said a voice, not from the thug standing before him, but coming from the speaker on a webcam sitting on a scarred metal table in front of him. The table also held a white sock that bulged at the toe, a semi-automatic pistol, and a butane kitchen torch.

"Who are you?" asked Nonny. "Why did you take us?"

A chuckle emanated from the speaker. "Well, because you are a man of taste. . . literally. You are helping out the FBI and the woman from the FDA. You are interfering with my business. You will stop it."

"I won't," said Nonny.

"Well, we can do more damage to your uncooperative man there." The thug picked up the sock and swung it back and forth, the bulge in the toe about the size of a billiard ball.

"That will not make a difference."

"Really?" The voice rose in pitch to register surprise. "Hmm. I think I believe you. You are a determined man. Even ruthless. How about this? I know about the truck that leaves your buffet each night. I know you're violating federal law. I could contact the authorities."

Nonny had been staring at the floor, but he transferred a steady gaze to the camera. He said nothing.

The voice continued: "And I know where the truck goes. And if I were to reveal its destination, many women would be put in danger. Some might even be killed."

"You would do that?"

"It would be a business decision."

"If you made that business decision, I would find you and kill you. That would not be a business decision."

"There is an outside chance you would be successful. But the women would still be dead."

Nonny stared silently at the camera before quietly answering. "If it means keeping the women safe, I will no longer cooperate with the FBI."

"Wise decision. But you know, I'm not sure I trust you. Perhaps there is a way to solve the problem of your exquisite ability to taste food permanently. Mr. Balicki, if you please."

The thug moved so that he was in the camera's field of view and nodded. He took up the kitchen torch and flicked it on, its pencil-thick blue flame hissing to life. He reached his huge hand out to grasp Nonny's face, wrenching his jaw open.

Chapter 10

"The two bodies were here when we escape the room," said Abadi. His voice was muffled by speaking through a swollen face as he regarded the bloody floor in the bare room where he and Nonny had been held. He surveyed the scene through one eye, the other swollen shut. "Looks like somebody drag this one out. Blood is smeared."

"Do you think he was alive?" asked Chun, carefully avoiding the smeared trail of blood leading out the door.

"Maybe not. When I wake up from being beaten, he is trying to burn Chef's mouth with torch. I kick him in side of leg, collapse his knee. His leg almost come off. Then, when he is on floor, I kick him in face. When I stop, he has no face." Abadi began to tremble, backing against the wall, leaning on it for support, his head down. Tears streamed down his face from his one open eye. "I kill him. I kill that man."

Lou put her arm around him, comforting him. "You did right, Daoud. You saved both of you," she said. Then, to Chun: "Can I take him now. He needs to recover."

"Just a few more questions. Daoud, what about others? What about the gun?"

"After guy I kick is laying still, I break plastic cuffs. . . ." Abadi rubbed the bandages covering the bloody welts on his wrists. ". . . I know there are others. . . two others on other side of door. So, I pick up gun, and I just start shooting through door. I hear a scream. When noise stop, I free Chef and open door. There is one body on floor, so

I had killed that man, too. But other guy must have run away. I hear the car leave, so I know we are safe. We go outside and look for phone."

Wearing latex gloves, Chun carefully unplugged the web cam, following its cord out the door and to a small table that had likely held a laptop computer. Nonny sat there, across the narrow hall on a folding chair, staring at the wall.

Lou emerged from the room, her arm still embracing Abadi. Nonny stood hesitantly, then approached Abadi and put his arms around him. Abadi chuckled.

"Hey, what's so funny?" asked Lou.

Still in Nonny's embrace, Abadi said, "Chef hates to touch people. He must like me."

Nonny backed away, a faint smile on his face. The smile faded as Chun emerged from the room, beckoning to three white-garbed, masked, capped lab technicians to take over.

"The man on the computer knew about the food tests I did on the restaurant samples," said Nonny quietly. "How did he know?"

"Leafy, you might have a leak," declared Lou.

"What did he say exactly?" asked Chun.

"He talked about me tasting food. He knew about Lou and the FDA."

Lou shook her head. "Well, we got to figure out where the leak is, that's for sure."

"And he knew about the truck, and the women, and that they could die."

"Nonny, what the hell are you talking about?" asked Lou.

"I will have to show you. I have been doing something illegal."

***

"Where is Balicki's body?" asked Dunst. He stood at the floor-to-ceiling windows of the condo, looking out over the glittering lights of the Las Vegas strip. The deep thrum of noise from the strip penetrated even the thick glass. He held a glass of red wine up to the light, contemplating its rich amethyst hue.

"In the desert," said Mutante. He limped forward a few steps from the entrance hallway into the living room, hindered by the bandage around his thigh that covered the bullet wound that Abadi had given him. A spot of blood had seeped from the bandage and through his pants.

"Balicki was stupid. Leaving the gun on the table. And the other one . . . Montegna?"

"He was wounded badly."

"How badly?"

"He is in the desert, too."

"Fine. And you? The doctor took care of you?"

"Yes. He says the bullet did not hit anything vital. The muscle will heal." Mutante said the last sentence with some emphasis. He knew it was important for him to remain fully functional and useful. Dunst and Diana had no use for those who weren't.

"There was no chance you were seen?"

"No cameras in the area. And when I went back to get Balicki's and Montegna's bodies, the chef and his man were gone. And, they hadn't had time to call the police."

"What happened to the chef?" asked Diana. "We only wanted him threatened, not injured. It would draw too much attention." She stood at the kitchen counter using a mother-of-pearl spoon to scoop caviar into a crystal bowl. She placed the bowl onto a bed of crushed ice, arranging the toast points and garnishes around the silver tray.

"No, he was not injured" said Mutante. "As you told me, Balicki was only to scare him with the torch."

"Do you think he got the message about the women?" asked Diana. "Do you think he will stop cooperating with the FBI?"

Mutante shrugged. Reading people's intentions was beyond his ability.

Diana set the caviar on the glass side table near the window and took up her own glass of wine, sitting down on the couch. "Well, our warning needs to be emphasized. One of the women . . . perhaps more . . . need to be . . ." She did not finish the sentence.

She did not need to. Mutante nodded, turned, and left.

***

"*Down with Big Meat!*" whispered the Veganite to bolster his courage as he hauled his portly frame out of his car. The paunchy, middle-aged man in the sports jacket and wide-brimmed hat took a deep, nervous breath to steady himself.

In the service of his cause, he'd never done anything like this before. He would be branded a terrorist after this attack, but he knew his quest was just. He was an eco-warrior, he told himself, and his guerrilla action today would help bring the Veganites the worldwide attention they deserved.

He mentally reviewed his plan of action. Brigham Baltazar had given the eco-warriors a menu of possible attack modes. Each carried a different likelihood of success, different risk of capture, injury, or even death. He had chosen one of the most aggressive, knowing that he would almost certainly be caught. But it would certainly accomplish his aims.

Now for *step one:* He pushed through the glass door of the Steak MegaMonster Restaurant in Topeka, Kansas. He was enveloped by the repulsive—to him—smell of cooking meat. The stench acted to steel his resolve. In his sports jacket, he looked distinctly out of place in the restaurant. The other diners were beefy, carnivorous types in t-shirts, sport shirts, and jeans.

He asked for a table that had a view of the entire room. It was also near the entrance for ready escape and positioned ideally for video, with the light from the street at his back. He ordered a beer, which he did not drink. Then he ordered his steak, disgusted at the idea that he would have to stoop so low. But his action that day would redeem him.

Step two: He called up the video conferencing app on his phone so it would transmit the scene to Brigham Baltazar. His leader would post the video of his and the other eco-warriors' actions. He propped up his cell phone using a stand, so its camera would have a clear view of the room and its crowd of dinnertime customers—soon to be justifiable victims of their own lust for animal flesh.

Step three: He told the server—a pleasantly plump smiling woman who would not be smiling long—that he'd left something in his car. And he had.

He went outside to where he had parked his car so it wouldn't be seen from the restaurant. He'd also scouted out where the parking lot cameras were, so he wouldn't be seen preparing for his action.

He hauled the battery-powered backpack sprayer out of the trunk, opened its top and poured in the contents of the two containers. They would mix with the ice water in the sprayer tank to produce the dilution he wanted. He hurried through the next steps, knowing that the gustatene binary combination would quickly begin degrading.

He took off his dress shirt to reveal a red t-shirt with the logo of the Topeka Pussycats softball team. Then he shrugged on the heavy backpack sprayer and draped the cape over it, to hide the huge hump the tank made on his back. He put on his respirator, testing its seal. He didn't want to suffer the same effects that the restaurant's diners would.

Then he donned the cutesy Pussycats mascot head, which he'd made to fit over the respirator. The diners would not dream that such a comical "Super Pussycat" character was about to drive them to manic hunger.

The respirator and the mask were stifling, but he'd spent time wearing them to avoid letting claustrophobic panic overcome him. Walking carefully to avoid tripping in the cumbersome mask, he made his way back to the restaurant and entered. Inside the entrance, he launched into the happy-dance that he had practiced in the mirror. He held the wand of the sprayer at his side as he danced his way into the restaurant.

The girl at the front podium smiled, and some of the diners giggled. Others applauded the mascot of their local team. He was making the right impression—a good sign that he wouldn't be stopped in his mission.

He danced his way down the row of tables, asking for high-fives and getting them.

He reached the door to the kitchen, whirled around and held up the wand, pushing its trigger. A full-on blast of yellowish liquid spewed from its tip, drenching the diners, who sputtered and shrank back. Striding toward the front door, he slashed the wand back and forth over the crowd, causing them to shriek and duck under the cascade. But it was too late for them. They had been fully dosed.

He willed himself not to run because he wanted to make sure that the full four gallons of gustatene mixture were emptied into the restaurant. No sense wasting perfectly good drug.

He reached the front of the restaurant to see the young hostess, standing wide-eyed and gape-mouthed. He gave her a full shot of gustatene. He jiggled the tank back and forth, feeling that there was still some left.

He planted his feet, as diners rushed the door. A huge potbellied man with a thick gray fringe of hair encircling his bald head rushed toward him, and he brought up the wand and sluiced the liquid directly into his face. He paused, temporarily blinded.

"WHAT THE HELL KIND OF SHIT IS THIS?" demanded the man, backing up two steps.

Then, charging toward him was a huge man wearing a Steak MegaMonster t-shirt, apparently the manager. He would not be so easily stopped. He slammed into the eco-warrior driving him to the floor and onto the backpack tank. The eco-warrior rolled over and kicked at the manager. He yanked off the pussycat head, shrugged his way out of the spray tank harness, leaped up, slammed open the glass door, and dashed away around the corner. He reached his car, leaped in, started it up and sped away. He tore off his respirator mask.

His face was wet, and an unfamiliar taste dribbled into his panting mouth. Suddenly, he was ravenously hungry! Horrifically, maddeningly, insanely hungry! The wild spray he'd spewed during his wrestling with the customer had doused him, too! Immersed in his hunger, he recalled the last sensory perception of food. It was the aroma of meat! *He needed meat! He could smell the same aroma coming from nearby!*

***

"Chef, what are you doing here?" Asked the round-faced middle-aged woman. She was smiling, but her tone was one of mild accusation. She stood in front of the locked metal gate to the garden apartments in the anonymous Las Vegas suburb.

Chef was silent, so Abadi answered her, his voice still muffled by his swollen, bruised face. "We know it is not good for us to come here. But we need to show these people this place. They need to know how Chef is helping here." He gestured at Chun and Lou standing beside him.

The woman shrugged in amiable resignation. "Well, okay, fine, come in," she said to the group. "Let's get you off the street." She gestured urgently with a pudgy hand as she unlocked the gate and escorted them through it and along a winding path among the two-story rows of apartments. "I'm Amy. I'm the manager, and kind of a den mother to the girls. C'mon into my place. We'll talk."

They entered Amy's ground-floor apartment to find themselves in a living room transformed into a security center. One wall was covered with flat-screen monitors showing video feeds from cameras around the complex. A burly man in a black polo shirt sat at the monitors, a pistol on his hip. He nodded briefly at them before going back to scrutinizing the feeds.

"So, what is this place?" asked Lou.

"It is a refuge, a haven, for endangered women," said Amy. "Thanks to Chef Nonny—"

"My mother," interrupted Nonny. "Thanks to my mother."

"Of course," said Amy, nodding her head vigorously. "Johanna Ciotti was our angel. She and Chef Nonny established this facility where we can protect endangered women. Let them heal. Help them start new lives."

Chun walked back and forth in front of the video feeds, scanning them, shaking her head in puzzlement. "So, I don't understand why there's something illegal here."

Abadi answered. "Some of these women are in such danger that they cannot leave here, even to shop for food. They were rescued from human traffickers, from violent husbands. So, Chef has arranged to secretly bring food from the Gourffet to feed them. Each night a truck comes. The driver knows to make sure he is never followed. Each night food is delivered. The food could be tracked if it were ordered from a commercial company or delivered from the food bank. So, it is delivered here illegally, off the books. We are breaking law. Embezzling. If the Grand Forum management found out, we would be fired, prosecuted."

"So, this is your secret?" asked Lou. "Your deep dark secret? Hey, not a bad secret to have."

"Some are in the country illegally, so this is violating immigration law," said Nonny. "Others were beaten by husbands. I am asking you to keep this secret."

Chun smiled in sympathy. "Look, we've got a Victims Services Division that can help these girls if they were trafficking victims. They can testify, and we can help them get new lives. And if it was domestic abuse, we can work with local cops."

"They are too afraid," said Nonny. "We can talk to them, but first you have to figure out how the people who took us knew about them and the food deliveries. And you need to find out if they know where this place is."

125

Well, I'm not INS, so their legality is not my concern." Chun paused for a moment, then declared, "Actually, I just decided that these girls are all witnesses to an FBI investigation. So, if the INS comes calling, tell them to contact me. Lou what do you say?"

"Yeah, well, I'm not INS either. And normally, I'd feel it necessary to contact the local health department about the food violation. . . being FDA and all. But, hey, I'm kind of irresponsible, so nah, that ain't gonna happen."

A thin, dark-haired girl dressed in a flowered shift came through the door and stopped, wide-eyed. She turned to go.

"It's okay, Therana," said Amy gently. Then to the group. "Therana is from Turkey. She's just joined us. If you don't mind, I need to see to her."

"Of course, of course," said Abadi. "We will go now."

He and Nonny led the way back along the walkway flanked by gardens of desert succulents to the waiting cars. Nonny climbed into his limousine, but Abadi hung back. He smiled with some difficulty because of the swollen face, and spoke quietly to Chun and Lou.

"I will tell you sometime about his amazing mother," he said. "She made him what he is. She died only a few years ago. She was his angel."

With that, he climbed into the limousine, and it pulled away. Chun and Lou followed in the standard-issue dark blue FBI sedan. Chun's phone sounded and she checked a text message, uttering a curse.

"Terror attacks with the drug!" she exclaimed. "In several places. Looks like this stuff has been weaponized!" She was scrolling through reports from the FBI field offices, so she took little note of the black SUV that passed them going toward the apartment complex. Its side windows were tinted, so she would not have been able to make out the driver.

***

The sobbing, groaning, and whimpering of the bleeding victims of the Steak MegaMonster restaurant attack were an audible accompaniment to the flashing lights of the dozen ambulances parked there. Hazmat-suited technicians washed down the drugged people staggering from the restaurant. Others struggled against the plastic cuffs that bound them, as the drug's residual effects still drove them to seek to gnaw chunks from their fellow victims.

The technicians were herding the victims into a white tent just outside the restaurant door and bandaging the gashes and bite wounds on their arms, necks, and heads.

Periodically, one of the ambulances would speed away, siren blaring, carrying a victim whose wounds were diagnosed as serious.

Standing at the edge of the crowd was the one person whose expression was one of quiet pride rather than shock. The blue-uniformed Shawnee County sheriff was satisfied that his deputies had done their job well. The terrorist behind this despicable attack had been apprehended immediately. Of course, it had been relatively easy to identify him. His very public havoc had triggered a 911 call to the Burger Bazaar near the steak restaurant.

The deputies had wisely kept their distance when they entered the burger joint. After all, he was madly snatching up hamburgers and stuffing them, wrappers and all, into his mouth, all the while growling like an animal.

It had taken two taser jolts to put him down, writhing and moaning.

The sheriff, a stout, balding man with a nevertheless commanding presence, turned away from the desperate scene of men, women, and children being washed down and treated. He walked over to the white SUV holding the perpetrator.

"Mirandized?" he asked the deputy standing beside the vehicle, not waiting for the answer. He knew the answer. He leaned down to the prisoner, who was slumped, head down in the back in handcuffs.

"Please, wash me," whimpered the man raising his head. His face and clothes were smeared with the remnants of the hamburgers he had devoured when he had been apparently dosed with the same substance he had sprayed into the restaurant.

"Son, did you get a taste of your own . . . medicine?" asked the sheriff wryly.

"Please!" the prisoner pleaded. "I ate *meat!*"

"Sorry, son, you are evidence." Then to the deputies surrounding the car: "FBI will be here in a bit. They're bringing their techs. Meantime, don't touch him. If you did, go see the hazmat folks, get decontaminated. I don't want any of you gentlemen ending up in some restaurant scaring folks and gobbling food, like this guy."

A deputy approached, holding a cell phone inside a plastic bag in his blue-gloved hand.

"Found this in the restaurant. The girl at the front said she thinks this guy set it up before his attack."

The sheriff took the bag in his own gloved hand and peered through the plastic, seeing that the cell phone inside showed a moving image. It was of the live scene.

"Damn!" he declared. "This thing is still live!"

***

The Shawnee County sheriff's frowning face loomed large on the monitor in the Veganite safe house. His quiet voice belied his fury. He said, "Don't know whether somebody is watching this, but we are going to catch you and prosecute you, just as we will this man."

The video scene swung around to reveal the slumping eco-warrior sitting in the back of the squad car, his chest heaving in suppressed sobs.

Brigham Baltazar stood in the safe house looking over the shoulder of his lieutenant Alex Teo. Teo was displaying six separate scenes on the wall-sized screen, depicting video from the six targets they had hit.

Baltazar smiled in satisfaction. "So, he was caught. Great! How about the others?"

"Looks like. . . ," began Teo, scrutinizing the screen for a long moment. "Looks like four of them were caught . . . at the Steak MegaMonster in Topeka, the Carnivore Carnival in Fort Worth, Steve's Beefarama in Fresno, and the Steak in the Hearth in Omaha."

"Okay, contact the other two. Tell them to turn themselves in. Get all of them lawyered up. The trials will be a showpiece for our cause." He modulated his smile only slightly. "Any injuries to our people?"

"Well, not really, as far as the coverage shows," said Teo, scanning across the video windows. "The Topeka operative apparently dosed himself by mistake. Then he invaded a hamburger place and was devouring the food. Had to be dragged out."

"How about media coverage?"

"All the networks. Live stand-ups. The 24-hour cable nets have their experts all over it."

"Okay, post our videos. That'll—"

Teo interrupted. "You don't want to know about injuries to the victims?"

Baltazar shrugged. "Necessary casualties of our higher cause . . . saving humanity from the ecological disaster of industrial farming, the meat Mafia."

"Yeah, okay," said Teo, shrugging his shoulders. He set about editing the videos that had streamed from the attacks. They depicted hunger-maddened crowds of diners bellowing, groaning, attacking one another, gnawing at each other's bodies.

His brow furrowed, Baltazar began to pace back and forth in the study of the safe house, his long-legged strides making only a few steps necessary for the circuit. "You know this is only the beginning," he declared.

"This was damned big," said Teo, clicking on the computer mouse to post the videos. "It will have an enormous impact."

"Not big enough." Baltazar stopped in his pacing, viewing the videos as their hits mounted into the tens of thousands only minutes after posting. He shook his head. "This is nothing. We're going back to the drug dealer. I've got a far, far bigger action in mind."

Chapter 11

"**I**s he still alive?" asked Diana, nudging the drug dealer Boudreaux's inert, bloody form with the toe of her Manolo Blahnik tan suede pumps. She was careful to choose a portion of Boudreaux's body that was free of blood. She wouldn't be able to clean blood from suede, if past experience was a guide. She held her shoulder bag fastidiously behind her, as if Boudreaux's blood spatter would somehow migrate upward to its leather surface.

"Of course he's alive," said Dunst, who had been sitting, legs crossed, in an armchair in the warehouse. They were enclosed in a wall of shipping crates, making their meeting private. Dunst also had been careful to situate the chair out of range of any possible blood splatter.

Behind him stood the nine other lieutenants in their cartel. The six men were variously dressed in polo shirts and khaki pants, suits and ties, and the saggy, wrinkled garb of street punks. The three women were more elegantly attired, given that their customers tended toward the well off. They wore pants suits whose elegant draping marked them as designer clothes.

All were dead silent, wearing grim expressions after having witnessed the horrific beating of Boudreaux.

Dunst gestured to Mutante, who was using Boudreaux's body to wipe blood off his gloved fists. "Bring him around. Sit him up."

Mutante doused a rag with ammonia and shoved it under Boudreaux's nose. The husky man jerked and grunted, his one unswollen eye opening wide at the shock. Mutante hauled him up and leaned him against a crate. Boudreaux slumped against it, his legs splayed out, showing his sneakers stained with his own blood.

"Mr. Boudreaux, are you conscious enough to talk?" asked Dunst. "I would like Miss Vodkonen to hear your story directly from you."

"Mmmph," replied Boudreaux.

"I'll take that to be a 'yes.' Please tell her what you told me."

Boudreaux made several unintelligible grunts before he was able to form words. "I did not know what those people would do with the drug," he said in speech slurred from being formed by swollen lips. "They said they had restaurants. The boss, he says his name is Malcolm Baker. He says he is head of the restaurant chain. He paid me what I asked, and I delivered the product. That is all I know."

Diana crossed her arms and shook her head, frowning, her gold earrings swinging with the movement. "And you didn't think to check out his story?"

"That's exactly what I asked," said Dunst.

"He had the money," said Bourdeaux. "Please. He had the money. You didn't tell me I had to check customers' stories."

"But now you know, correct?" asked Dunst.

"Yes sir, Mr. Dunst," came the pained, muffled reply.

"And you saw the result. That our operation was seriously compromised by all the publicity surrounding this group, the Veganites, mounting these attacks."

"Yes, sir."

"And now you know there will be consequences for not being careful."

"I do. I do."

Dunst gave Diana a look that asked an unspoken question. It was one that Diana knew could be answered with a nod "yes" or a shake of the head "no."

After a long moment staring at the sagging, bloody Boudreaux, Diana nodded. Leaning against one of the stacks of crates, her arms crossed, she asked "Can they trace you?"

"No. No. Absolutely no."

"And can you contact them?"

"Yes, but I won't. I won't."

"Actually, we do want you to contact them," said Diana. "We want you to make sure they understand that any further problems they present for us will result in . . ." she smiled slightly, as she used Dunst's term ". . . consequences."

"I will. Yes, Miss."

"And make it a video call. Show them your face."

Boudreaux began to sob with relief, his body shaking. His whimpering echoed in the warehouse.

Dunst rose from the chair, turning to Mutante, who was removing his blood-soaked gloves and donning a sport coat over his massive frame. "Take him to our doctor." Then, he turned to Boudreaux, who had managed to stifle his sobs. "Mr. Boudreaux, you committed an error, but we have decided not a grave error." He smiled wryly at the pun. "So, we will continue to employ you, should you so agree."

"Oh, yes, Mister Dunst. I do so agree. I *do* so agree."

"We will not pay you your usual salary for a month. Do you find that fair?"

"Yes! Fair! Thank you!"

"And your money will be distributed among your colleagues, as some restitution for having failed them."

Boudreaux could only manage a nod, leaving his head hanging, as he slumped to the concrete floor.

Diana turned to the mute group of lieutenants, pulling from her shoulder bag a tablet computer in a thick, leather case. She opened the case, and tapped the screen, scrutinizing it for a long moment.

"We have had an exceedingly good quarter," she began "Except Mr. Boudreaux, of course. So all of you will receive bonuses amounting to twenty percent of your salary." An appreciative murmur arose from the group, but Diana held up her manicured hand, turning to one of the men. "Except for Mr. Blanchard. Our accounting showed that you have embezzled one hundred and twelve thousand dollars from us over the last six months." She unzipped a small pouch in the computer case.

Blanchard, dressed in a suit and tie, raised his hands in protest, beginning "But, Diana, I—"

Before he could finish the sentence, Diana pulled a small, nickel-finish Glock 19 pistol from the pouch and fired two rounds into his forehead. The cracks of the pistol shots reverberated in the warehouse, and Blanchard's head—now with two closely spaced bloody holes—snapped back, his body slamming into the concrete floor with a dull thud. The others leaped away from his inert body, holding their hands high to show they were not reaching for weapons.

Dunst rose from his chair, shaking his head and smiling in tolerant amusement at his partner's impetuous action. He would remind her over dinner that they could have conned Blanchard into emptying his bank account before killing him. He nodded to Mutante, who nodded back, signaling that he would take a trip into the desert that night.

Expressionless, Diana slid the pistol back into the case and zipped it up. She closed the financial program on her tablet, and prepared to leave. But then she turned back, bending over a trembling Boudreaux. "Please find out as much as you can about these Veganites. Use our investigator. We may have to deal with them at some point."

***

Lou was still damp from the shower, wearing a terrycloth robe, her long hair stringy-wet when she answered her hotel room door. She saw that Abadi's still-swollen face held a stricken expression, as he stood outside the door.

"You couldn't tell me over the phone what you wanted?" she asked.

"No, no, is a terrible thing that has happened, and I needed to talk to you, to persuade you."

"Of what?" she gestured for him to come in and sit on the desk chair in her cramped room. She sat on the bed and took up a towel to dry her hair. "Where's Nonny?"

"He is at apartments. *Girls were taken! Four.*"

"Oh, my God, what happened?"

"People . . . thugs . . . broke through gate and overpowered guard. There were four girls outside . . . Elena, Jocelyn, Veronika, Natalia. They were trafficked girls. Men take them."

"Did you call the police?"

"No no no! We do not trust. Girls would be identified. Word would get out."

Lou picked up her cell phone. "I'll let Chun know. It's an FBI case, anyway."

"Again, no no no! We ask ourselves now how thugs know about girls, about apartments, also knowing just how Chef and me are working with FBI. We think even more there is an FBI leaker. And also, girls still afraid that if they are officially found, agent Chun will have to deport them. FBI bosses will make her."

"But I don't get it, then. Why are you coming to me?"

"Nonny trusts you. I trust you. We want you to find girls."

"Y'all know I'm an FDA person, right? I find bad vegetables, tainted meat . . . stuff like that."

"Nonny says you are . . . what does he say . . . *relentless.*"

"Well, not exactly the compliment I would like from him, but I'll take it." Lou bowed her head in thought, still drying her hair. "Um, why didn't Nonny come and ask me himself."

"When they take girls, thugs put our guard in hospital. Nonny is making sure he is okay. Besides, he say he does not want to be alone with you. He says you are a distraction."

Lou chuckled. "Well, that's an improvement on 'relentless.' Look, I tell ya what. I'll monitor all the data coming in. I'll see if there's any sign of the girls. We know it's the same drug dealer who took y'all. I'm sure there'll be some connection that I can trace. I'll go in now."

"*Oh, thank you! Thank you!*" exclaimed Abadi, leaning forward and taking Lou's hand.

Lou shook her head, frowning. "But I must tell you, if I get anything, Agent Chun will have to know. She'll make sure they're rescued; she'll take care of the girls, I can assure you."

"Okay, if you can assure me."

"Listen, I gotta ask something. About your chef. He's a genius, I know. But his . . . how can I say this? His nature . . . well, I'll just ask. He's an aspy, right?"

"Ass-what?"

"Asperger syndrome."

Abadi frowned in indignation. "Chef is not syndrome! He is brilliant Chef, wonderful man! He is—"

"Hey, I'm not insulting him or demeaning him," declared Lou. "A friend of mine had a brother like him, a wonderful man. Nonny is an amazing person. I'm just trying to understand him better."

Abadi's expression softened. He smiled amiably and shrugged his burly wrestler's shoulders. "Chef is unique person. He had hard upbringing. He never tell me anything about it. But his friends did. His father was cold to him because he didn't understand him. After his father die, it was only him and his mother, Johanna. She had family money, and when she saw that he loved cooking, she take him all over world, showing him all about how crops are grown, meat is produced, great restaurants are run. And she make sure he got into best culinary school . . . in New York. And she make sure they understand that he is so special. When they gave him problems, she was real pain in ass to them. He so love her, he name his restaurant after her."

"Well, she sure saved him. Clearly, cooking makes him happy. And rich."

Abadi laughed heartily, shaking his head.

"What's so funny about him being rich?" asked Lou.

"He *was* rich. Then virus pandemic hit and close down his restaurants. He wouldn't lay anybody off. He pay them out of his own pocket. That take a lot of his money. The rest he give to food banks. He even mortgage his house. Now, he is finally coming back."

"That must have made him happy, helping everybody."

Abadi struggled to his feet, wincing at the pain from the beating he had taken. "You want to make him more happy? Find the girls."

***

"What was the holdup?" asked Chun, shooting a disapproving glare at the newly arrived Tate. "Did you have better things to do?"

"It took time to find the truck carrying the chemicals," said Tate, sitting down at his desk across from hers in the FBI field office, smoothing down his suit coat. "I had a shit load of footage to go through."

"But you found the warehouse?"

"Well, I traced the truck to a road where it apparently turned off the highway, but I couldn't trace the back roads."

"And you went out to look for it."

"Just got back. There are a few big warehouses out that way, but I couldn't be sure which one was the one."

"Why didn't you get some other agents on it?"

"Everybody was busy."

As Chun continued her annoyed glare at Tate, Lou emerged into the office, walking down the long row of desks at which sat the dozen FBI agents making phone calls or bent over their work.

She continued past Chun's desk, nodding for her to go to the conference room. Once there, she shut the door and perched on the table.

"I gotta be straight with ya, Leafy. I had a visit from Daoud Abadi. He said four of the girls at the condo had been taken. But he didn't want me to tell you. They're still freaked about what they think is a leak."

"Jesus, that's terrible! So, what do you want me to do?"

"Well, whatever you can to find them without, y'know, alerting anybody who might be a mole."

Chun paced the room for a long moment before answering. "I just can't accept that there's a mole in this office. Maybe somewhere along the information chain, but surely not here."

"Don't mean to be rude or anything, but that's what a tight-ass would say."

"Yeah, well, rudeness aside, it's not tight-ass to trust your colleagues. They've all been FBI agents for a long time."

"So you're saying long-term folks can't be moles? But, Leafy, you follow the clues, the facts. That's what got you your nickname. The fact is, the bad guys know about stuff they could only have learned about from a mole."

Chun took a deep breath. "Yeah, well, let's proceed with caution on accusing anybody, but also on keeping key information to a need-to-know. Tate's zeroed in on the area for the drug lab. So, that might be where the girls are, too. But in any case, I'll poke around with the Vegas police, see if they've had any chatter about kidnappings. I gotta guy in vice who's got CI's on the street who will put out feelers without making anything formal."

Lou chuckled at what she was about to say. "Okay, you know those two, Nonny and Abadi, are going to be huge pains in the patoot. Can you let them come along if you do a raid? They could be useful. They know all the locals. Maybe they'll recognize somebody."

"I'll light a fire under Tate; get the boss to let me flood the area with agents. We will goddamned well find that lab! And we will goddamned well go in!"

Chapter 12

"Your rats ready?" asked Chun. She did not look up from the display screens in the crowded FBI mobile command post. The screens showed video of the cinderblock warehouse that agents had pinpointed as housing Kane's drug laboratory. The FBI had commandeered a nearby factory for their assault, under cover of darkness driving their hulking truck-like command van in. At the same time, agents had fanned out under the shroud of night to place surveillance cameras.

Next to Chun, Tate sat watching monitors showing constantly shifting scenes from the body cameras of the SWAT team.

Lou peered into the four wire cages containing pairs of white rats, which were busily nosing about. "Yup, my guys are ready to work," she replied.

"Or try to eat each other if they get drugged," said Chun. "Give them to the team, then."

Lou stacked up the cages and hauled them out of the vehicle into the factory, handing them over to the Technical Hazards Response Unit team dressed in yellow hazmat suits. The THRU team joined the similarly garbed FBI SWAT team members who would breach the target. They assiduously checked one another's hazmat suits, as they boarded two dark blue armored assault vehicles. They would be extremely cautious, given the news footage they had seen of the mayhem in the restaurants, where the drug-soaked diners had attacked one another.

Lou walked over to Nonny and Abadi, who stood fidgeting beside their limousine.

Abadi demanded, "Anything? Any sign of the girls?"

"Chun says surveillance hasn't shown any movement outside the warehouse since last night," said Lou. "So, nobody for you to identify."

Said Nonny, "But the police believe they might be there."

Lou patted the worried chef's shoulder in sympathy. "Yeah, but only possibly. Agent Chun's contact only said that word was around that the women had been taken and that the kidnappers had taken them out of town."

"Do they know who took them?"

Lou shook her head. "Seems to be freelancers, like the ones who took you. Out of town guys. And this place . . ." Lou gestured in the direction of the target warehouse. "They still don't know whose it is. Ownership is hidden by shell companies within shell companies within shell companies."

The roar of the assault vehicles starting their engines filled the factory, and Chun emerged from the command van to join Lou in climbing aboard the second assault vehicle, slamming its rear steel hatch shut. The factory overhead door rattled open, and the tracked vehicles accelerated out into the morning desert sun, swerved, and sped down the narrow road. Following closely behind was the truck marked with the FBI logo and the sign "Mobile Forensics Laboratory."

A mile farther and the caravan reached the anonymous-looking warehouse, its parking lot empty of cars. The assault vehicles lurched to a halt and the SWAT team swarmed out of them and toward the warehouse's steel door. One of the SWAT team took aim with a combat shotgun and with a single blast exploded away its lock.

Chun and Lou stood outside, listening intently on their radios to the terse messages among the team members as they poured into the warehouse.

"Are the girls there?" asked Nonny, who appeared beside them with Abadi.

"Get the hell back!" exclaimed Chun. "I told you to wait at the staging area."

Abadi snorted. "Seriously? You tell Chef something and you expect him to obey?"

Chun listened to her earpiece for a long moment and declared, "Nobody's there so far." Then, she issued an order for the THRU team to enter just as the warehouse's overhead door rattled open.

"How are my rats?" asked Lou. "I gotta get in there and see what the fu. . . . what's going on."

Chun held up her hand in caution, still listening. After several minutes, she nodded. "Your rats are good, and the team sees no evidence of contamination. She radioed Tate to report on any activity around the warehouse. Finally, she nodded to Lou. "Let's go in." She turned to glare at Nonny and Abadi. "If you so much as look like you're following us, I will handcuff you to a vehicle."

Abadi shrugged and cocked his head in mute agreement. Nonny said nothing, his gaze riveted on the warehouse overhead door.

Chun and Lou sprinted through that door to find the SWAT and THRU teams ranging about the sprawling, darkened interior.

Lou scrutinized the analytical machines, declaring, "Gotta be easily a million bucks worth of instruments here. Somebody has deep pockets."

She moved quickly over to rows of lab benches littered with the shards of smashed laboratory glassware. She frowned as she picked her way gingerly among the debris, glass crunching beneath her boots. She inspected a row of six-foot stainless-steel tanks. "Whoa! They were doing large-scale production of whatever it was," she declared.

Finally, she reached the chemical storage area, studied the labels on blue drums, and moved on to shelves holding smaller containers, also scrutinizing their labels.

"*Mother. . .!*" she exclaimed, stopping herself.

"What?" asked Chun, who had just arrived with the THRU team. They began meticulously taking swab samples from the smashed glassware, placing each sample in a labeled tube.

"These are different chemicals than we knew about," said Lou. "This stuff . . . " she gestured at the shelves of brown glass bottles and plastic containers". . . means they were doing a different synthesis. . . a new compound, a different one."

"Did you find the women?" came Nonny's voice, as he and Abadi rushed past them into the warehouse's interior.

Lou and Chun followed them, Chun scolding, *"Goddamnit, I told you—"*

Behind them, a thundering explosion burst from the barrels launching a cascade of flaming liquid. Clouds of thick smoke rolled outward enveloping them, choking them. The blast drove them to the debris-littered concrete floor, cut off from the entrance. Chun was the first to rise. She shouted instructions into her communicator for the THRU team to evacuate, then turned to the others. "BACK! BACK!"

One of the THRU team members had been blown down, his suit erupting in flames, as another patted them out. He dragged the technician toward the door, just as the flames spread blocking any exit for Chun, Lou, Abadi, and Nonny.

One barrel after another erupted in flames, driving the group, choking and gasping, deeper into the warehouse. They retreated farther, with Abadi stopping to clutch the unconscious hazmat-suited body of a THRU technician, hauling him along with them. They reached the back of the warehouse, which was piled floor-to-ceiling with cardboard boxes.

Lou choked out, *"It'd be good to have ideas for getting the hell out about now!"* over the roaring crackle of the spreading flames.

"Working on it!" exclaimed Chun, issuing instructions into her radio.

"I hear something!" shouted Nonny, who had retreated to the back wall. *"I hear something!"* He turned to the stack of boxes, pausing only a moment before beginning to yank them down, heaving them away. Abadi joined him.

Lou scanned the warehouse. "There are rooms along the rest of this back wall. I'd bet there's rooms behind these boxes. Somebody stacked them up to hide them." She bent to help Nonny and Abadi, and they uncovered a row of locked doors.

Nonny moved along the doors, stopping at one to begin to kick at it. Abadi motioned him back, slamming against it with his thick body. It didn't give.

"Back," commanded Chun drawing her pistol and firing three rounds into the doorknob. The blasts reverberated above the crackling of the flames, as their heat grew to a searing intensity. Abadi launched his body against the door again, and it careened open. They entered to find a large office, and cowering in a corner were four sobbing young women. Nonny and Abadi helped them to their feet and led them out to face the looming, roiling flames that were relentlessly advancing, hemming them in.

"So, Leafy, got a plan?" asked Lou as they shrank back against the office door, the heat growing to an unbearable intensity.

Without replying, Chun moved along to a section where the offices ended and the warehouse's back wall began. She shouted into her radio, "BREACH FORTY FEET FROM SOUTHEAST CORNER! NOW!" She waved the others back toward the offices. Lou ducked away back into the office that had held the women.

The back wall exploded inward with a cascade of cinderblocks, as an assault vehicle rammed through. Its back door slammed open to reveal a SWAT team member, waving them in.

Chun herded the others through the door, as Abadi grabbed the unconscious THRU technician by the shoulders, and hauled him in. But Chun didn't enter, leaping out to peer back through the thickening smoke.

"Where the hell is. . . ," she began, then plunged away. She reached the office to find Lou stuffing a garbage bag with files from the office file cabinet.

"*Will you get the hell out of here!*" she commanded.

"Yeah, yeah, I'm just—"

"You're *just* about to get yourself barbecued is what!"

"Okay, okay!" Lou dragged the bulging garbage bag out of the office just as the cardboard boxes that had hidden the office burst into flames.

The two of them plunged, hacking and gagging, into the vehicle, and Chun slammed the door, burning her hand on its hot metal. The vehicle accelerated out of the burning warehouse, speeding away to the growing sounds of sirens.

Inside, Nonny and Abadi were comforting the whimpering girls, as Lou slumped against the plastic garbage bag. The interior reeked of smoke, as the passengers periodically suffered fits of coughing.

Chun glowered at Lou, shaking her head. Lou shrugged and gave her an embarrassed grin. A mask of black soot surrounded her nose and mouth, and her hair was singed.

"Never did like to leave trash," she said.

"Yeah, well, you would have been incinerated right along with it."

Lou opened the bag and rummaged briefly through it. "But this ain't trash. These are lab notes, shipping records. We are going to find out what the *schnitzel* these people have been up to."

*****

Amid the melee of the warehouse breach and explosion, Tate clutched the burner phone below the counter in the command van, so the other agents couldn't see it. He could feel the phone vibrate insistently, as it had done twice in the last ten minutes. The damned phone was like a leash the drug dealers had put on him. Diana Vodkonen had given it to him, insisting that it be the only means to contact them.

"I'm going out," he told the other agents sitting at their consoles. They looked at him with some surprise that he would leave his post. "I've got to go see if everybody is all right." He tinged his voice with a note of urgency. He rose from his chair, slipping the phone into his jacket pocket. "Just got to make sure," he said.

He exited the van and circled around out of sight of the other agents in the factory that was the staging area. Fortunately, he thought, they were busy tending the wounded and loading ambulances. He hit the button to call one of two numbers on the phone, the other linked to the detonator in the warehouse.

He listened for a moment, then said, "Yeah, I set it off. And yeah, it took out the building." He listened for another long moment. "Everybody was where you wanted them. The bait was there. Listen, I can't help it that they got away. I did my job." Listening again, he frowned. "Look, this was above and beyond. *Way* above and beyond. I'd better see a big goddamned bonus."

An agent appeared around the corner of the van, and Tate startled in surprise, saying into the phone, "Honey, I'm okay. Everybody is okay. Just don't worry. I'll see you tonight." He ended the call, shrugged, and grinned at the agent. "Guess they can't help but worry, right?"

***

Lou sat cross-legged on the floor of the FBI van, her singed mop of hair wildly askew, her face still soot-blackened. She hauled sheaves of papers from the garbage bag that had not left her hands since they had arrived back at the factory. She gave each handful a cursory fan-through before depositing it on the van floor beside her.

Chun, however, had managed to wash her face after checking on Nonny, Abadi, and the girls. That face registered a frustrated grimace, conveying her frustration at trying to persuade them to go straight to the hospital to be examined.

"I don't know who's more aggravating, Daoud or Nonny," she declared. "They're so damned bullheaded."

146

"Nonny's an aspy," said Lou absentmindedly, not pausing in her examination.

"Asperger? Ah, that explains a lot."

"Well, ASD, to be more accurate. Autism Spectrum Disorder. And remember, Nonny saved Abadi's life. So, Abadi will do anything for Nonny."

"Yeah, true," said Chun, starting up the van. She had just put it in gear when the passenger side door opened and Tate climbed in. Chun nodded at him, her brow furrowed in puzzlement. "You're not staying to monitor the after-action?"

"I need to find out from you what went down in the warehouse . . . . If there's anything I need to be doing to move the investigation along."

Shrugging, Chun eased the van out of the factory and directed it down the long desert road toward the freeway into Las Vegas.

"Succotash," muttered Lou, bent over the papers. "Interesting stuff here."

"What do you have?" asked Tate, twisting around.

"Lab notes, chemical orders, and such. Yeah, like I saw in the drug lab, there were some different chemicals than the bulk ones we'd traced." She began to mutter to herself ". . . aromatic compounds . . . esterification . . . Sn2 reaction . . . substituted acetylene . . . Grignard reagent. . ."

Finally, she sat up, took a deep breath and allowed herself one drawn out "Shhhhhiiiitttt!"

"Now now, remember your resolution," scolded Chun, smiling.

"Yeah, well that cuss was warranted. Kane is synthesizing something totally new. Says in these notes he called his original stuff gustatene. It was a binary. . . two drugs mixed together to activate. Tough to disseminate. Heat labile. The new drug looks like a single compound. No mixing, just spray the crap all over. It's his new drug, his new weapon."

"Well, then your 'shhhiiittt' was indeed warranted," said Chun.

***

Mexican drug lord Eladio Campana laughed heartily, as Mutante and three of Campana's henchmen dragged away the two grunting men and two moaning women from the dining table. The test subjects strained to continue their mad gorging on the plates of rice and beans dosed with gustatene. They were hauled out of the sprawling apartment that Campana kept in his *maquiladora* factory complex a few dozen miles south of the US border.

Campana watched the ravenous people go, shaking his head. "So, they act *loco* like the people I see in the news videos," he said. His squat, barrel-chested body was encased in a black silk shirt and white pants. Thick black hair framed his round face, which was adorned with the emphatic punctuation of a luxuriant mustache. His grin showed white teeth against dark, tanned skin. "Seeing the people going *loco de hambre* in the restaurants was very entertaining. But that is not something I want to be involved with."

He took a bite of steak and a sip of wine in a crystal goblet. Beside him rested his trademark pistol, a fifty-caliber titanium gold Desert Eagle with Bengal Tiger stripe pattern and a monogrammed mother-of-pearl handle.

Dunst smiled winningly. "Ah, my friend, I would never bring you a proposal that would fail to make you a *lot* of money and would be absolutely foolproof."

He leaned back and took a healthy drink of his wine, raising his eyebrows in appreciation. "The attacks in the restaurants were unfortunate. They were carried out by terrorists who have nothing to do with us. My salesperson did not check out who we sold to. But the incidents did show how powerful this drug is that our Doctor Kane has made."

Campana flipped his hand dismissively and smirked sarcastically at his own head chemist, a slight, balding man sitting beside him, who himself smiled faintly. "But this is not cocaine. This is not heroin. This is not a drug that people would buy. . . to take to get high."

Diana Vodkonen, sitting beside Dunst, answered: "No, but it is an additive that food companies, restaurants the world over, would pay enormous sums for." She leaned toward the drug lord, raising her eyebrows and cocking her head. "Eladio, imagine not needing any distribution network, no street pushers. We could make this drug in large quantities and sell it to them for huge profits. "This man . . ." she nodded at Kane, who sat beside her, mute and stone-faced. ". . . is a scientific genius."

Campana, known as El Campesino, or "farmer" for his humble roots, wiped his lips and stood. He picked up his pistol and walked over to the apartment's glass wall that overlooked the factory floor. He cocked his head in amused skepticism.

"Señor Dunst, señora Vodkonen, I know you are desperate for a new base, since your laboratory up north was raided. Perhaps you are overselling?"

Dunst spread his hands and cocked his head in a dismissive gesture. "It is true that we need facilities such as yours. And we come to you because you are the best. And we have had a warm and lucrative friendship with you for years. But there are lesser businessmen we could also partner with."

Campana grunted. "Perhaps you mean Hernández? He is retired. I retire him." He turned his attention to Kane. "So, what do you have to say for yourself, *El Genio Científico?*"

Kane stiffened and placed his hands on the table. "Sir, I have developed a comprehensive simulation of the human gustatory system—"

Campana interrupted. "What do you have to say about this drug you have developed? The one that drives people crazy mad for food."

"Well, the people in the restaurant were given large doses. In microgram doses it makes foods have an irresistible taste."

The slight, balding man rose from his chair and whispered to Campana, who held up his hand.

"Ah, my own *científico* tells me that your chemical has flaws. For one thing, it is . . ." he turned to the slight man, who prompted him. ". . . heat labile. Not good for transport and selling. And it does make food taste wonderful, which is nice. But I want a drug like cocaine, heroin. One that people must have!"

Kane nodded, his expression brightening. "I have recognized those problems. I have designed a new molecule. A molecule that will not break down under heating. And, this molecule not only affects the taste receptors on the tongue and the receptors of the gustatory system in the brain. It has an entirely new effect. It mimics the hormone ghrelin that triggers hunger in the appetite center, the hypothalamus."

Dunst answered. "Eladio, this is a drug that we can sell in vast quantities to the food companies, to the restaurants. And, Eladio, it is *legal*."

Kane shook his head. "Well, it needs to be tested on animals, then on humans, I—"

"Not to worry," interrupted Campana. "I have many test subjects." He gestured out the window at the factory below. He looked expectantly over at the slight, balding man.

Campana's chemist finished his examination of the papers. He looked up and nodded.

Campana holstered his pistol. "And what do you call this new drug?"

"Gustatene X," said Kane. "GX for short."

Chapter 13

C hun smiled sympathetically at the four young women, declaring in Romanian, "*Sunteți in siguranta. noi vă protejăm și vă oferim noi identități ca martori.*"

Smiling back, Elena answered for the other three, also speaking in her native Romanian. The women sat in the FBI conference room table dressed in new colorful print dresses given them after their rescue from the burning warehouse. While the others in the room could not understand the reply, the smiles on the girls' faces conveyed their emotions.

"What did you tell them?" asked Nonny. He sat next to the girls, not having left their side since they were rescued.

"I told them that they were safe, and that we will protect them and give them new identities as witnesses," said Chun. "I'd recommend that you get them an immigration lawyer. They've got a slam-dunk case for asylum."

Nonny shot a brow-furrowed glance at Abadi, who immediately understood his mission. He left the room, cell phone in hand, to call Nonny's lawyers to assemble a legal team to advocate for the girls.

"But they've got to cooperate fully," said Tate, shaking his head in doubt. "We've got to remember that they might have ulterior motives."

Lou gave Tate an annoyed look. "Yeah, survival. That's a real bad ulterior motive. Let's concentrate on getting their stories and letting them get on with having better lives."

Added Chun, "To be blunt, those drug dealers didn't expect them to survive that blast, or us for that matter. So, I'm sure they didn't care what those girls saw. So, they're a valuable asset."

For the next hour, Chun, Lou, and Tate questioned the girls about what and who they had seen at the warehouse.

The four—Elena, Jocelyn, Veronika, and Natalia—eagerly gave information. *"Da, asta sunt ei!"* exclaimed Veronika when shown photos of Oskar Dunst and Diana Vodkonen.

"Bingo," said Chun, explaining to the girls in Romanian that they had identified the people behind their kidnapping.

Abadi returned to report that he had recruited a team of immigration lawyers who would make sure the girls' asylum claims were well established. With him came a slim, middle-aged woman who introduced herself to the girls in Romanian as their interpreter. They chattered happily among themselves for a moment.

The interview complete, Tate stood and said, "Let's get them to a safe house. I'll make sure they're settled in."

Nonny declared emphatically, "You may have a safe house, but I will make sure they are in a *safest* house."

"Look, we can't just let you take them somewhere you *think* they'll be safe," said Tate. "We'll have agents watching them, we'll have—"

"You'll have to account for a leaker," interrupted Nonny. Tate's expression became stone-faced. "Are they free to go?" asked Nonny.

"Of course," said Chun. "We just want to be sure of their safety."

Abadi loosed a hearty chuckle. "Chef knows people who can make sure girls are safe. He has made some pretty tough people very happy with his cooking. And they will stay with girls."

Nonny stood up and, through the interpreter, told the girls that they were leaving. As they left the room, Abadi remained behind to relay to him any further information that Chun, Lou, and Tate might want to give.

"So, where are they off to?" asked Chun.

"Nobody will know except Chef . . . and of course pilot of the jet."

"Jet, eh?" asked Lou. "I remember you talking about a jet. He must be doing pretty well to afford that."

"Oh, its use was offered in gratitude," said Abadi.

"Wow, somebody must really be grateful," said Lou.

"A billionaire give him use of one of his jets whenever he needs. Chef made the billionaire's mother cry."

"Um, that warrants a little explanation," said Lou.

"Billionaire was from Iran, and his grandmother . . . his mother's mother . . . had died tragically in Iran-Iraq war. Nonny found out that billionaire's mother was very sad. She told Nonny that she missed her own mother's wonderful Ash-e Reshteh. It is a noodle soup with all kinds of spices, eaten to welcome the Persian new year."

"So, he made her the soup?"

"Oh, it was much more complicated than that! Her mother had not given the recipe, and it involved all kinds of exotic local spices. So, Nonny spent months traveling around Middle East to find the exact spices her mother used in soup. That was why he came to my restaurant in Iran and ultimately save my life. He test and test recipes until he find the exact recipe. It was so perfect, the billionaire's mother cried, she was so happy. It was a memory of her mother she could hold on to. So, billionaire tell Nonny, 'You take a plane whenever. You go anywhere you need to go to find your recipes, to make your perfect foods to make people happy.'"

"An angel in flight," laughed Lou. "An eccentric angel, but an angel."

With that, the group filed out of the conference room to follow up on the leads from the girls' interviews. Tate excused himself to run errands, and once he was in his car, took out his burner phone and typed in a four-word text message.

"They suspect a leak."

***

Campana smiled contentedly, as he strutted down the block-long assembly line of workers bent over their workbenches. When he had first entered the factory, the babble of convivial conversation had echoed in the huge space. His appearance brought an abrupt blanket of silence to descend. Now, the workers, mostly women, pointedly kept their heads down, inserting parts together to assemble toy robots and dolls.

They sat in five long assembly lines in the cavernous, fluorescent-lit factory fitting the parts of the toys together and packing them into brightly colored boxes. At the end of the rows, men stacked the boxes on wooden pallets, swathing the stacks in plastic shrink wrap.

As Campana led the group—Dunst, Diana, Kane, and his chief chemist—along the row, his hand casually caressed the bare back of one young woman. She stiffened, but also did not look up. Trailing the group, one of Campana's men bent down and whispered into the girl's ear. Her shoulders slumped, and her hands paused in her work, trembling.

"This is a very fine *maquiladora*," declared Campana. "I have it in the name of a shell company in US, so it is not connected to me. So, we can ship our toys all over America." He chuckled. "We even make profit on our toys!"

He reached the back of the factory, where a metal wall held only an overhead door and a smaller entry door. Campana pushed through the small door into another large room where more workers, all men with pistols on their hips, were also packing the cardboard toy boxes and loading them onto pallets. However, the contents were not toys but tightly wrapped bundles of white powder. A forklift moved the shrink-wrapped pallets to the overhead door, where a bearded, tattooed man in a red baseball cap spray-painted a small red X on the top.

"We have a very efficient shipping system," said Campana, as the overhead door opened, and the forklift hefted the X-marked pallet into the main factory, trundling away toward a distant loading dock.

"Very impressive," said Dunst. "But this is not exactly what we need, in terms of a facility." He glanced over at Kane, giving him a reassuring raised-eyebrow look.

Kane's expression was grim, as he eyed the huge drug-shipping process.

"Oh, do not worry, *mis amigos*," chuckled Campana. "This arrangement is just to show you what security your operation will have. Your laboratory will be behind this room." With that, he led them to the shipping area's back wall and through a door into a gymnasium-sized laboratory containing twenty-foot-long rows of research benches, a multitude of analytical instruments, and in the back, a phalanx of stainless-steel vats connected by a network of pipes.

"Okay, this is more like it," said Dunst.

"We had used this for production. Your *científico* will now work here," said Campana. "He will have any instruments he wishes. I will give him whatever *tecnicos* he needs to help him. And we have equipment to scale-up production." Campana turned to talk directly to Kane. "You can live in the apartment. My men will take you wherever you want, bring you anything you want. Food, drink . . . women."

"I will give you a list . . .," said Kane, then clarified ". . . of *instruments*."

Diana strode down the row of laboratory benches, then returned, smiling at Campana. "It is a very impressive facility, Eladio. And I'm sure it will be sufficient for Doctor Kane's research and for production. But boxes of powder will not be the product we will wish to ship to our customers. It will be liquid."

"Ah, my dearest Diana, did you not enjoy the wine we had for lunch? It was from one of my wineries. I ship my chardonnay, my tempranillo, my dolcetto, north to be bottled. I ship it in bulk—in sealed flexible tanks. The tanks are themselves in shipping containers on rail cars and trucks."

"And will the tanks hold enough for our purposes?" asked Diana.

Campana spread his hands and laughed. "*Señora*, each container holds two-hundred-and-fifty gallons of liquid. I am sure that will be sufficient!"

***

"According to plan," exulted a pleased Brigham Baltazar, as he mouse-clicked on coverage of the court arraignments of the Veganite attackers. The videos showed their lawyers all spouting the group's assertion that their guerrilla actions had aimed to save the Earth from climate change by reducing carbon dioxide.

"Yes, it all seems to have gone according to plan," echoed Alex Teo, pulling up a chair so he could see the screen.

"And now we get more ambitious," said Baltazar. "We will launch a mission on tens of thousands of people. And with our next action, the whole world will see the existential dangers of consuming animal flesh, of allowing carbonized farming. But we need more gustatene. Much more."

His computer beeped, signaling that his first of a series of video chats was online. The image of the drug dealer Boudreaux appeared on the screen. But it was not the face he had seen at the door to his hotel room.

"Jesus!" exclaimed Baltazar. "What the hell happened to you?"

Boudreaux's face was a swollen, purple mass, with one eye swollen shut. One arm was covered in a blue cast.

"*You* happened to me you son of a bitch," he declared flatly. "You lied to me and this is what happened. If I could find you. . ." He let his voice trail off.

"I *am* sorry that we deceived you, but it was necessary for the security of our operation."

"Your goddamned operation almost killed me."

"We want to make it up to you. We want much more gustatene. We will pay a premium price, since you know what we want it for."

"You will pay *no* price. My bosses, they say we will not sell anything to you. Not the old stuff, not even the new stuff. I double-cross them, I get much worse than this." He touched his swollen face.

"New stuff? You have an improved chemical? What does it do?"

Boudreaux jerked his head in a gesture of disgust at himself for revealing the existence of a new compound. "I am not telling you anything more. But I tell you what. You tell me exactly what you are planning, maybe I can convince my bosses." Boudreaux's unswollen eye opened wider at the prospect of new intelligence to ingratiate himself with Dunst and Vodkonen.

"We don't discuss future operations. I will tell you, we want amounts of hundreds of gallons. And if you have a more powerful agent, we will still want hundreds of gallons."

"If you don't tell me, you will get shit!"

Baltazar leaned closer to the screen, a faint conspiratorial smile on his face. "Mr. Boudreaux, it looks like your employer has treated you badly, and with no respect. Our group has considerable funds. You can name a price for your . . . well . . . your consulting service. You don't have to actually sell any of this new chemical. You just have to give us information on how we can get our hands on it. *Any* price, Mr. Boudreaux. Enough to make you wealthy." Baltazar's voice lowered to a whisper. *"How does seven figures sound?"*

Boudreaux's long pause told Baltazar that the offer had an impact.

"I will go now," declared Boudreaux abruptly, and his face disappeared from the screen.

Teo asked, "Do you think he'll agree?"

"I think we put a bug in his ear. Next step, let's see how plans are coming." Baltazar checked the time displayed on the computer screen. "Our man should be available now."

A moment later, the slim, sharp-featured face of a young man in a backward baseball cap appeared on the screen. In the background was a large topographic map. The two greeted each other warmly, and Baltazar asked, "How did the scouting go?"

"All elements look entirely optimal," said the young man.

"The target?" Baltazar remembered not to use any specifics, should his communication be tapped.

"Soft target. I checked air traffic control in the area, and it's outside any high-security zone. I'm sure I can spoof my way in. There's lots of routine civilian traffic in the area on the operation days."

"And the helicopter?"

"We can breach airfield security, either by stealth or by force."

"You're sure a helicopter is the way to go?"

"Absolutely. 'Copter has better maneuverability, better targeting. And the rotor wash will disperse the agent downward."

"And the payload capability?"

"Fifty gallons."

"That's not much."

"That usually covers about two-and-a-half acres of crop spraying. That's about the size of the primary target, right?"

"Yeah, well, still it's not much capacity."

The pilot chuckled and said, "Ah, but we steal both the spray 'copter *and* the support tanker with its roof landing pad. We position the tanker near the primary. I bring the 'copter into the primary, spray its load, and pandemonium ensues. In the confusion, I navigate the 'copter to the tanker, land, refill, and take another run at the primary. Or if I can't do that, I hit a secondary. We develop a priority list. Since the bird is so maneuverable, I'd bet I could get in multiple runs before the authorities figure out what's going on and mobilize. Then, I just set the copter down where there's good escape routes, and take a pre-positioned vehicle, and we're gone! Across the border and out of reach."

"We?"

"Yeah, of course it's a two-man job. Didn't you get that?"

"And that means—"

"Two fees. A hundred grand. . . each."

Baltazar shook his head emphatically. "That's ridiculous!"

"You won't get anybody better than us. My buddy, he was my gunner in the Apache I flew in Iraq."

"Two hundred thousand dollars?" Baltazar shook his head again. "And you'd want half that up front for an operation that could easily totally fail? It's off. We're going in another direction."

The pilot held up his hands to stop Baltazar from ending the call. "Wait a sec! Okay, just wait a sec! How about doing an incentive deal? I've got such confidence that we can do it, that I'll just ask for a modest up-front payment. Say, twenty-five K each. Then, when we hit the primary, you pony up another twenty-five each."

"So, you're saying you'll get more for—"

"For a second run, another fifty each, since the risk goes way up. Then fifty each again for subsequent secondaries."

"So, you could come out with one hell of a lot more than two hundred thousand dollars."

"Yeah, and you could come out with one hell of a bigger impact for your cause."

"Yes, well, it means the risk of getting shot down goes way up, you're getting caught, and—"

"Listen, pal, we flew our Apache over mountains in Iraq in the middle of the night under fire. I can do this mission easy and not get caught."

***

"Nice joint," declared Lou, standing in the living room of Dunst's abandoned penthouse in the Sheer Towers. The view through its floor-to-ceiling glass wall overlooked the sun-drenched Vegas Strip. The glimmering animated displays advertising superstar entertainers showed vividly even in the sun. "Guess being a drug lord pays pretty good."

"Yeah, those two live a good life by ruining others' lives," said Chun. She moved to begin meticulously sorting through drawers in the condominium bedroom with her small, blue-gloved hands.

From elsewhere in the sumptuously appointed penthouse came the voices of other FBI agents scouring the rooms for clues to the whereabouts of Oskar Dunst and Diana Vodkonen.

"What do you know about them?" asked Lou, following her into the bedroom.

Chun continued her search as she spoke. "Dunst is the extremely black sheep of a prominent German family. He basically took over the European drug market by killing off his competitors. He decided to expand and moved to Vegas after he got the permission of his supplier, one of Mexico's biggest drug lords, Eladio Campana."

"And Vodkonen?"

"Total sociopath, absolute genius. Adopted from a Romanian orphanage where she was neglected, beaten. Like other sociopaths, she became a perfect mimic, able to convince people of whatever response they wanted to see. When she came to the FBI's attention, we interviewed relatives of the foster parents she lived with until college. They said she seemed sweet as sugar unless something set her off. Then she could turn violent."

"Why didn't you interview the original adoptive parents?"

"They died in a house fire, along with her stepbrother. Nobody suspected Diana, since she seemed so genuinely heartbroken. Emphasis on *seemed*. And she suffered minor burns, too, but escaped. But then it came out that three months before, she had persuaded the couple to write her into their will. Since the stepbrother died, too, she inherited everything, which is why she could afford Wellesley, MIT, and Stanford. Apparently, she burned through her inheritance and wanted more. So she moved to Vegas, where she was suspected of fleecing gamblers, hacking computers, even killing for hire. Then she met Dunst, a match made in hell."

"So, you think we'll get 'em?" asked Lou, who had moved to the bathroom to begin sorting through the vials of prescription drugs in the medicine cabinet.

"Only if we're real damn good and real damn lucky. So far, we've found records of three houses here in the US, a condo in Paris, one in Rome. We've got teams on all those. But hell, they could have places elsewhere under other owners."

"Any travel records?" asked Lou, moving to a bedside table to rummage through it.

"We're pretty sure they've got a jet at Henderson airport. Our sources say they've gone out there quite a bit. But whatever they're flying is registered deep in a shell company, so we haven't got a clue where they went."

"Well, you've got those terrorists . . . those vegetarians . . . who bought the gustatene for their attacks."

"Yeah, the Veganites." Chun moved to the other bedroom, going through the closet, sorting through racks of shimmering designer gowns and designer silk pantsuits. "We've got the ones who committed the attacks, but they're not talking. Homeland Security is trying to charge them with as much stuff as possible. But after all, they only committed assault and battery, although they did drive people to harm each other. But they're basically brainwashed cult members, and they have no motivation to give up their leader. He's the one who actually dealt with the drug dealers."

"You know the leader?" asked Lou.

"Yeah, Brigham Baltazar. A typical charismatic cult leader. Been on our radar for years. Big ego. But we haven't found him yet, he—" She stopped, staring down at Lou, who had flopped down on the floor and was scooting under the bed. "What the hell are you doing?"

"The maid hasn't come yet," said Lou, her voice muffled by the bed clothes. "So, there were some stain rings on the bedside table, like a glass had been set there."

"And what does that mean?"

"Sometimes, when folks have to take a pill early in the morning, they don't like to get out of bed. They keep their water glass and pills on their bedside. And when you're sleepy, you sometimes drop—" she paused for a long moment, abruptly exclaiming "*Hah!*" She squirmed her way out from under the bed, not bothering to brush off stray dust bunnies clinging to her clothes. She held up a single pill, scrutinizing it.

"You've got something?"

"Oh, yeah. When people drop pills where they're hard to get, they often just leave them. And maids don't clean under beds. If my memory of pill shapes and colors serves me, this is an antipsychotic, a pretty common drug."

"So, it can't be traced?"

"Not the pill, but the pharmacy can. I'd bet she filled this in her name. We'll start canvassing the local pharmacies and work our way out. Given that they were working with a Mexican drug lord, I'd bet that at one time she filled it in a Mexican pharmacy. Pills are cheaper down there, and even rich drug lords like to save money. We've got a target search area!"

"You mean like a whole country?"

"I can narrow it down. I've got a buddy in the Mexican drug agency. We used to smoke weed together in college. He'll help me trace where the prescription was filled."

Chapter 14

"Very tasty-smelling," said Eladio Campana, breathing in the aroma of the posole Mexican stew. "Perfect for testing GX. Has it been dosed?"

"Not yet," said Kane. He held a flask of the yellowish liquid that was gustatene X. They stood in the kitchen of the apartment over the *maquiladora* factory.

"Ah, *bueno*," said Campana. "I would like some of this myself, but I do not wish to be an experiment." Campana ladled a helping of the spicy pork and hominy stew into a bowl and took up a spoon. "If they see me eat it, they will be less suspicious. We will get better result, no?"

"Sure, fine," said Kane. His slumping posture and haggard face told of two months of nearly round-the-clock research. It had been motivated not only by his own obsession with proving his theories. He had also been driven by the constant, looming presence of the hulking guards who shadowed him from the apartment to the laboratory. And by the need to report to the slight, balding man, who was Campana's chief chemist.

The chemist now stood beside Campana, and he asked in an indefinable European accent. "What dosage do you plan?"

"Well, since I haven't been able to do sufficient animal—"

"What dosage?" interrupted the chemist.

"Approximately a microliter per liter dilution."

"Will that be sufficient?"

"As far as I can tell. I'm using much less than with the original compound. The old gustatene was the equivalent of a firecracker. GX is more like nuclear."

"So, it could be cut considerably."

"I . . . well . . . I don't . . ." Kane shrugged, his voice trailing off.

"Let us proceed in any case."

Kane used a glass pipette to measure droplets of GX into the two-gallon pot of simmering stew. "GX, of course, is not heat labile," he said as he pipetted, his voice brightening at the chance to recite his achievement. "It's a very sturdy structure. I was very pleased with how I could achieve the physiological effect on the rats and dogs even after exposing the compound to extreme heat, and even acidity."

Voices filtering from the apartment's large dining room led them to enter it to see the arrival of Dunst, Diana, and Mutante. Still slurping the stew he carried with him, Campana greeted them and signaled to his men, who left the room. They appeared shortly with four men and four women from the factory. Their expressions were wide-eyed with anxiety, their postures cowering.

"Ah, my friends, we will feed you this fine posole today! It is a *gracias* for your excellent work!" exclaimed Campana, raising his bowl. The men and women made appreciative noises, but with dubious expressions.

Campana's men seated them at the table, and placed large, steaming bowls of the stew before them. They began to slowly eat the stew. But after only a few spoonfuls, blissful smiles rose on their faces, and they began to utter appreciative sounds between bites. Their eating grew more eager, transforming into a devouring of the stew, a raising of their bowls to beg for more.

Campana nodded, and his men complied, hauling the large pot of stew in, setting it on the table and ladling more into the bowls.

"Mis amigos, comed todo lo que quiered!" exclaimed Campana. *"Llenad tus estómagos!"* He turned to Diana and Dunst. "I tell them to eat all they want."

As the men and women grew even more urgent in devouring the stew, Dunst said, "This looks like before," said Dunst. "I don't see a difference."

"Oh, GX is a huge difference," said Kane. "For one thing, I put it into a boiling liquid with no apparent degradation. And for another, I used far, *far* less than with the binary gustatene. And it's a single molecule. And the new molecule not only makes the food's taste irresistible. It makes people hungry for it."

Groans began coming from the people eating the stew, as they slumped back, panting, their stomachs distended.

"What's going on here?" asked Diana. "They look terrible."

"Probably just the dosage," said Kane, his voice rising slightly in defense. "They'll be fine."

"Sure, sure, no problem," said Campana, signaling to his men to haul the gorged, lethargic people out of the room. "This was excellent test. We begin production immediately."

"But how?" asked Kane. "We can't possibly scale up production in the lab. We don't have the facilities."

"Ah, again no problem." Campana gave a knowing look to Dunst, who nodded his head in approval. "If you look out window at night to the west of here, you will see many big lights. That is chemical plant I own. It makes many chemicals, including drugs that *señor* Dunst, *señora* Vodkonen sell in US. It can easily switch to making your compound in large amounts. Just give . . ." He stopped and turned to the slight, balding chemist, who continued:

"We'll need you to give us the ingredients, the formula, and the synthesis procedure. Our engineers will scale up, configure the reaction vessels, and so forth."

For the next hour, they planned delivery schedules, strategies for selling GX, and logistics for shipping large quantities. The planning was done over much toasting of their success, and even Kane managed to celebrate his success.

They were interrupted by one of Campana's men, who whispered something to his boss. He shrugged and said "*No hay problema. Haz que se vayan.*" The man nodded and left.

"What's the problem?" asked Dunst.

"Oh, the people we feed, they don't seem to be getting normal. Drug not wearing off."

"I need to see them," said Kane urgently. "I need to know whether it's a dosing problem. There may be some physiological reaction that—"

"Too late," said Campana, with a dismissive wave. "The people they have left."

***

"Miss me?" asked Lou. She stood grinning in the doorway of Nonny's house, wearing a backpack, tattered jeans, boots, and a t-shirt that said "Spread Hummus Not Hate."

"It's been sixty-three days since I saw you," said Nonny, with a faint smile.

"So, you did miss me. Invite me in."

Nonny backed away from the door, and Lou sauntered in and dropped her backpack by the door.

Saying nothing, Nonny headed back to his sprawling kitchen with its professional Wolf stove and array of mixers, blenders, pasta makers, and other appliances. Standing at the large marble-topped kitchen island, he proceeded to carefully add ingredients to a stainless-steel mixing bowl.

"Making dinner?" asked Lou.

"Developing a new recipe," said Nonny. "It's an idea I had for a Persian pomegranate and walnut stew. It's a vegan version of a Persian chicken dish called fesenjan."

"Vegan, eh?" So is that my influence?"

"Yes. And Daoud's." Nonny kept his head down, concentrating on his mixing.

"Well, great. Then I'll stay for dinner. So, how are the girls? Last I saw you, you were taking them away in the jet the billionaire let you use because you made his mother cry."

"They're all in witness protection. Elena is at a university. Jocelyn is in high school. Veronika is working as a translator. Natalia is also going to school, too, and is with a family as a nanny."

"And you trust that they're safe?"

"I have friends watching over them."

"Friends? Nonny, these drug dealers that are after them are dangerous."

"So are my friends."

"Like, maybe the family Natalia is nannying for?"

"Former CIA. Both the father and mother."

Lou found wine glasses and chose a bottle of wine from Nonny's wine cooler and opened it. She poured herself and Nonny both glasses. She raised hers. "I propose a toast, to our new upcoming collaboration."

Nonny raised his glass, but also his eyebrows. "What do you mean?"

"Here's the deal. We've been chasing those two motherfu . . . those two scum all over the world, literally. They've got houses, a yacht, airplanes . . . all kinds of hiding places. We've gotten close, but every time we think we've got them, they slip away."

"It's that leak in the FBI."

"Yes, certainly, so I had an idea for an off-the-books op. Just you and me."

"What do I know about 'ops'?"

"Okay, in my research, I realized that one of the key traits of those two is that they only dine in the best restaurants. I did some research, and I found out that they've been to three-star restaurants in Brussels, Paris, Mexico City, and other places. I even have data on what they ordered."

"So, what can I do?" Nonny's voice raised a notch in pitch. He took a drink of his wine and looked at Lou expectantly.

"You analyze the dishes they ordered. Figure out their food preferences. Then ask your contacts at the best restaurants that meet those preferences to be on the lookout for those two."

Nonny said nothing for a long moment, pouring the ingredients from the mixing bowl into a pot simmering on the stove. He stirred them in. "Daoud will help. He can put it all into the computer. We can look for patterns."

"But only him. We keep this totally quiet."

"Totally quiet," agreed Nonny, stirring.

Lou poured a full glass of wine and took a long drink, then a long breath. "Look, you need to know more about me." She took another drink. "I'm a southern belle who turned out to be a clinker. A Savannah debutante gone wrong. My folks had it all planned out that I'd get some lame-ass degree in art or something that would make me eligible to be a good southern wife. But I disappointed them. I went to Georgia Tech and got fascinated by chemistry. I lived and breathed chemistry."

She paused to see Nonny's reaction, but he continued to stir.

"Okay, that's my education. As for my love life, I've had my share of boyfriends. I'm easy to get along with, and I think pretty easy on the eyes. And by the way, I'm really good in the sack. But most of my boyfriends broke it off. I think most didn't understand my passion, how I'm driven. I mean, jeez, I've got tatts of molecules on my back! But I think you do understand that passion. I know we're a lot alike."

Nonny placed the lid on the pot, adjusted the flame, and looked in her direction. "So, you're telling me all this because. . .?"

"Because you are a very sexy man. Very, *very* sexy. And I can tell we are physically attracted to each other. So, at some point, we are going to have some major lovemaking." She slid off the stool and fetched her backpack, pulling out a red paperback. "I know you like recipes. This book has lots of recipes for terrific sex."

She flipped through the book, revealing page after page with yellow highlighter markings and marginal notes. "I've marked key parts. Pay special attention to chapter fourteen. There's a list of recommended. . . um. . . appliances. So, check it out, sport." She slid the book across the kitchen island.

Nonny smiled, reached over, and picked it up.

***

Diana Vodkonen, her svelte, oiled body minimally covered with a string bikini, lounged back in the deck chair looking out on the azure Sea of Cortez. A warm breeze wafted through the villa, bringing a scent of ocean. She held up the snifter of amber AsomBroso tequila to the sunlight and swirled it, watching the pearl-like droplets clinging to the glass. She took a sip, letting the complex tang of the liquor suffuse her mouth.

"Remarkable," said Dunst emerging from the shade of their villa outside Cabo San Lucas. "I just talked to Campana. It's only been a week since the test, and they're well on their way to having a production plant running. He says we'll have all the GX we need for a bulk sale in a month or so. You ready for the meet?"

"I'm still thinking," she answered lazily. She put down the snifter and picked up the barrel to her pistol, giving it one last swab and mating it to the slide. She finished assembling the pistol, tested its mechanism with a click of the trigger, then slapped in the clip and chambered a round. Finally, she screwed on the silencer.

"That doesn't look like thinking," said Dunst. "That looks like preparation."

"Just in case. And I was thinking, as well."

Dunst chuckled. "Well, good. Every time you are thinking, somehow, we end up making more money than we expected. What are you thinking about?"

Diana took another sip of tequila. "I did an analysis of GloboChem's finances, their product line, and their market. I factored in how GX might increase that market if it was added to their products."

"And?"

"We can charge them forty million for the first shipment."

"Excellent. And if we can't come to terms?"

Diana casually waved the pistol at the direction of the marina where their yacht was docked. Dunst shrugged in tacit agreement. The yacht had been used numerous times to transport bodies to final disposal in the open ocean.

After a lunch prepared by their chef, they sipped tequila until the hulking Mutante appeared, a signal that their guests had arrived. Diana went upstairs to change, while Dunst instructed Mutante to let them in.

Shortly, GloboChem executive vice president, Engineered Food Products Division Gabriel McAndrews stood before them with his security chief Joseph. They looked as stolid as the marble pillars of the living room. McAndrews wore dark slacks and a dress shirt, with a yacht tan that fit well with the Mexican Riviera, Cabo San Lucas. Joseph had made no concession to the resort, wearing a tan suit, his eyes hidden beneath small round sunglasses.

Behind them, Mutante escorted the chef and the house servants away out the villa's front door. He reappeared, staring pointedly at Joseph.

"Your man does not need to be here," said Dunst, spreading his hands and smiling. "We have adequate security."

"Nevertheless . . ." said McAndrews, giving Dunst a cold stare.

"Tell you what. Let's have both our men take their ease in the library, where they can enjoy refreshments while we talk business."

McAndrews was silent for a tense moment, finally nodding his assent; and Mutante and Joseph silently vanished.

Diana appeared, stepping down the stairs from the second floor, barefoot and wearing a sky-blue silk pant suit, and carrying a leather briefcase. She opened it on the coffee table, facing away from McAndrews.

"So, are you ready to make a lot of money for your company?" she asked, smiling.

"We are already doing well, and we're not really sure you can help us," said McAndrews. "You see, we analyzed the sample of binary gustatene you gave us. We believe we can reproduce the components ourselves. However, that would give us some . . . well . . . logistical problems. It would be problematical for us to manufacture it secretly in our own facility. So, we're actually here to explore your supplying us with an amount consonant with the twenty million dollars we invested in your venture. And perhaps a modest additional payment for more."

"Oh, but you are so behind the times, sir," said Dunst. He placed on the coffee table a vial of pale-yellow liquid. "You see, Doctor Kane has developed a much-improved single compound, gustatene X. It is far more potent, it triggers hunger, and it is impervious to cooking."

"We are working toward such a compound ourselves," said McAndrews tersely.

"I doubt it," said Dunst. "In any case, we are supplying this sample for testing purposes only. Should we find that you are attempting to duplicate it. . ." Dunst didn't finish his sentence. He didn't need to. He was sure McAndrews recalled their conversation on his plane. He turned to Diana. "I think you have some figures to persuade Mr. McAndrews of our proposal?"

She took her tablet computer out of the briefcase and tapped it several times. "You have invested twenty million with us. For another forty million, we can supply two tanks of two-hundred-and-fifty gallons of GX each. It can be diluted at least a thousand times to make the final additive. Given that the demand for your food products would skyrocket because of the increased consumption by customers, I calculate that GX would increase sales perhaps half a billion dollars. An excellent return on investment."

"A substantial risk I am not willing to take," said McAndrews, standing up. Diana placed her hand inside the briefcase, her gaze at him steady, cold. McAndrews stood in front of the fireplace, shaking his well-coiffed head. "We would have to figure out how to transport the compound to our facilities. How to introduce it into the product. Then, of course, there were the terrorist acts, which drew attention to Doctor Kane's work." He stopped abruptly and stared at Diana with her hand in the briefcase, his eyes widening slightly at a realization.

Said Dunst, "We will handle the terrorists, the Veganites. They will shortly no longer be a problem. And we will deliver the compound to your central manufacturing facility for dispersal."

"So, your decision?" asked Diana.

McAndrews continued to stare at Diana, with a glance toward the library where his security man was sequestered. "Uh . . . I'm sure we can work it all out," he said abruptly. "We quite commonly adjust the recipes for our product. We'll simply tell our production managers it is a flavoring. We don't need to detail the ingredients of any so-called natural flavoring."

Diana took her hand out of the briefcase and gave McAndrews her tablet. "I assume you came prepared to transfer the sum."

***

"*Dear God, what have you done to them?*" Kane choked out, gagging at the stink emanating from the dog cages. The kennel was in an isolated metal building down a dirt road on Campana's estate in the brown rolling hills above the city. But the kennel's row of low cages held, not dogs, but ragged, moaning people—three men and four women—clawing desperately at the wire mesh. The men were naked except for soiled shorts, and the women wore tattered dresses.

"We did nothing to them," said the slight, balding chemist. "It was your compound. It hasn't worn off."

"What do you mean?" asked Kane.

"Watch." The man nodded at two guards, who moved down the row of cages, quickly opening each door and pitching in chunks of meat. The men and women grabbed the meat and began to wolf it down, grunting as they ate.

"I don't understand," said Kane. "I just don't—"

"It did not wear off!" exclaimed the chemist.

"Maybe it will," said Kane. "Maybe I just used too large a dose." He stopped, his brow furrowed. "There were eight people before."

"A man died. See, they will gorge themselves until their bellies are so full they can't eat any more. Then they just collapse unconscious until they wake up to eat more. The man just died from some kind of gut problem."

"It's the dosage," said Kane, as if to reassure himself. "It's just the dosage. It didn't happen with the dogs, or the rats."

The chemist shook his head. "Dogs are pure carnivores. They evolved to gorge. You wouldn't have noticed it with the dogs. And the rats are obviously not humans."

"No, it's just the dosage," said Kane, backing away from the sight of the people crouched on the filthy concrete floors of the cages, gnawing on the meat, grunting as they ate. "Has to be the dosage. They'll be better soon. I'll check my data. They'll be better soon."

One of Campana's men hauled out a hose and began to wash out the cages, sluicing the human waste into a drain.

***

"Wolves don't stray far from their territory," said Abadi, turning his laptop around on the coffee table in Nonny's living room. "I figured these wolves didn't either."

"Not wolves," said Nonny, fresh from his restaurant, still dressed in his double-breasted white chef coat and dark slacks. "Jackals."

Beside him sat Lou, her bare feet folded beneath her on the sofa. "So, you found them with the food?" she asked. "Looked at what they were eating at restaurants to see where they might be hiding?"

"No, it was their liquor," answered Abadi. "When they were in restaurants in Mexico City, and even in Paris or Rome, the woman liked to order tequila. Specifically, AsomBroso Reserva Del Porto. It's one of the most expensive tequilas, about three thousand dollars a bottle. It comes from Portugal. So, I went to the source. I give the man at the distillery a lot of money. I ask him where they ship bottles recently. I am betting she want her own bottle."

The doorbell rang, and Nonny answered it to see Chun and Tate. He scowled at them, demanding, "What are you doing here?"

"I asked them," said Lou. "If we want to catch these people, we need some big dogs. That means FBI. My FDA is not particularly strong on strong-arming."

"I don't trust them," said Nonny, still glaring at the two.

"Look, Nonny, we have to trust somebody. Let them in."

Nonny backed away from the door, and Chun and Tate entered, Chun saying, "Nonny, you do need us."

"We *do* need them, Chef," said Abadi. "Just look at my data. There were six bottles of the tequila sold in Mexico. The jackals, as you say, would not stray far from their business. Five bottles were sold in Mexico City, but one was in Cabo San Lucas. That is kind of place these people would want to be. That is place we need FBI to get to."

"Remember, we're pretty sure they have a yacht, but we haven't found it," said Chun. "It's registered under some shell company. We need to contact the DEA. . . get them to put a FAST team on it."

"FAST team?" asked Nonny.

"Foreign-deployed Advisory and Support Team. They work with foreign governments to set up raids," said Chun.

Tate had been silent, but now he said, "I'll take care of the DEA. They'll get the Mexican *federales* involved to organize a raid."

"Then, we go to Cabo," said Abadi.

They all stood to leave, but Lou remained folded up on the couch. "Nonny and I have some literary business to attend to," she said smiling. "We've started a book club."

Chun gave her a puzzled look, but Nonny's emphatic march to his front door and opening it made it clear that they were to depart.

When they were alone, Lou asked, "So, have you done your reading?" She pursed her lips and raised her eyebrows teasingly.

"I have," said Nonny, beginning to unbutton his chef's coat.

"Including chapter fourteen?"

"Yes, and chapter eighteen, as well."

"Ah, chapter eighteen," declared Lou. She reached up to make sure her ponytail fully secured her mop of hair. "A *very* good chapter. A real workout. I'll need my hair well out of the way for that chapter. You did advanced work!"

***

"You have failed, totally and utterly," said McAndrews, crossing his legs and taking a sip of his coffee. He sat on the sofa in his executive suite at GloboChem's Philadelphia headquarters, with Joseph standing beside him.

Carson Hayworth's haggard face showed a three-days' growth of stubble that rendered his carefully shaped beard less defined. He slumped in the chair across from McAndrews. He had just come from the airport on an overnight flight after being summoned from Las Vegas yet again.

"I don't understand what you mean," said Hayworth. "We analyzed the gustatene sample. We found out how to synthesize it. We can contract with an outside company—"

"Gustatene is old news," said McAndrews. "I have just met with our so-called *partners*." He said the last word with disgust. "They said that Kane has progressed to an entirely new compound, gustatene X, with far superior properties. Properties that make it a very useful additive to just about all our products. It's powerful and heat-resistant."

"Well, if we could get a sample—"

"We can't. But even if we could, you with all your resources, all your manpower, should have been able to come up with it. We have poured millions into your laboratory."

"But Kane was already so far ahead of us," said Hayworth pleadingly. "His computer model was so far advanced. And he wouldn't give his data to us."

"But he was willing to go to work for a drug dealer. Frankly, I don't see much of a future for you here at GloboChem. That is, unless you show progress toward a potent, sturdy version of the compound." MacAndrews rose and went to sit at his desk. "And now, I have a meeting." He began typing on his laptop until Hayworth roused himself with some effort and was escorted out by Joseph.

Joseph returned, saying, "You didn't give him the sample they gave you?"

"You may recall what the thugs said. If they find out we're trying to make it ourselves, there would be unfortunate consequences. But if Hayworth manages to come up with a similar compound independently, and if we've bought forty-million-dollars' worth of their compound from the thugs, they'll be placated."

"What would you like me to do?"

"Monitor his activities. I don't trust him." McAndrews leaned back in his chair, pulling the vial of yellow liquid from his coat pocket and contemplating it. "And I've got to figure out a way to test this stuff."

Chapter 15

"*Oh Dios mío, no me mates!*" the maid begged, falling back against the wall, as the helmeted, masked, black-uniformed Mexican federal police burst through the front door of the Cabo San Lucas villa. Others swarmed in through the back patio, assault rifles raised.

Shouts from the men of "*Claro!*" echoed through the villa, as they went from room to room and up the stairs to the second floor. The plump middle-aged maid was hauled sobbing into the living room and made to sit onto the couch. She was joined shortly by another younger maid, who had been brought down from upstairs.

"*¿Dónde están?*" commanded the helmeted sergeant, shouldering his assault rifle. "*¿Donde han ido?*"

Chun and Tate appeared beside him wearing bulletproof vests bearing white FBI initials.

"They do not know where the people went," said the sergeant to them.

"*No te haremos daño. Te protegeremos. Sólo dinos,*" said Chun softly. Then to Tate: "I've reassured them that they'll be safe if they tell us."

But the tearful maids both shook their heads and hung them in fear.

As Abadi and Nonny appeared to stand next to the villa's stone pillars, Chun sat down beside the women and began to quiz them in Spanish. After many questions, she reported, "The two left yesterday. She thinks they left on a boat, but she doesn't know which one."

Abadi found the credenza holding the liquor bottles, rummaged through it, and held up a round sculpted bottle a third filled with amber liquid. "The AsomBroso Reserve," he announced triumphantly. "Our detective work paid off!"

"We can also get clues from their provisioning of the boat," said Nonny. "They would have bought exotic foods." He led Abadi toward the kitchen.

Chun and the Mexican sergeant began calling Mexican port masters in an attempt to track Diana and Dunst; while Tate began a search of the rest of the house.

Lou pointedly joined him, saying, "It would be good to have a second set of eyes."

After an hour, they gathered in the living room to compare notes.

Said Chun, "This marina was a bust. We did get video of them entering the marina, but there were no cameras on the docks near the big yachts. The owners want privacy. So, we can't find out which boat they were on, especially since it's the high season and boats are leaving all the time."

Lou and Tate reported back a frustrating lack of clues from the villa's rooms to the pair's. "Fancy clothes and stuff, but no notes or other records," said Lou.

"I have better luck," said Abadi, "We check the trash. We find their chef's shopping list. Exotic foods." He read the list: "He buys spices like saffron, cardamom, pure vanilla. Japanese Wagyu beef, veal, pheasant. Canary melons. Exotic cheeses like Cremona provolone, Grand Suisse Gruyere, imported French Brie."

Nonny sat silently, staring straight ahead for a long moment. Without looking up, he said. "I know what recipes he plans to prepare. But he doesn't have all the ingredients. He would have to order them. Some are very rare." He looked around for a piece of paper and a pen, scribbling a list and handing it to Abadi. "We will contact purveyors of exotic foods and find who orders these." With that, Abadi and Nonny left to take their billionaire benefactor's jet back to Las Vegas.

Chun dispatched Tate to visit the marina to compile the video and to meet them at the airport. And after spending another hour questioning the maids and double-checking the villa, Chun and Lou settled into the back of the car that would take them to the airport.

"So, you and the chef, eh?" asked Chun with an intimate smirk.

"Yes, me and the chef," answered Lou, cocking her head.

"So. . . ?"

"So what?"

"How is he as a. . . y'know?"

"As a lover?" Lou turned toward Chun, leaning back against the car door, grinning beatifically. "Well. . . he's not just a *culinary* genius." She chuckled. "True, he is really into food. I mean, jeez, our safe word is 'Julia Child.' But he is *quite* talented beyond that. And, it turns out, he is a wonderful guy. Durnit, Leafy, I'm in love!" She willed herself to emerge from her wonderment. "Okay, I shared. Now it's your turn. You're married, right? You've never talked about your husband."

"He's an artist. Doctorate in art history from Yale. I met him at a gallery opening of his in New York."

"Ah, so an artsy-fartsy type, right? Sensitive, delicate."

"Well, not your average artist. After we'd gone out a couple of times, he invited me to another kind of show he did. He paid for college as a dancer."

"What, ballet? Modern dance?"

"Um, actually, exotic. He was a male stripper."

"Wow! You mean stuff-a-dollar-in-his-G-string-type stripper?"

"Yup," said Chun. "He even did private dances. As a cop, fireman, and such."

"And he's . . ." Lou flexed her arms to make muscles.

"Yup, he's buff."

Lou smiled, but that smile abruptly faded. Her expression turned grim. "The mole. It's either you or Tate. I hope it's not you. If it is you, I will get you."

Chun shook her head. "I'm not the leak."

"Yeah, you would say that. But I'm making a risky bet that it's not. I'm going to make a play. When we're on the plane with Tate, I'm going to plant a false lead. You just follow along."

Chun nodded somberly, and when they climbed aboard the FBI Gulfstream jet, Tate was waiting. Lou took out her cell phone, checked her messages and uttered a satisfied "humph!"

"Got something?" asked Chun.

"Yeah. My buddy in the Mexican drug agency traced the woman's prescription to the pharmacy." She scrutinized the text. "It's the *Farmacia Superior* in Mazatlan. He says he'll get down there day after tomorrow to get their records. That'll give us a location where the Diana woman has her drugs delivered. We'll nail 'em!"

***

"Hayworth has gone rogue," warned Joseph, consulting his tablet computer. He passed the tablet to McAndrews, as they sat in the limousine on the way to Philadelphia International Airport.

"What am I looking at?" asked McAndrews, peering at rows of phone numbers on the tablet screen, some highlighted in yellow.

"The first highlighted numbers are Hayworth's calls to a lawyer for a Veganite defendant. The rest are to a burner phone. We can't trace the burner to a person, but I did access its call records. They showed calls to the other lawyers for the Veganites, as well as half a dozen other burner phones.

"Your conclusion?" asked McAndrews.

"That Hayworth first reached out to the Veganite lawyer. The lawyer gave him a number central to the Veganite organization, either the leader's or a higher-up."

"Your recommendation?"

"Neutralize Hayworth," Joseph said in a matter-of-fact tone.

"Okay," said McAndrews, thinking for a long moment before reaching into his jacket pocket and handing Joseph the vial of GX. "This needs to be tested for efficacy. See if you can accomplish both objectives. Be creative."

***

"First off, do you got the money?" Boudreaux asked Baltazar over the video link. "You get nothin' from me unless I get the money." On the computer screen, his face still showed remnant swelling and purplish bruises from the beating Mutante had given him. "I told you I want a million. I ain't greedy."

"Of course you're greedy," chuckled Baltazar. "But I did agree to the amount. But only if you give me specifics on how to get the shipment of the new drug. I'll give you half when you give us the details; half when the operation is successful."

"Okay, the stuff they're shipping is called GX, and—"

"We know about GX," interrupted Baltazar. "We have a source in GloboChem. We know about its properties. We need you to tell us how it's being shipped."

Boudreaux paused and stared, mute for a moment, recovering from the discovery that he wasn't the only information source. "Yeah, well, pay the half right now, I give you the info."

"Agreed." Baltazar called up the Veganite bank account in the Cayman Islands and transferred half a million dollars to Boudreaux's account in the same bank.

On the screen, Boudreaux paused, peering at his own bank record. Satisfied, he said, "Okay, there are two shipments, separate routes, two-hundred-and-fifty gallons each. I'm just gonna tell you about one. So, your hit will look like a random highjackin'. If you took both trucks, they'll know it came from inside. Can you make it look like a hijacking?"

"Our operatives are good actors. The drivers will think they're blindly going after the cargo."

"Yeah, right, okay." Boudreaux proceeded to give Baltazar the Mexican border-crossing point, day, and time. "That's all you get. You have your people follow them from the border, okay? If you intercept the truck right at the border, they'll know you knew the route."

"What's the destination?"

Boudreaux loosed an acid laugh. "You think I'm nuts? None of your business. You don't need to know. Like I don't need to know what the hell you plan to do with that stuff."

"Oh, you'll know when it happens," said Baltazar, touching the computer key to end the connection.

Chapter 16

"Just what the hell did you think you were doing?" asked Diana over the cell phone.

Holding the phone that Diana had given him close to his ear, Tate backed against the wall of the lobby of the FBI building, peering around. He replied in an urgent whisper. "I couldn't reach you. They said they were going to raid the pharmacy in Mazatlán where you got your prescription filled. I had to do something. So, I contacted a guy who's done work for us in Mexico to steal the records. I told him it was confidential FBI business. So he broke in, and—"

"Did he find any records?"

"No."

"That's because I never had a prescription filled in Mazatlán." Diana's measured tone conveyed a smoldering rage.

It took several seconds for Tate to realize what had happened. He felt a wave of nausea roil his gut, and he slumped against the wall, amid the people coming and going in the lobby. He had been trapped! They knew he was the mole! Panting in fear, he managed to pull himself out of his fog of fear to hear Diana's voice on the phone coolly cursing his stupidity.

"Look, you've got to help me!" he managed to choke out. He realized that a woman walking by had heard him and was staring. He tried to manage a nonchalant smile. He failed.

"Help you do what?" she asked.

"Get out! Get away! I'll need . . ." He paused, realizing that he hadn't even thought about what he would need. He tried to develop a strategy. "Okay, I'll need a passport, credit cards, all in an alias name. I'll need to get to a non-extradition country. I'll need more money. I'll need—"

"*Okay, okay, just calm down,*" said Diana. "Are you on speaker?"

"No, of course not."

"*Now listen very closely.*"

"Okay," he answered. Diana had begun to speak in a low voice, so Tate held the phone tight against his ear.

The cell phone detonated with a resounding crack that shattered Tate's skull and spewed his skin, brain, and bone across the lobby. It splattered the walls and floors with red splotches and showered a young woman nearby, who spread her blood-flecked hands in shock, screamed in horror, and lurched away, retching. The sickening smell of burned explosive and charred flesh permeated the lobby.

Tate's nearly headless body slumped to its knees, blood spurting from its severed neck, then toppled forward onto the marble floor into a spreading crimson pool.

***

"Nobody else can come in," said Joseph to the security guard at the door to the executive dining room in the GloboChem Dallas factory. The guard nodded and stationed himself outside. Joseph turned back to Hayworth, seated at a table overlooking the factory floor, with its long row of two-story stainless-steel vats. Workers moved among them, dwarfed by the huge tanks. They were checking dials, adding barrels of ingredients, and hauling hoses to fill or empty the vats with the company's dressings, sauces, condiments, and other food products. As the lunch hour arrived, the floor was emptying of workers.

"So, why are you here?" asked Hayworth.

"Not to worry," said Joseph, sitting down and adjusting his suit coat. "Mr. McAndrews just wanted to correct what he told you in Philadelphia. He was upset then. He wanted to reassure you that we have every confidence in you and your team. He just wanted me to get a sense of your progress, so he can report knowledgeably to the board."

"Yeah, well, I don't have a lot of time. I'm just here checking on the lab tests they're using for quality control."

"Sure, sure, I understand. That's why I thought we'd just have a quick lunch, and I could get an update."

"So, you flew all the way to Dallas for this? We could have done it over the phone."

Joseph shrugged and smiled. "Hey, the boss says fly to Dallas, I fly to Dallas. I had sandwich-makings brought in. Let's just grab a quick bite and talk."

He rose and went to the cold buffet, beginning to make himself a roast beef sandwich on a roll. Hayworth hesitated a moment, then followed, also assembling a roast beef sandwich. They returned to the table, but Joseph immediately got back up. He took his sandwich to the buffet and spooned a healthy amount of pickle relish onto the sandwich. He then filled a bowl with the pickle relish.

With his back turned to Hayworth, he poured into the pickle relish a drop from the vial of yellow liquid McAndrews had given him, stirred it with a plastic spoon, and put the spoon in the relish.

"I just heard that they introduced this new pickle relish," he declared, bringing his plate and the bowl back to the table. "I had some yesterday, and it's amazing."

"I hadn't heard that," said Hayworth.

"You wouldn't. Mr. McAndrews wanted to introduce it as a premium product." He pointed at the factory floor. "See that third vat? That's full of the pickle relish." He pushed the bowl at Hayworth. "See what you think. Actually, Mr. McAndrews will want your opinion, in terms of quality control." Joseph took a healthy bite of his sandwich.

Hayworth uttered a noncommittal "hmm," and spooned some relish onto his sandwich.

185

"So, what should I tell the boss?" asked Joseph. He stared expectantly at Hayworth as Hayworth took a bite of his sandwich and began to outline the progress of the effort to develop a GloboChem version of GX.

After eating half his sandwich, Hayworth was saying, "So, we're thinking that—" But then, he interrupted himself. "This sandwich . . . this relish . . . it's . . ." He spooned a mound of the relish onto the remaining portion of the sandwich. He took a large bite.

"You were saying?" asked Joseph. He had stopped eating his own sandwich.

But Hayworth didn't answer. He was now taking large bites of the sandwich. His expression had grown blank, his gaze distant. He finished the sandwich and sat for a long moment. Then he grabbed the bowl of relish and began to spoon it into his mouth, then tilting the bowl and shoveling it into his mouth with his hand.

"Umm," he moaned. "It's . . ."

Joseph pointed out the window to the factory floor. "The third vat, Carson. The third vat. It's full of relish. The relish you just ate. The same wonderful relish."

"*Oh. . . yes. . . God!*" breathed Hayworth, turning his gaze to the window, lurching to his feet and stumbling out the door past the guard.

Joseph remained seated, to make sure he wouldn't be implicated in what was to occur. The guard would witness Hayworth leaving the dining room on his own. The security cameras would record Hayworth crossing the factory floor on his own and climbing the metal stairs to the catwalk overlooking the vats. They would capture him throwing open the metal cover to the large vat on his own. And leaning down to scoop handfuls of the green relish into his mouth.

"That's a good boy," whispered Joseph to himself. "Just go for it. Just go for it."

Hayworth was now crouched low over the vat, using both hands to shovel relish into his mouth. Abruptly, he dived forward into the vat, disappearing for a moment before flopping to its green gelatinous surface. Joseph could see that he was struggling, but he couldn't really tell whether Hayworth was trying to get out or trying to ingest yet more relish. Actually, it didn't matter if it achieved the objective. The guard couldn't see the vat from his post. And when Joseph scanned up and down the factory floor, he saw that the nearest worker was a hundred yards away and hadn't noticed Hayworth.

After about a minute, Hayworth stopped moving, his body floating inertly in the thick sea of relish.

Joseph threw Hayworth's sandwich and the relish bowl into the trash, made himself a cappuccino, and sat back down at the table, sipping it slowly. After fifteen minutes, he rose and went to the door.

"I guess Mr. Hayworth went to check some product," he told the guard. "Our meeting is done, so folks are welcome to use the dining room." Joseph checked his watch. He just had time to get to the airport for his flight.

Chapter 17

"C'mon, *compañero*, I ain't eaten all damn day!" exclaimed the pudgy trucker with the frizzy beard, sitting in the passenger seat. "We got a whole day's drive to Vegas, and I need to eat."

The white unmarked box truck had just spent two hours in the long line of other trucks at the Mexican commercial border crossing. Finally on US soil, the driver—a wiry man with an unruly head of long, thinning hair—impatiently accelerated onto the highway. He grumped, "You just gotta deal with bein' hungry. Campana says we deliver this load fast, so we go like rabbits."

The pudgy trucker continued to complain until the driver, also suffering hunger pangs, swerved the truck onto an exit and into the broad asphalt parking lot of a truck stop with a huge lighted sign that said "Truck Stop."

They climbed out, walked quickly into the neon-lit café, and sat in a booth. They opened menus, ordering as soon as the waitress came.

"Happy now?" asked the driver.

"Gonna be, once I eat," replied the pudgy trucker.

They were waiting for their food when two young women slid into the booth across from them. As did the other truckers in the cafe, both of the men took very appreciative note of the women. One was a slim blond with flyaway hair whose red shorts revealed long tanned legs; the other was a petite long-haired brunette whose halter top revealed a shapely chest and whose own shorts revealed smooth, creamy skin.

"Shit! Shit! Shit!" exclaimed the blond. "What the hell are we gonna do?"

"I dunno. Those bastards!" answered the brunette.

"How much you got?" asked the blond.

"Just what was in my pocket," said the brunette. She dug in her shorts and pulled out several crumpled bills. She spread them on the table. The waitress arrived, and the women frowned, scrutinizing the menus. They ordered enough food to fit their pocket-money budget.

The truckers' hamburgers arrived, and they began to eat, but despite the hunger, they were paying more attention to the two women than to their food.

"They took my purse with my phone, but you've got yours, right?" the blond asked the brunette.

The brunette pulled her phone out of her pocket and stared at it, shaking her head. "Yeah, but it's dead." She looked around, her almond eyes wide with anxiety and leaned across the aisle to the truckers. "Say, do you guys happen to have a charger that would work with this phone?" She held up her phone.

"Well, lemme see it," said the driver, reaching out to take the phone. He examined it, concluding, "Yeah, I've got an adapter in the truck."

"Oh, we would be sooooo grateful if you'd let me charge my phone! Y'see, we were robbed. These guys were giving us a ride from Mazatlán. We agreed to pay them, and we camped our way up. But we got here, and we got out of the van, and the bastards just drove off with all our money and our stuff!"

"Sure, sure, sure," said the pudgy trucker enthusiastically. "Always happy to help ladies in trouble."

"Well that's really nice of you," said the blond. "And calling us ladies! We ain't never been accused of that!" She laughed a musical laugh.

The driver leaned over to his partner, whispering, "What the hell are you doin'? We got to get this cargo delivered. You know what would happen to us if we were late?"

The pudgy trucker whispered back, "C'mon, these *chicas* are hot, man! You see the *tetas* on that one? And we'll make up time. It'll be fine."

After the two women finished their own plates of tomatoes, toast, and hash browns, they followed the men out to the truck, climbing inside.

The blond giggled, and said, "We sit boy-girl-boy-girl! I don't wanna sit by her. I'd rather sit between you handsome guys!"

The two truckers eagerly agreed, and as they nestled together in the truck were acutely aware of the girls' young, nubile bodies.

The brunette plugged her phone into the charger and began to punch in a call. "I'm gonna call my brother," she said. "My folks would have a shit-fit if they found out." Then, into the phone: "Brent, it's me. Yeah, we're back in the US. Listen, Brent, we got robbed. Shit, they took everything! We're fine, we're fine. Listen, can you send money?"

She then turned to the truckers. "Where you guys going?"

"Vegas," answered the pudgy trucker quickly, ignoring the driver's frown.

"Can you take us there? We'd pay. A thousand apiece! Seriously!"

"Sure, sure," said the pudgy trucker quickly, noting that the driver's frown had faded, and he had nodded in agreement, eyebrows raised in anticipation.

Twirling her hair with one hand, the brunette spoke into the phone again. "Brent, we got a ride with some. . ." she paused and grinned knowingly at the two men ". . . very nice elderly ladies. So, wire ten grand to Western Union in Vegas. And for chrissakes, don't tell Mom or Dad!" She ended the call, and said to the truckers, "We're good to go."

The driver leaned back in his seat and gave the blond a long appraising look. "So, you were in Mazatlán?"

"Yeah," said the blond. "A long spring break."

"I like your tatt," he said, eyeing one just above the blond's left breast. It was the outline of a heart, with the top forming a green V. One arm of the V sprouted a leaf. "What's that one mean?" He patted the tattoo.

"Oh, that's a vegan symbol. We're both vegans. Show yours, Jenny."

The brunette pulled up her halter top to show the same tattoo just below her left breast. "I've got more tatts you can't see," she said with a suggestive smirk.

"So, you no like meat?" asked the pudgy driver.

"Oh, *some* meat!" laughed the blond.

The driver chuckled, but then with an accusing frown, said, "Look, how we know you're gonna pay us. You might just leave us when we get to Vegas?"

The blond cocked her head saucily and placed the driver's hand on her left thigh and the pudgy trucker's hand on her right thigh. "How about we give you a down payment? Or like a tip?"

The brunette giggled and exclaimed "Lizzie, I hope it's more than a tip!"

"You got protection?" asked the blond.

"You got a big blanket?" asked the brunette, while placing the pudgy trucker's right hand on her thigh. "Find somewhere quiet. Like down a road or in a field."

The driver instantly started the truck and removed his hand from the blond's thigh just long enough to shove the truck into gear. He gunned the truck onto the highway and drove for several minutes before seeing an exit that led to a side road, which in turn led to a dirt road. He drove the truck out into an area thick with desert brush. He parked the truck and started to climb out, but the blond stopped him. She gave him a long kiss and placed his hand on her chest.

Dennis Meredith

"Let's foreplay a little bit first," she declared. "I like slow."

The brunette had done the same to the pudgy trucker, saying "I like to take it a bit slow, too. And make sure you got protection."

The pudgy trucker flipped opened the glove box and took out a handful of condoms. The brunette giggled and kissed him.

After some minutes, the brunette lowered the truck's window and paused. "Okay, Lizzie, let's give these boys what they deserve." She opened the door and climbed down from the truck, and the pudgy driver followed.

"Let me get the blanket—" he started to say, but stopped, finding himself staring into the barrel of a pistol held by a muscular young man with a buzz cut, wearing a t-shirt, cargo shorts, and sneakers. The man had come up the road behind them.

"Open the back, shithead!" declared the young man.

"Do what he says," the pudgy trucker heard the driver say from the other side of the truck.

"*You bitch!*" spat the pudgy trucker.

"You sucker," replied the brunette.

His hands raised, he walked ahead of the young man around to the back of the truck to see the driver on his knees, his hands behind his head, a gun to his head. The gun was held by another taut-bodied young man with a ponytail.

"You really *don't* want to do this," said the driver.

"Yeah, like, we very much *do*," said Ponytail.

The pudgy trucker swung the back doors open to reveal a large plastic tank, its liquid contents sloshing slowly back and forth. The blond girl climbed inside and inspected the tank.

"What's in it?" asked the muscular man.

"Whoa! Label says it's wine!" exclaimed the blond.

"Wine? Awesome sauce! Ought to be worth a shitload!" exclaimed the muscular young man.

192

Ponytail pulled a fistful of white zip ties out of his pocket. "Let's tie these dudes, put them out in the brush, change the plates and go get us a payday! Lizzie, go get the van."

"*Estúpido idiota!* Do you know who owns this cargo?" asked the driver.

"*We* own it, bitch!" replied Ponytail.

***

"That deranged monster," spat Chun, shaking her head. She stood in the blood-spattered lobby of the Las Vegas FBI field office holding up three plastic evidence bags. They contained the shredded bits of what was once a cell phone. Faint traces of pink on the bags' inside told of their history of blasting through the brain of deceased FBI agent Rydell Tate.

The blue-shirted Evidence Response Team was still scouring the lobby for further clues to the blast that had killed Tate.

"So, this was Diana Vodkonen's doing?" asked Lou.

"Certainly," said Chun handing off the bags to an ERT team member. "We've had agents going through her history . . . y'know, college, grad school, and so forth. Those who knew her said she was a total sociopath. She manipulated people, used them in despicable ways. But they also gave her props for being a brilliant engineer."

"So, how do those parts help us find her?"

"I'd bet that phone contained a little chunk of C-4. The forensic people might be able to trace it. The detonator would likely be specially built to fit into the phone. And the internal pieces just may contain her fingerprints, or maybe whoever she had build the device."

"And, of course, the boys are here," said Lou, peering out the glass front windows of the lobby. Chun followed Lou's gaze to see Nonny and Abadi standing outside, peering impatiently past the guards.

Chun and Lou joined them, and Abadi declared, "It was him who was mole? It was Tate? I thought it might be him. And now he is dead. Will you be able to find the people who he worked for?"

"Well, we can try to trace his movements,' said Chun. "And we can try to trace the money he was probably given. But I'll bet it's in offshore accounts. We don't have access to them."

"I know people," said Nonny.

"He does know people," said Abadi, nodding knowingly.

"Another billionaire whose mother you made cry?" asked Lou.

"Something like that," said Abadi. "Food can have a strong influence on people."

Said Nonny, "I can trace his money if you give me as much information as you can about where Tate has traveled . . . like to the Caymans or Cook Islands."

"But we have more important news," said Abadi. "Did you know that Carson Hayworth is dead?"

"No shit!" exclaimed Lou, forgetting her no-swearing pledge. "Holy mother—." Then she remembered it.

"It was in Dallas. He was in one of the plants on business. He drowned in a vat. It was an accident."

"Yeah, right," said Chun. "We'll damned well see about that."

***

"Very nice," said Diana, crossing her legs and scrutinizing the screen on her laptop. She ignored the vista of the sun-dappled open ocean, as the one-hundred-twenty-foot yacht motored smoothly through the mild chop.

"See something you like?" Dunst was seated with her, lounging in the shade of the covered sky lounge cantilevered above the stern deck. He held a glass of merlot in his hand, watching the sunlight reveal the wine's rich purple-red hue.

"It seems there was an explosion at the FBI field office in Las Vegas. It seems there was a fatality."

"Your gadget worked."

Diana gave him a scolding frown. "Gadget? That was a precisely engineered device. A shaped charge triggered by a digital code."

"Now, my dear, please do not take my jest as implying any aspersions cast upon your technical skills," chuckled Dunst, holding up his glass in a toast.

Diana's frown faded, and she closed the laptop. "I accept your apology."

"And will you please not make my own phone one of your lethal, engineered marvels?"

"Not your phone. But all the phones we're giving our associates. They are another matter."

"And you have all their detonation codes. Why not share them with me?"

"Because you are impulsive," said Diana, taking up her own glass of wine. "And brutal. You would kill our associates just for the fun of it."

"Pot, kettle, black," he teased. "But your fireworks in Las Vegas. Now our people will know what happened and decline your offer of a free phone."

"They won't find out. As usual, the FBI will keep its investigation confidential. The phones will continue to be a useful management tool."

Diana had ordered lunch from the chef and began to eat her conch ceviche salad when her satellite phone beeped. She answered, listened for a moment, then put the phone on speaker. "Say again," she instructed.

It was Boudreaux's voice. "The damn shipment was hijacked. I mean one of the shipments, she is gone. But just the one. The other one made it to Vegas."

"Who took it?" asked Dunst.

"We don't know. The truck just didn't show up in Vegas."

"What happened to the drivers?"

"They're just gone. They may have taken the truck. Me and Campana's guys found out they were eating in a truck stop, talking to some girls. They went off with the girls in the truck."

"Did the hijackers know what was in the truck?"

"Maybe. They knew that it came from the chemical plant, not the winery. I'll let you know if we hear from them, like asking for ransom or something."

Said Diana, "Get that shipment back, whatever you have to do. And if you find the drivers, put them in the desert. The girls, too." Diana ended the call and took a final bite of her salad. "I have an appetite," she said coolly.

"For more than lunch, my dear?"

She stood, luxuriantly stretched her lithe, bikinied body, and headed for her suite. "Send that steward with the tattoos, then come by yourself in an hour or so."

***

"We may have found Baltazar," declared Chun, sitting in the seat of the FBI jet, scrutinizing her laptop. "His travel records had him in Vegas, but then they lost him. He likely switched identities. But we're trying to trace his calls and ping the phones, but given that everybody's using burners, it's not easy."

"So, we go to Dallas," said Lou, strapped into the seat across the aisle, with her white-socked feet propped up on the seat across from her. She had just ended a call on her cell phone.

"Yeah, that's the best play until we know more. This GloboChem scientist, Hayworth's, death is just too weird to be an accident. You saw the security footage. As a food scientist, what's your take?"

"Yeah, weird is the word. It's not normal practice in sampling a vat to take off the cover and just lean down like that. Contaminates the vat. Best practice is to use an extension to take bulk samples and put them in sterile containers. He didn't have any of the paraphernalia. Something was clearly wrong with the guy."

"What do you think an autopsy will show?"

"Frankly, I think we're looking for gustatene or some version of it. That's gonna be damned tough to detect."

"So, you think GloboChem is implicated in using the stuff?"

196

"I'd bet money they've got something going on. Especially because of what Abadi just told me." She waved her phone in the air. "Him and Nonny said there's rumors around the restaurant business there of some kind of new food additive coming into Vegas. They're runnin' their sources now to find out."

Chun's cell phone emitted a musical tone, and she swiped the screen to take the call. She listened for a long moment.

"When?" she asked into the phone. "Oh, shit!" she exclaimed, ending the call.

"Something happen?" asked Lou.

"I'll say. A crop-dusting company north of San Diego just reported a helicopter and support tanker truck were stolen. Out there, they use 'copters to spray avocado groves. The 'copter does a spray run, then lands on a platform on top of the tanker truck and refills. The local police reported it to our field office because it smelled like a terrorist plot."

"You think it's Veganites?"

"So, okay, let's say you're Brigham Baltazar. You get your nut-case terrorists to release some bad stuff in a bunch of restaurants and get all kinds of publicity. But you've got this ego. You want to go bigger. I've just got a hunch this is 'going bigger'." Chun left the seat and hurried forward to the cockpit, calling back, "We're diverting to San Diego."

Chapter 18

"So, they recovered?" asked Kane, staring into the empty kennel cages on Campana's ranch. He had to fight to keep from choking at the overpowering odor of bleach permeating the tin building. The cages had been scrubbed, the concrete floors power-washed.

"They did recover," said the slight, balding chemist. "I told you there was nothing to see here; that you didn't need to come. They got better, we gave them a lot of money for participating in the test, and we sent them home."

"But they were like animals before."

"Oh, certainly, you saw them when they were having bad episodes. But like you said, it was the dosage. We've told all our customers that they need to dilute the compound heavily. It actually made them quite happy, given that they got a lot more active ingredient for their money."

"I need to see the subjects," said Kane. "I need to take blood samples. I need to see how the GX was metabolized. . . whether there are any dangerous breakdown products in the body."

Campana's chemist paused for a long moment before answering. "That won't be possible," he finally replied. "The subjects were not local. We didn't want to use our own people. They have returned to their towns."

"But I saw—" Kane started to say. He recalled seeing two of the women on the factory line.

"They were not local," interrupted the chemist.

Kane clenched his hands, took a deep, tremulous breath, and declared, "Then get them back. This is really critical. GX could be poisonous."

"I'll see what I can do. But we want you back in the lab. We want you to streamline the synthesis. We've got it running at about sixty-five percent efficiency in the plant, but we think you can make it better."

To emphasize his point, the chemist stepped to the door of the tin building and opened it, standing there expectantly.

"I need them back," Kane said, but less emphatically. Squinting against the bright sun streaming through the door, he stepped out and into the dirt parking area around the building. As he walked to the waiting SUV, and as his eyes adjusted to the sun, he realized that areas of the dirt were stained black. He had seen such stains before. He knew what dried blood looked like.

Nausea began to overwhelm him, and his legs began to give way. He put out his hand against the side of the SUV to steady himself, to fight the urge to vomit. He wanted to cry.

"*Vamonos,*" commanded the chemist. "You will go back to your lab." A beefy guard in a cowboy hat with an automatic pistol in his holster hauled open the SUV door and stood watching Kane with a dead-eyed stare.

***

"*Half the goddamned shipment?*" exclaimed McAndrews, pacing the thickly carpeted floor of his office in Philadelphia. He sat down in his chair and leaned into the computer screen showing Joseph's face. "*They lost half the shipment?*"

"And they apparently have no idea who took it," said Joseph, his shaking image revealing that he was walking along a tourist-crowded, sun-blasted sidewalk in Las Vegas.

"Do three things," instructed McAndrews. "First, make damned sure Dunst and the Mexicans plan to supply us with the two-hundred-fifty gallons that they lost. Second, divert the shipment headed to the factory in Dallas to Vegas. Third, tell the new research director there that he is to prepare a range of diluted solutions for field testing."

"You think Vegas is the right place? After all, that's where the first attacks happened."

"It's the perfect place," McAndrews shot back. "We've got the lab there, and we've also got retail customers to give test batches of dosed product. But what makes Vegas really perfect is that the authorities are already on alert for anything unusual. If we can manage to field-test without detection, we know we can go national, hell *international*. There's billions in market share at stake here."

"And if the research director says he doesn't want to do it?"

"Two things," said McAndrews. "First, tell him the order came from me." A smirk rose on McAndrews' face as he added, "Second, ask him if he'd like to try our new pickle relish."

***

The pilot crouched down to inspect the helicopter's undercarriage and the long booms jutting out each side that held the spray nozzles. "This is helo to base, you on station?" he asked over the cell phone.

"*Affirmative, helo,*" came the reply from his buddy. "*I'm at landing site. You got a clear approach when you want to come in for a refill.*"

The pilot stood up, turned his baseball cap around backward, and scanned the clear sky. He saw no sign of any police or other aircraft that would signal he had been detected. He didn't expect any. They had stolen the helicopter and tanker truck under cover of darkness. And, he had flown the helicopter to a remote hangar in a rural field, his buddy following in the tanker truck. Together, they had pumped GX from the plastic tank in the hijacked box truck into both the helicopter and the tanker. They had done so wearing respirators and protective suits, thoroughly washing each other down afterward.

After the tanker truck departed, the pilot had monitored the police radio bands. Surely, the theft had been reported, but he heard no indication that the police knew where the helicopter or the truck were.

He spoke into the cell phone. "You frosty?"

"Yeah. I put a tarp over the back of the truck. Makes it look like just another freight-hauler. Gunny, you are cleared to kick the tires and light the fires!"

Turning his cap back around, the pilot climbed into the helicopter and flipped the switches to bring its turbine to life. With a resonant whine, the rotors began to spin up until they produced a gale of downdraft that whipped at the grass of the field.

The pilot placed his feet on the pedals, gripped the joystick-like collective and gave it a twist.

"Pulling pitch," he announced into the cell phone. "See you on the flip side. Out."

He throttled up the turbine, and the helicopter lifted smoothly off the grass. He worked the controls to pitch it forward, sending the craft accelerating to sail over the brush-covered, rocky landscape. The helicopter was no Apache, but he knew he could make it skim low over the terrain. He felt the same kind of thrill he'd felt when flying into battle.

And as with his attacks back then, they would never see him coming.

***

"What a crap shoot! What a fu—. . . *fluxing* crap shoot!" Lou almost forgot her non-swearing vow in the heat of the moment. "How the heck do we know this is the target? And what am I here for?"

She zigged and zagged her way among the crowd in the noisy, cavernous concourse of San Diego's Petco baseball park. Trying to keep up was a stadium security guard, his portly frame stuffed into his uniform. They threaded through the milling people, who chattered excitedly and bought drinks and food, eager to see their Padres play. After all, the team stood at the top of the league standings, with the promise of making the playoffs.

Chun had set up a monitoring site at Camp Pendleton Marine Base north of San Diego. Lou heard her scolding voice in her earpiece. *"Close call on the language, girl. There are probably children around you."*

"Yeah, yeah, language," Lou replied. "But I gotta ask again, what am I here for?"

"Because, like I've said, the big crowd, open air makes it the most likely target."

"Yeah, okay, I'll go watch the sky and wave at the terrorist when he flies over."

"Just keep an eye out. He might have an accomplice there. And you're the best person to deal with the effects of the attack."

"How about the military guys you're with? They ready?"

"Pendleton has Super Cobras in the air. If they find him, they'll track him."

"Yeah, but for God's sake do not shoot him down!"

"No, they took your advice. Wouldn't want whatever he's carrying to rain down on the city. Oh damn!"

"What?" asked Lou, pressing the earpiece more tightly into her ear to hear over the crowd noise.

"They got him on radar. He's headed your way!"

***

The pilot grinned in satisfaction, as he pushed the control stick forward to bring the helicopter down to skim low over the car-clogged freeway toward downtown San Diego. His maneuver was triggered by hearing warnings from air traffic control to set down and that he was being tracked. And that he would be shot down. But he knew that any of the military helicopters would be far behind him, up north.

He'd only had to modestly change his mission plan. Now, he would make his spraying run, then set down at a parking lot heliport near the border. Then, he'd catch the trolley to the border, walk over to Tijuana, and begin to spend some of the money that would pour into his bank account. He picked up his cell phone.

"Leave the truck," he instructed his buddy. "Head you-know-where, and I'll meet you."

"*Roger that,*" came the reply. "*Outta here.*"

He grinned again. The you-know-where was their favorite Tijuana hotel and bar. They would have a high old time before heading farther south to a non-extradition Caribbean island.

He put his finger on the switch that would sluice a spray of his liquid cargo onto the crowd, mentally rehearsing the maneuvers that would send him banking away to escape.

***

"God, these poor people," breathed Lou, as she and the guard emerged from the concourse and into the stands. She shook her head, as she looked out across the crowd of men, women, and children happily chattering and eating during the pregame show.

"What's gonna happen?" asked the guard.

"A shitstorm. . . almost literally," she said, scanning the sky.

On the field, a buzzing swarm of quadcopter drones performed an intricate aerial ballet. They swooped, rose, and dove, creating a changing panoply of formations in mid-air—the Padres logo, a baseball player, and an explosion.

"Drone show?" asked Lou.

"Yeah, they do a pre-game performance and a post-game light show," he said.

As Lou watched the drone aerobatics, her grim expression slowly morphed into an impish smile. "Where are they controlled from?"

"There's a skybox on the top level."

"Take me there!" She clapped the portly guard on the shoulder, urging him onward back onto the concourse and to the nearest elevator.

"Leafy, you there?" she asked into her earpiece.

"*Yeah, the guy is about three miles out. The Pendleton 'copters aren't gonna catch him! You gotta get out of there if you're going to be effective after the attack!*"

"Is there somebody there who knows about 'copters."

"*Everybody here knows about helos.*"

"Ask them how drones could bring down a 'copter so it didn't crash."

"*You means drones with missiles? We don't have any.*"

"No, no, the little ones."

Lou heard Chun talking to multiple people in the background. She came back with an answer: "*They said it's impossible. A little drone can't bring down a helo.*"

"How about a hundred? They've got them here." Lou and the guard emerged from the elevator into a hallway lined with doorways to the stadium's skyboxes.

Now Chun's conversation was longer, and the voices in the background were arguing. She replied: "They say just *maybe* you could. Never been tried before. They say try to maneuver the drones in above the helo, so the downdraft will suck them into the blades."

"Won't that shatter the blades and crash it?"

"Probably not. The blades are tough composite with metal edges. The blades would shred the drones, but the blades' aerodynamics would be messed up. The pilot would have to land. It might be a hard landing, but not a crash."

"*Cool!*" Lou reached a door that the guard pointed to. She told the guard "Stay outside. Don't let anybody in. This could get messy."

She entered the small skybox to see a pudgy young man with an unruly bush of hair and wearing a t-shirt. He was hunched over two laptops set on a counter overlooking the field. His hands gripped two joysticks flanking the laptops.

"Hey, how are ya'?" asked Lou brightly.

The young man startled and peered around at her. His round face was decorated with a sparse, unkempt beard. "You can't be in here," he muttered, turning back to the laptop. "I'm doin' a show."

"I know, dude. I need those drones."

The man turned back to her, glaring and declaring, "No way!"

"Yes way! Look, there's a terrorist who's going to attack with a helicopter. The drones could bring him down."

"Again, no way. I'm calling security." The man reached for a phone.

"You want security? He's just outside the door. I'm with the government. Show me how to pilot those drones."

"Get the hell out. You're going to make me screw up and lose my job."

Lou's expression morphed into a dark scowl. How could she possibly enlist this young man's cooperation? A desperate strategy dawned on her. He was a young man, and she knew that young men liked. She would do it. Hell, she'd done it drunk at Mardi Gras to get beads thrown from the parade floats. She could do it sober here to save thousands. She stepped up beside the man, as he peered intently out the window at the drones performing on the field.

"I'll show you my boobs!" she announced.

The young man jerked upright. He turned toward her, his eyes wide. "Um. . . uh. . . well. . ." Was all he could manage to stammer.

Lou gripped the bottom of her t-shirt and raised it just enough to reveal her belly button. "Dude, you'd get a good show."

"Uh. . . uh. . . uh. . .," the man continued to stammer, licking his lips nervously. After thirty seconds of stammering, he made a decision. He launched himself out of his chair, backed against the wall, and waved at the laptop, gesturing for her to take over.

Lou stripped off her t-shirt revealing her breasts and her tattoos and sat down at the controls. She scanned the wide screen of the laptop. It showed a diagram of the drones' shifting formations and a collection of images from their cameras.

"Chun? You there?"

"*Yeah,*" she heard in her ear piece. "*I heard it all. Seriously? That's how you're working him?*"

"Yeah, well, whatever it takes. Can you give me a heading toward the 'copter?"

"*North of you at twenty-eight degrees, speed ninety knots.*"

Lou turned to the man. "Okay, show me how to maneuver the drones to intercept. I need to go to a twenty-eight-degree heading. And show me how to use the cameras."

"Okay, but, uh, ya gotta let me feel them," he said, his eyes riveted on her chest.

Lou glared back at him. "You touch my ta-tas and your nuts won't see daylight ever again. Now tell me how to guide these things."

"Well, then I won't—"

"Look, you help me and I'll get the guard's handcuffs and cuff you, so you can say I made you do it. If you don't help, I'll say you were an accomplice. But if we stop the attack, I'll make sure you're hailed as a hero."

His gaze not leaving her chest, the doughy young man shrugged and instructed, "Touch the button on the left screen that says 'phalanx mode.' That'll put them in formation. The control panel on the right screen shows their altitude, speed, and heading. Use the joysticks to pilot the whole formation."

Lou hit the button on the touch screen and grabbed the joysticks. On the field, the drones ceased their ballet and shifted into a square formation, lofting into the sky.

"Yeah, baby!" exclaimed Lou. Peering intently at the screen, she said to the man. "Help me navigate to that 'copter, dude. If I miss it, the shirt goes back on."

***

Two minutes to payday, the pilot declared to himself. Now, he was skimming the helicopter over La Jolla, following the freeway south toward Petco Park, keeping as low as he could. Again, he touched the switch that would unleash the cargo, to make sure he could smoothly mount the attack before diverting to his landing spot and an escape.

He did a quick check out the helicopter's canopy to confirm that there were no other aircraft shadowing him. Nobody to spoil his target run.

He had just spotted the tower at SeaWorld when a deafening blast of debris slammed into the canopy from above. He flinched and jerked his head upward as a swirling maelstrom of plastic and metal shards spewed from the whirling blades ricocheting against the canopy like the bursts from a machine gun before flying away, driven downward by the rotor wash.

The helicopter began to shake, first only slightly, but then becoming a teeth-rattling vibration.

"*Shit! Shit! Shit!*" he exclaimed as the craft veered wildly to the left, and he gripped the controls to steady it. But the helicopter would not obey, as another fusillade of debris slammed into the cockpit.

He had no choice! He would have to try to put down or crash! To his right were the broad lawns of Mission Bay Park, so he wrestled the careening helicopter toward it.

The goddamned palm trees! Their tall trunks jutting up throughout the park would shatter the rotor blades, likely sending them slashing into the cockpit ripping him apart. Panting with fear, he managed to just pass over them, wrestling the helicopter downward toward a broad grassy lawn. People below scattered, fleeing the looming machine careening down from the cloudless sky.

The helicopter slammed to the turf with a bone-jarring impact, its damaged blades jerking the aircraft crazily back and forth as they spun down.

The pilot tore off his harness and tumbled out of the cockpit, picking himself up, and running as hard as he could to escape. With luck, people's shock at seeing a helicopter crash to earth would give him some chance at becoming just another anonymous visitor to the park.

No such luck. A black-and-white police car hurtled across the lawn, its lights flashing, its siren blaring. It lurched to a halt and two cops leaped out, drawing their pistols.

"*Down! On your knees! Hands behind your head!*" one bellowed.

The pilot complied, his head bowed. His payday was not to be.

***

"Clear out now!" exclaimed Baltazar, glaring at his computer screen. "They got him!"

"Who?" asked Teo. The small, wiry man had just come in from the kitchen of the safe house.

"The pilot. It's on the news. The helicopter was brought down, he survived, he's in custody."

"Well, they can't find us, right?"

"No, he doesn't know where we are directly, but they'll have his computer. They'll eventually trace our communication to here. Pack as much as you can, put it in the car, and let's go to the other safe house."

"How about the others?"

"Right. . . the others." Baltazar typed out a quick warning to the Veganite operatives and punched a button to send the email. He unfolded his lanky frame from the desk and began to stuff papers into a large satchel. "I think if we—"

He was interrupted by a beep from the computer signaling a video call was coming in. He sat back down and opened the window to see Boudreaux's worried face.

Before Boudreaux could speak, Baltazar said, "We've seen the news. We're getting out. We won't let the authorities get us."

Boudreaux cackled. "Man, they are the least of your worries! Dunst and the bitch are onto you! You gotta make yourself really, really scarce. Get out of the country."

"We appreciate the warning," said Baltazar.

"Oh, I don't give a rat's ass about you. If you get caught by either the cops or them, you gonna give me up, that's for damn sure. Me, I'm taking a vacation."

***

"You got your shirt on under there?" asked Chun, looking dubiously over Lou's shoulder through the faceplate of the yellow hazmat suit.

Lou, also dressed in a hazmat suit, did not look up from her task of taking samples around the downed helicopter. "Yes, Leafy, I'm wearing my shirt," she replied wryly, patting her chest. "I only show the girls when strategically necessary." Taking samples required some precision in the bulky suit. And she had to carefully duck below the craft's splintered rotors.

Chun had just arrived at the large grassy lawn of Mission Bay Park guarded by a squad of FBI agents, all in hazmat suits. She had donned her own suit and ducked under the crime scene tape that cordoned off the area.

"Yeah, well, the FDA brass wouldn't much like your strategy of weaponizing breasts," she warned. "Any leaks from the tank detected?"

"Not so far as we can tell with just a visual inspection."

Lou finished taking samples with cotton swabs, placed the last in a vial and stood with the rack of vials. She beckoned a hazmat-suited Technical Hazards Response Unit member, who stood near the FBI's mobile laboratory truck. He came up, took the samples, and left to disappear inside the truck.

"We'll get a read pretty quick from gas chromatography about area contamination," said Lou. But I'll want to take bulk tank samples back to the lab for full analysis. I need to figure out, not only the structure of this stuff, but the bioactivity." She carefully unscrewed the filler port on the helicopter's large plastic tank, pipetting its yellowish liquid into sample tubes.

A male voice behind them said, "We'll be taking samples, too."

They turned to see a man arriving in an army-green isolation suit, his face obscured by an oxygen mask. He was holding a sample case.

"Colonel, good to see you," said Chun. "Meet Lou Baumgartner, FDA."

"And you are?" asked Lou.

The man waved his gloved hand clumsily. "I'm with the Army Chemical Corps. Flew out here the minute we heard about the attack."

"Damned good to have you, colonel," said Lou. "From the size of this tank, this threat has gone from a small-scale terrorist plot to chemical warfare."

"It gets worse," said Chun. "I just got off the phone to the people in the San Diego field office who are interrogating the pilot. He's very happy to cooperate. He told them where a tanker truck full of the chemical is."

"How much?" asked Lou.

"Two hundred gallons," said Chun.

"Dear God! That shows a horrific potential!"

"What do you mean?" asked Chun.

"The amount used in the first attacks could have been made in a lab. A quantity of hundreds of gallons means somebody has a factory. If tanker-sized loads of this stuff get in the wrong hands, God knows how bad it will get!"

Chapter 19

Eladio Campana tapped the side of the stainless-steel tank with the barrel of his pistol and chuckled in satisfaction. Beside him stood his slight, balding chemist; and standing nervously before him was Edwin Kane.

They stood in Campana's sprawling chemical plant set amid a sprawling, empty terrain of desert hills. The plant consisted of rows of the two-story tanks connected by a welter of pipes and covered by a high, metal, open-air roof. Around them, workers hauled blue plastic drums of chemicals to the tanks and raised them on forklifts to catwalks overlooking the tanks. As they poured the liquid and powder contents into the tanks, the complex tang of organic chemicals filled the air, lingering in the still, dry warmth beneath the roof. At the far end of the plant, hazmat-suited workers were piping end-product into large plastic tanks in the backs of trucks.

"My engineer say you get ninety-two percent efficiency with production," said Campana. "That is good. What do you do next?"

Kane took a deep tremulous breath. "Well, I need more biological testing. I need to understand the effects of GX—"

"I mean to make it better." interrupted Campana. "More concentrated, so we can dilute it down even more for more profit."

"Um . . . uh. . . the thing is, we don't understand long-term effects, like how permanent the effects are on people. We shouldn't send it before we do that. From what I can tell, the test subjects—"

Campana laughed derisively. "Test subjects? They are of no consequence. Let me tell you what we do now. We ship big samples all over the world. To my *compañeros* in Europe, Asia. They see how they can sell it to customers . . . food makers and others. . . legally! It is not illegal after all, you see! There is no law, so they can make much money with no fear of the law! And with this plant, we can make thousands of gallons!"

"You can't do that! You don't know—"

"*I don't know? I don't know?*" The drug lord's expression grew furious, and he chambered a round into the large gold pistol, clicked off the safety and jammed it against Kane's skull. "*You do not tell me what I do not know!*"

***

The petite, snow-white-haired woman smiled warmly when she opened the door of the remote cabin to see Dunst and Diana.

"Oh, it was so lovely to hear from you!" she declared brightly, her blue eyes sparkling. "It has been too long. You come right in, and I'll tell Cam you're here."

The two drug dealers entered, and Dunst placed a large box wrapped in flower-print gift paper on the table by the door. "We can't stay long," he said. "We want to limit our stay in the US as much as possible."

The woman announced their presence to her wife, Cam; and another petite woman with a pixie haircut emerged, also smiling, from a back room. She said, "Oh, when Sharon told me you were coming, I was so pleased!" She made a brow-wrinkled, mock frown. "Now, Sharon has made her special lamb, so you must at least stay for dinner or you will hurt her feelings."

Diana showed a rare smile, declaring, "Oh, we *know* what happens when Sharon has her feelings hurt."

Sharon and Cam ushered the two into their cozy living room, whose floor-to-ceiling windows revealed the bucolic surroundings of their leafy, wooded acreage. Cam proceeded to pour a cabernet wine from a decanter, and the four engaged in convivial conversation, while Sharon arranged the food dishes on the kitchen island. The delicious aroma of roast lamb wafted through the room, as they got up to fill their plates. Accompanying the lamb were fresh sauteed string beans from their garden, fluffy mashed potatoes, and fresh-baked asiago cheese bread.

The four had an amiable dinner, chatting about their travels; and after a dessert of homemade blackberry cobbler, and a move to the living room for coffee, Diana said, "Okay, you need to open your gift, Sharon." She signaled for Dunst to fetch it, and he hefted the box onto their coffee table.

Sharon gingerly removed the gift paper, saying "Oh, I know it's me being cheap, but it's such pretty paper. Maybe I'll use it in my decoupage." She opened the box and chortled merrily in surprise.

"What is it?" asked Cam.

"You really didn't need to," said Sharon cheerily. "You two are such sweeties! She pulled out a stubby-barreled weapon with a large ammunition drum."

"Is that?—" began Cam.

"Yes, it's an M32A1 grenade launcher! I've thought about getting one, but I just couldn't find a source."

Said Diana, "We knew about your rotator cuff problem, and we knew what it was from."

Sharon smiled sheepishly, cocking her head back and forth. "Yes, I was throwing overhand too hard, and Cam scolded me that I should throw grenades underhand."

Cam gently patted her wife's knee. "I know how frustrated you were, not being able to go back into the field. You do like explosions, sweetheart." Then, to Dunst and Diana, "This has been such a lovely evening, it's a shame we need to get to business. I know you two want to get going. How many?"

"Thirteen. . . probably," said Dunst.

"And who are they?"

"They're called Veganites. They compromised our business, and they are likely to continue to do so."

Sharon took out a notebook and a pen and began to take notes. "Do you have names, locations?"

Dunst handed her a thumb drive. "Here's all we have. Some of them are public, like the terrorists on trial now. We also know the leader is a guy named Baltazar."

"It's a big order," said Cam. "Tell you what. Given that you've been such reliable clients, I think we can give you thirteen kills for the price of twelve." She looked over at Sharon, who nodded in cheerful agreement. She continued: "At a hundred thousand each, that's one point two million. However, should the number go up, we'll have to add a hundred thousand per task."

"And that includes everything?" asked Diana.

"Absolutely. As before, our subcontractors will handle tracking them down and neutralizing them."

Said Dunst, "If at all possible, we'd like most, if not all, to look like accidents."

Her lips pursed, Sharon nodded slowly in agreement, as she took notes in graceful handwriting in a monogrammed notebook. "We'll have our people do recon, and we'll give you an assessment of what's feasible. As you know, it's more of a bother to simulate natural deaths than just to do drive-bys. But we do like the lower profile. And so do our subs."

Said Cam to Diana and Dunst, "You have our account number from past contracts. Please deposit six hundred thousand, and we'll get started."

Sharon began to close her notebook, when Diana held up a hand to stop her. "Unfortunately, we have another task for you," said Diana. "And we prefer it not be handled by your contractors. We wouldn't want knowledge of it to get out into the contractor community."

"You want us to handle it personally?"

"Yes, and of course, there would be an additional premium for your personal services."

Sharon smiled sweetly. "Well, I suppose we can go into the field, especially for valued clients like yourself. Who is it?"

Diana took a sip of wine before answering quietly. "It's our own man. Boudreaux. He's had an influx of money. We have people who watch foreign transactions that might interest us. He had quite a large sum deposited into a new account. And one of our shipments was hijacked under circumstances that implicate him."

Said Dunst, "And we'd just as soon it not be known that someone so high in our organization has betrayed us so brazenly and escaped. It's not good for confidence. So, an assassination by a rival group would look better."

"Indeed," said Sharon. "Say a hundred and fifty thousand and we can make it look like another group did it. I do hope it's in a nice part of the country. Cam and I could use a bit of a vacation."

"Agreed," said Diana, and they all stood, the two women warmly hugging Dunst and Diana, with Diana showing the cool response of a sociopath.

As they prepared to go, Sharon smiled sweetly and held up a hand to stop them. "Not so fast. You absolutely must take food for the road. Please let me fix you a box. I'd bet your chef isn't with you. And restaurant food can be so impersonal." She bustled into the kitchen to pack containers, as Cam, Dunst, and Diana stepped onto the porch to enjoy the cool mountain breeze whispering through the pines.

***

Watching the rats slam violently against the walls of their plastic bins, writhing and squeaking, as they fought for food, Lou shook her head in disbelief. She allowed herself a string of curses that would have brought a reprimand had she uttered them in the presence of colleagues.

A knock on the door of the FBI lab, and Chun entered. "Well, what're the results?"

"You ever heard of forever chemicals?"

"They don't sound good."

"Well, they're industrial chemicals that don't break down in the environment. When they're released in wastewater, they go up the food chain to be consumed by people in all their foods. They cause diabetes, infertility, cancers. . . all sorts of bad stuff."

"You're saying that this chemical is that?"

"No, but the same principle. We finished structural analysis of the samples from the helicopter. It was damned hard. It's a hellishly complex compound. But it shows that Kane built a totally new gustatene-type molecule whose bonds don't break down in the environment, like plastics. And it also persists in the body."

"Bottom line?"

Lou pointed to the bloody rats fighting for food pellets. "They got just a small dose. Basically, the molecule stuck in their brain, on the neural receptors for hunger. They became insatiable. They went crazy eating."

"What happens to them eventually?"

Lou went over to a rack and pulled out a plastic bin. A morbidly obese rat lay inside, inert, panting, its beady eyes glassy. "If you give them unlimited food, they gorge until they almost kill themselves, then drop into a coma. Once they excrete the food, they start all over again. They'll probably die from the metabolic overload or intestinal blockage."

"Jesus," breathed Chun, shaking her head.

"Imagine tons of this chemical getting out into the environment. Imagine it getting into people's brains and just sticking there."

"People would. . ." Chun couldn't finish the sentence.

"People would become compulsive binge eaters until they died either from the long-term consequences of obesity, or more gruesome deaths from burst stomachs or blocked intestines."

"And it would be addictive?"

"Oh, yeah, like cocaine, like heroin. At first, people would just want the food that contained it. But their hunger would persist, and they'd go nuts and go after all foods. And the drug would persist in the environment, so it would spread."

"*Jesus!*" exclaimed Chun again, now more emphatically. "That would be disastrous."

"And it gets even worse."

"How could it possibly be worse?"

Lou leaned against the wall, her head bowed. "Well, the hunger receptors are pretty much the same in all mammalian brains."

"You mean. . .?"

"Out in the environment, not just rats would be affected. . . going mad with hunger. We're talking mice, dogs, cats, pigs, cows, bears. . . *every* mammal. Agent Chun, we're talking a global biological catastrophe."

Chun stared at Lou in stunned silence. She was brought back from her shock by the sound of her cell phone. She took a deep breath and answered the call.

"Where?" she asked the caller. "How bad?" She ended the call, shaking her head.

"What happened?" asked Lou.

"That was the Vegas police. It's happening on the Strip, all over Vegas. The cops thought they were just drunks, but they're not. There are mobs of crazy people roaming around gorging on food! The cops are calling them food zombies."

Chapter 20

A dull thump sounded in the FBI assault vehicle, as the huge, slavering man threw himself onto the truck's hood. Inside, Chun jerked in surprise, as the man thrust his face against the windshield, trying to peer inside.

"Keep going," demanded Chun in the passenger seat, but the driver slowed to a stop, blocked by abandoned cars and trucks, some smashed, others smoking.

In the back, Lou and five SWAT team members watched with stunned amazement the mad scene outside the window on Las Vegas Boulevard. A throng of berserk people staggered along the sidewalks of the Las Vegas Strip, their eyes glazed with an insatiable hunger. A young woman wrestled with an elderly man for a bag of potato chips, her hair an unruly mop, her teeth bared in a snarl. A fat man in a stained t-shirt and cargo shorts squatted on the sidewalk, his back against the wall of a restaurant, gnawing on the remains of a steak. He held it close to him, guarding it against others circling him like wolves stalking prey, trying to steal his prize.

Even through the vehicle's thick armor plate, they could hear the steady roar of roiling mob's anguished voices, punctuated by howls, growls, and shrieks.

"We can't keep going," said the driver, trying to see around the man sprawled on the hood. "Road's blocked by cars." Peering out the windshield, Chun nodded in agreement.

"Take the sidewalk," she directed.

The driver swerved the huge truck onto the sidewalk, but immediately found its path blocked by the staggering, wild-eyed people.

"Ideas? Anybody?" asked Chun, but the people in the back were silent, except for Lou.

"I think I could clear the way, but I got to go outside," she said.

"No! Too risky," said Chun. "Let me try something." She pulled out her pistol, opened the side window and fired into the air.

At the sharp crack of the rounds, the crowd shrank back, their dull gaze turning to the truck, but only for a moment. Then, they resumed their maddened quest for food.

"Okay, let's retreat and regroup," said Chun. "We can't risk—"

"Oh, hell no!" exclaimed Lou. "We've got to reach Nonny! Lord knows what's going on at that buffet!"

"The operational parameters dictate—"

"Screw operational parameters! They could be in deep trouble."

"Look, I have to consider the risk-benefit assessment for this mission," said Chun.

"How about this benefit?" asked Lou. "Nonny knows more about the food industry in this town than anybody. He is absolutely the best bet for finding out how these zombies got started. And from there, we could figure out how to help them."

Chun hmphed in annoyance, turning back to the SWAT team. "Okay, let's try to clear the way," she said, directing the men in their helmets and riot gear to pile out of the rear hatch of the hulking truck and deploy around to the front. They first hauled the large man off the hood, dragging him onto the car-clogged street. Then, they began to move down the sidewalk ahead of the truck, rousting people out of the truck's path, allowing it to inch slowly forward.

But their efforts were thwarted. An ominous, low muttering arose in the crowd, with the growled shouts of *"Food in truck!"* passing from one person to another like a virus, until it became a mad incantation.

The prospect of food drove the crowd to surge forward, grunting and panting, and reaching out to claw at the truck. A middle-aged woman clutched the truck's side door, straining to wrest it open. On the other side, a teen-aged girl hammered her small fists at a window, shrieking.

The crowd began to swarm the SWAT members, forcing them to their knees. Engulfed in writhing bodies, the men struggled to free themselves, unwilling to use their weapons on the people who were piling onto them demanding any food they were suspected of having.

"Back in the vehicle!" shouted Chun over her radio, and the men managed to shove their way through the crowd, wrest open the assault vehicle's rear door and retreat inside.

"Jesus, they think we've got food in here," said Chun.

"Well, actually we do," said Lou. "I figured we might need an incentive, so I brought some along." She hauled out a cardboard box and tore it open. "I thought you might have a problem with me bringing these along, Leafy, so I didn't mention them."

Chun twisted around in her seat to see Lou hauling out brown packets from the box and stuffing them into a tote bag.

"Are those MREs?" she asked. "Oh, hell no! You're not going to—"

"Yup! Meals Ready to Eat!" exclaimed Lou. "Tasty, nutritious, and just the bait to lure the food zombies out of the way!"

"Goddamnit, get back—" Chun began but she was too late. Hauling the tote bag with her, Lou flipped open the truck's overhead hatch and climbed up to perch on the roof, dangling her legs in the hatchway.

"HEY, Y'ALL!" she bellowed, pulling a pouch out of the bag and waving it in the air. "*I got ham and bean stew!*" She sailed the pouch into the street out of their path, and the mob reacted as one, scrambling off the sidewalk to retrieve it as it fell between two abandoned cars. "*I got barbecue sauce with chicken! I got beef stew! I got pasta marinara!*" As she hawked the foods, she pitched the pouches away into the street, clearing the sidewalk ahead of people. The truck accelerated forward, and Lou grabbed a handhold to keep her balance. As the vehicle advanced, she threw more food pouches into the street. Below, the SWAT team pulled more pouches from the box and passed them up.

"*Parting the zombie sea!*" she shouted triumphantly.

She was so intent on the action in front of her, she didn't notice behind her a thickly muscled young man in a t-shirt and jeans grab a handhold on the back of the assault vehicle and haul himself up. His expression one of crazed hunger, he threw his thick tattooed arm around her neck and jerked her backward.

Inside the truck, one of the SWAT members saw her legs begin withdrawing and grabbed her ankles. The others realized what was happening and threw open the rear hatch, trying to climb up to reach the assailant.

"*Gimme!*" grunted the man. "*Gimme all the food!*"

Now he had one arm around Lou's neck choking her, and the other wrapped around her chest. Lou felt her consciousness waning. She waved the tote bag in front of him.

"Dude, I got energy bars," she choked out. "I got corn nuts. C'mon, just take 'em."

"*Inside!*" growled the man, beginning to claw his way over Lou's body to reach the open hatch. "*More better food inside!*" He shoved her away from the hatch, and she barely managed to remain atop the truck and not fall into the surging crowd below. The SWAT members had begun clambering over the top, but the man had reached the hatch opening. They knew if he made it inside, his mad thrashing could cause serious injury.

Lou pulled herself up and managed to reach out to hook her hand over the man's belt to slow his crawl toward the hatch. She shoved her other hand into the tote bag and pulled out one after another of small pouches of snacks that came with the MREs. She stuffed them into the man's back pockets, down his pants, and up his t-shirt, tucking it in to hold them.

She leaned over to the crowd milling around below, bellowing, "HEY, Y'ALL, THIS GUY HAS FOOD IN HIS POCKETS, IN HIS PANTS! COME AND GET IT!"

The people reacted immediately, three men hoisting themselves up onto the roof, grabbing the man, and hauling him down to the street. The crowd closed around him, tearing at his clothes, finding the snacks and gnawing them open. He was down to his underwear by the time they realized that they had harvested all the food on him.

Lou climbed back down the hatch, now keeping her body well inserted into it. She continued to pitch the contents of the MREs into the street, clearing the sidewalk.

Ahead of them, cylindrical steel posts across the sidewalk blocked their way.

Chun glared at the barriers, as if she could will them to part. "Everybody out," she said coolly. "We've got to fight the rest of the way on foot."

***

"TASER TASER TASER!" bellowed the casino guard, backing against one of the buffet tables of the sprawling Emperor's Feast Gourffet. Giving the warning was standard practice for cops preparing to tase a target. But the guard's tone was not standard because a massive, bare-chested, ravenous man was looming toward him, intent on the serving table that held remnants of the Gourffet's taco bar. The guard's trembling voice registered panic because the huge buffet hall was teeming with hunger-maddened men, women, and even children, all gorging on any food they could find.

The guard raised the black taser pistol and fired, launching the taser darts trailing their hair-thin wires into the man's hairy chest. He jerked and moaned and collapsed to the floor, writhing, his eyes harboring the blank stare that matched those of the others in the mob.

The guard wrestled the man onto his stomach and pulled out plastic cuffs from a sheaf on his belt, tightening them around the man's wrists. He knew he also had to bind the man's ankles because

222

the crazed people would try to get up the minute they were left alone. And many were, since the five guards couldn't keep up with the throngs of people storming the buffet.

"Are you okay?" asked a voice over the tumult. It was a human voice! Not the guttural sounds being made by the mob. The guard rose to see two people he recognized—the woman from the FDA and the one from the FBI. They were disheveled and breathing hard. Behind them, stood five men in tactical gear.

"Hell, no!" exclaimed the guard. "I got no more taser cartridges. And these. . . these. . . zombies keep comin'! I'm gonna have to just turn the place over to them."

"Can't do that," said Chun. "They'll hurt themselves and each other."

"Well, I'm damned well not gonna get close to them. They bite!"

"Look, we just made it through a huge mob of them. They only attack if you have food or attack them. Handle them right, and they can be taken down. And bites can be treated."

"Hell no they can't!" exclaimed the guard, hauling his beefy frame to stand up. "Look over there."

Across the room at the base of the salad bar lay a uniformed guard, trussed up and struggling to free himself from the plastic bands. His face was stained with food, his eyes glassy.

"What happened to him?" asked Lou.

"He got bit! At first, we thought, y'know, just get a tetanus shot, put a bandage on it, he'd be okay. Then he went nuts!"

Lou picked her way among the writhing, moaning bodies to the downed guard and crouched down to examine him. She managed to avoid his gnashing teeth to examine the bite marks on his forearm.

She stepped away, shaking her head. "Oh, jeez, I should have known."

Chun joined her, staring down at the guard. "How did he get that way?"

"One of two ways, both bad. Either whoever bit him still had some in their mouth. Or maybe it's excreted by the lungs or salivary glands and gets into the mouth. The stuff is so danged potent that even a little bit that gets into the blood stream through a bite will go to the brain and turn the victim—"

"Into a zombie?" asked Chun.

"Yeah, basically."

The guard holding the spent taser pistol stepped up beside them, saying, "Y'see? I'm outta here."

"Not a good idea," said Lou. "It's bad on the Strip, too. Cars crashed, ambulances stuck, mobs bustin' into restaurants. National Guard is on its way, but until then stay put. At least you got a defensible space. Tell me what you've seen."

"Well, it was like before here when that guy sprayed people's food. Customers were just eatin' like usual. Then they all started goin' nuts. Like they got superhuman and started goin' after the food. But the video footage didn't show anybody spraying anything. Only person not affected was her." The guard pointed to a young, dark-haired woman in shorts sitting on the floor, her back against the Mexican food serving counter. Her mouth was opening and closing, as if tasting food, but there was nothing in her mouth. She was peering around dully, but remaining quiet.

"Why is she calm?" asked Lou. "Did you tase her."

"Nope, she was goin' after the food there and suddenly just stopped."

Lou stepped over to the serving counter and peered up and down its length. She leaned down and examined the girl's mouth, seeing that her lips were smeared with red. Lou stood up, a grin dawning slowly on her face.

"What's so funny?" asked Chun.

"Not funny, just cool. I know how to stop their uncontrollable food seeking. It won't cure them, but it will quiet them."

"Jesus, how?" asked the guard.

Lou picked up a serving bowl full of salsa. "Hot sauce. When the girl started eating it, the spice overwhelmed her taste sensation, overloaded the brain's appetite center. . . temporarily, anyway. Help me with an experiment."

She fetched a spoon, and they returned to the bound, struggling man the guard had just tased. Lou directed the guard to hold his head still. He bucked and struggled and loosed an animal growl, straining to free himself. But when his mouth flew open, Lou spooned a glob of salsa into it.

"This is the really hot stuff," she said. "Let's see what happens."

A puzzled look rose on the man's face, and he began to smack his lips, protruding and retracting his tongue. He quietened down, laying still, his jaw opening and closing.

"Leafy, call the cops, the National Guard, tell them to use their pepper spray on the zombies. But don't aim for the eyes, squirt just a little into their mouths."

Chun stood up, pulled out her phone, and began to call. The guard grabbed the bowl of salsa and hurried away to share it with the other guards and the SWAT team, instructing them on its use.

"Got another idea!" exclaimed Lou. "Tell everybody to go to the grocery stores and get all the hot sauce they can find. The hottest possible. Dilute it so it's liquid enough. And get some of those big damn super-soaker water rifles. That way, they can squirt the zombies long-range without having to get close so they might get hurt. And without using up all their pepper spray."

Chun finished passing on the information, and the two had begun helping the guards subdue crazed feeders when Abadi appeared from the kitchen. His eyes wide, his expression was one of abject fear.

"Oh praise Allah, you are here! You must come! You must help!"

"What's happened?" asked Lou.

"It is Chef! He has poisoned himself!"

***

"I did not know he would do this!" exclaimed Abadi. His anguished gaze was directed at Nonny, who sat on the floor against one of the stainless-steel prep tables in the kitchen of Johanna's Restaurant, his hands bound behind him. His glassy stare scanned unseeing around the room. He uttered unintelligible gibberish.

"What the hell did he do?" asked Lou.

"When people started going nuts, Chef come here, and he know something was in the food. He knew it was in something we buy, like a spice or a sauce. So, he get samples of everything that come from outside suppliers, and he line samples up on table." Abadi pointed to dozens of dessert bowls lined up on the prep table, with labels inked on their sides.

"He tasted them?" asked Lou.

"He call me in. When I get here, he tell me what he will do. He say 'If I go crazy, you tie me up. And you figure out what make me crazy.' That is what happen."

"Didn't you try to stop him?"

"You don't stop Chef Nonny when he decides something. You know that."

Lou crouched down to stroke Nonny's head, taking care to stay clear of his mouth. "Oh, goddamnit, you dear, dear fool," she lamented. "Now you've gone and done it."

Chun moved down the line of dishes, inspecting their contents. "Daoud, can you figure out what dish did it?" she asked.

"I think this," Abadi replied, lifting up a dish that had been licked clean. "When he get to this one, he go crazy, so I tie him up."

Chun inspected the label. "Should've known. It's a sauce from GloboChem. They either developed some version of the new compound themselves, or they got hold of a supply." She took out her cell phone and punched in a number, saying, "I'm ordering a raid."

***

"What a lovely walk," said Sharon, as she and Cam strolled beneath the moss-draped oaks along the narrow trail along the Louisiana bayou. They breathed in its clean organic aroma.

"I'm so glad our target decided to come here, especially during this time of the year," answered Cam. "Are those shoes okay?" The two petite women, dressed in khaki pants and camouflage shirts, reached the edge of the bayou, with its still, brown waters, and took the path that followed its edge.

Sharon chuckled tolerantly at her solicitous wife. "I know you think I should not have brought new shoes. But the last pair I bought was comfortable from the start. Is that the cabin?"

"Think so," said Cam, now whispering. "I hope we got the right location information."

"Well, if we didn't, our informant won't get the second part of his payment," said Sharon. "And of course, his health would be severely compromised."

"Let's find a spot and set up. I could use a bite to eat."

They circled quietly through the thick green foliage of the Louisiana swamp, keeping an eye out for any sign of movement in the rusty-tin-roofed shack perched on stilts on the bank of the bayou. They reached the dirt road that led to the shack, warily crossed it, and found a grassy clearing with a line of sight to the shack about a hundred yards away.

Cam slung the duffel bag she had been carrying off her shoulder and shrugged out of her backpack. Sharon also took off the tan backpack she had been carrying. Cam unfurled a brown blanket and spread it on the ground.

They settled onto the blanket, and as Sharon pulled sandwiches out of her backpack, Cam zipped open her pack and pulled out the collapsible sniper rifle, snapping the stock open. She slid the barrel out of its sleeve and screwed it on, inserting the bolt into the rifle and gently clicking in the magazine.

As she attached the bipod, Sharon whispered, "Don't you want the suppressor, dear?"

"I think not this time," said Cam. I don't think noise will be an issue out here, once we engage."

Sharon began to eat half of her shrimp po'boy sandwich, holding it with one hand and using the other to hold the opera glasses, through which she monitored the cabin.

"That is his car," she said, as Cam began to eat her catfish sandwich. "Hope he appears soon. We do have that dinner reservation. I absolutely refuse to leave Louisiana without having a good gumbo."

"Oh, yes, lovely," said Cam. "And for me, crawfish étouffée."

They finished their sandwiches and settled in to watch the shack. The afternoon was muggy, but comfortable, and they saw a crane swoop low over the bayou in search of fish. Sharon managed to snap a photo of the graceful bird in mid-flight, proudly showing the image to Cam.

After two hours, the door to the shack opened with a scraping sound, and Boudreaux appeared. He opened the trunk of the white Honda, hauling out a bag.

"Cam, he's out," Sharon whispered, peering through the glasses.

In an instant, Cam was on her stomach, bringing the rifle to bear on Boudreaux. She made a slight adjustment for the distance, and squeezed the trigger. The sharp crack of the shot pierced the quiet of the swamp. Boudreaux uttered a surprised bellow, a sound followed by the slam of the shack's door.

"Oh, fudge," said Sharon. "I think he's only wounded. Can't see, though."

From the shack erupted a fusillade of automatic rifle fire, randomly tearing into the brush and trees surrounding the cabin, splintering wood, shredding leaves.

Sharon hunkered down, still watching through the glasses, and Cam maintained her steady bead on the cabin.

"Left window," whispered Sharon, and Cam zeroed in on it. After a moment, she loosed another round.

The rapid fire continued from the shack, followed by a shout. *"You ain' gonna get me! I got ammo and food, and I can take this all day!"*

Sharon shook her head. "Cam, we have dinner reservations. Can I? Please?"

Cam did not answer immediately, but sent several more rifle rounds slamming into the cabin's windows, wall, and door. Finally, without taking her eye from the rifle's telescopic sight, she nodded.

Smiling in satisfaction, Sharon opened the duffel and hauled out the grenade launcher, amid a blistering fire from the cabin. She rotated the launcher's spring-operated drum to cock it. She pulled out the fat, bullet-shaped grenades and inserted them into the six chambers.

"Need a better angle," she whispered amid the gunfire and left to sprint back across the road, keeping low.

After a minute, Cam heard the hollow thunk of a grenade erupting out of the launcher, the faint tinkle of shattering window glass from the shack, and the blast of the grenade erupting within the cabin. Four more hollow thunks were followed by the shattering explosions, the erupting shrapnel tearing holes in the cabin walls.

The gunfire ceased, and Sharon returned, now strolling upright. Cam stood and drew a semi-automatic pistol from her backpack, and the two warily approached the cabin.

"Oh, dear, I do hope the body's recognizable," said Sharon.

"Not to worry, sweetie. I'm sure there is some identifying mark. I'll take photos. And I've got a plastic bag. We'll take the fingers."

The shack's gray wooden walls were peppered with holes from the blasts inside, and the door was blown off its hinges. The sharp tang of explosive and the cloud of dust filled the air. Cam ducked in first, her pistol at the ready.

The shack was empty. A door on the bayou side was flung open, and they ducked through to see the distant figure of Boudreaux paddling furiously away through the cypress trees in the narrow skiff known as a pirogue.

Sharon hmphed in annoyance and raised the grenade launcher. She pulled the trigger to send the last grenade arcing high in the air on its deadly parabolic path. Its explosion blew a geyser of brown bayou water into the humid air.

***

"Do you all have photos of the suspects?" asked Chun into the microphone clipped to her bulletproof vest. Standing in the road leading to the GloboChem factory, she flipped through the images on her own phone—the roster of key GloboChem Las Vegas employees. They would likely yield the best intelligence if captured in the raid.

"I know you want the people," said Lou, standing beside her. "But we also need to get the stuff. You've seen what that crap does."

"Just stay within the operational parameters," said Chun, peering down the road at the warehouse through binoculars.

"Our parameters need to include stopping some hellish chemicals from getting loose, okay?"

Chun ordered the FBI SWAT teams to deploy around the building, and their assault vehicles accelerated down the road, to swerve into place on all sides of the gray, concrete-walled building.

At her signal, a SWAT member burst one of the doors open with a battering ram, and the first team members poured into the building. Shortly, the line of overhead doors began rattling open, and the other team members poured in.

Chun and Lou sprinted after them, as the team bellowed commands to shocked factory workers, who obediently dropped to their knees, hands behind their heads, eyes wide with fright.

"I see-em! Gotta get to the chemical!" exclaimed Lou, dashing ahead into the depths of the warehouse.

"GODDAMNIT, HOLD UP!" shouted Chun, but Lou was gone. Chun beckoned for three SWAT members to follow and ran after Lou.

Far down the long rows of barrels two hazmat-suited figures could be seen working beside a translucent tank. They were manipulating a hose that ran from the tank to a pump, whose outlet hose was stuck into a floor drain.

Lou flew toward them at full speed, tackling one figure by the shoulders, flinging him away from the tank and into the wall. The other figure bent down to the pump, reaching for its switch. Lou leaped onto him, wrestling him backward on top of her, locking her legs around his waist. The man slammed his elbow into her time after time, but Lou held on, reaching up with her hand and clawing at the figure's plastic helmet.

Chun and the SWAT members reached her, and the agents hauled the man off her and tore off his helmet. Lou groaned and tried to catch her breath after having been repeatedly elbowed in the stomach.

"He. . ." she began, but could not finish the sentence. She took a deep breath, and tried again. "He was going to pump that crap into the sewer. Vegas sends its treated wastewater to Lake Mead. It would have poisoned the whole West, then the whole ocean. It would have been disastrous."

"And if he'd had a gun, LC, that would have been pretty damned disastrous, too, right?" said Chun sarcastically. She turned to the man, who glared up at her, and began to smile. "I believe your name is Joseph," she said. "I believe you work for Gabriel McAndrews. And I believe we will have a nice long chat about what your company has been up to."

***

"Want to watch some TV?" asked Lou, as she entered the FBI's interrogation room. She hauled in a duffel bag and a laptop computer.

Joseph stared at her quizzically. He raised his hands in a gesture of puzzlement, his movement hindered because his wrists were handcuffed to the bar on the steel table. "Why would I want to do that?"

231

"Oh because there's lots of stuff going on. Really scary shi. . . stuff. Zombies, man, hungry zombies!" Lou set a laptop in front of Joseph and opened it to reveal live footage from the Strip showing National Guard troops wielding, not their rifles, but colorful plastic Super Soaker squirt rifles. They were aiming streams of liquid into the mouths of hunger-maddened men, women, and children. They were plastic-cuffing the confused, subdued people, loading them into vans, and hauling them away.

"Too bad," said Joseph coldly.

"*You* did that."

"A miscalculation."

Lou snorted. "Your 'miscalculation' caused a disaster, hurt people, even killed people. Now we need to stop that disaster. We need to know where you got that stuff. Who gave it to you? Where are they?"

"Sorry, can't help you. Let me call my lawyer."

"Right, of course. Due process. See, but I'm not FBI. I'm FDA. So, I'm not so much up on due process. Or suspect rights. Sooo, I get to do this. . ." Lou pulled a small translucent spray bottle from the duffel bag and set it on the table. The bottle was full of liquid. She then extracted a yellow hazmat suit from the bag. She sat down on the chair on her side of the table and began to pull it on over her jeans.

"What the hell are you doing?"

"Boy, I tell ya, those poor people who get dosed by the chemical go through holy hell. They suffer constant, agonizing hunger. It tortures them, drives them nuts. But, y'know, the thing is, they know what's happening to them. They are still coherent. Well, until they die a really horrible death from a burst stomach or an intestinal obstruction."

Lou stood and shrugged the hazmat suit up over her shoulders and zipped it up. She pulled the helmet from the bag and held it under her arm.

"What is all this?" demanded Joseph, his eyes widening. His gaze went to the spray bottle. "What's in that?"

Lou continued, smiling. "My point is that, let's say you'd gotten accidentally dosed with the stuff in the warehouse before we got there, and you turned into a zombie. Even though you were in agony with hunger, you could still tell us what we needed to know. And you *would* tell us because you'd know your information could lead us to an antidote to save you. And if it didn't, well, as you said, 'too bad.'"

"This is torture!" exclaimed Joseph. *"This is illegal! Where is the FBI? Do they know what you're doing?"*

Lou shrugged and put on the helmet. "Oh, those guys? They're off doing FBI stuff." Her voice muffled by the helmet, she said, "They said since I'm a scientist, I could interrogate you better to find out about the chemical, and labs, and such. Pal, you ready to become one of the Unfed? That's what I'm calling the zombies. Very funny name. But not so funny if you are one." She finished sealing the helmet to the suit and picked up the spray bottle.

"STOP! YOU CAN'T!"

Lou twisted the tip of the spray bottle to open it. She thrust it in Joseph's face, as he closed his eyes, clenched his jaw, and violently jerked his head back and forth in a desperate effort to evade the sprayer.

"I'd ask you to say 'ah' so I can get it in your mouth. But just breathing this crap in will do the trick. So, it doesn't matter. You got to breathe sometime, right?"

***

"OW, MAN! YOU TRYIN' TO KILL ME?" Boudreaux lay on his stomach on the surgical table, gripping its side, as the veterinarian extracted a needle-sharp piece of bloody shrapnel from his back.

"'Quiet!" commanded the veterinarian. "You're the one who said no anesthetic. There are people outside who can hear you."

"Yeah, well, I don't want no anesthetic because people outside might be after me. And I'm payin' you enough so it don't need to hurt."

The veterinarian, a slim man in his forties, paused, staring down at Boudreaux's shrapnel-shredded back, which looked like a bloody moonscape under the glare of the surgical lamp. "You didn't say anything about being hunted when you came in. Am I in danger? If so, you need to get out."

"Look, you get me patched up fast, I'm outta here, and you're not in danger."

"Three more pieces, and I can bandage you, and you can get out."

"Great." Boudreaux gritted his teeth as the last bits of grenade metal embedded in his flesh were extracted. After the veterinarian covered his back in bandages, he donned the sport shirt he'd had the man buy at the nearby thrift shop. He left the treatment room and edged up to peer anxiously out the front window of the veterinarian's office.

"Will you leave please?" pleaded the vet.

"Yeah, yeah, just let me call somebody first." Boudreaux took out his cell phone and looked up a local number. He called it.

"Hey, yeah, FBI? My name be Boudreaux. You know all dat shit goin' on in Vegas with the poisoned people? I know a lot about that. I got killers after me. Y'all come pick me up, you give me protection, I give you all you need to know."

***

"The good cop, crazy cop routine worked pretty good," said a grinning Lou, removing her hazmat suit outside the FBI interrogation room.

"You do 'crazy' just a little *too* well," said Chun, shaking her head. "You are a scary woman."

"You got everything recorded?"

Chun nodded, pressing a key on her laptop and bringing up the video of the interrogation room. It showed Joseph jerking his head back and forth in desperate avoidance, as the hazmat-suited Lou thrust the spray bottle in his face.

"*McAndrews!*" he exclaimed. "He's behind it at the company! It's called gustatene X, or GX. He bought it from Oskar Dunst and Diana Vodkonen, and it was made in a chemical plant in Mexico by a cartel. . . Eladio Campana's cartel. Now take that stuff away!"

Lou packed the hazmat suit back into the duffel bag, and Chun took notes from the video, as Joseph recited details about people and places. "He sure was afraid of a little water," said Lou wryly.

Finally, Chun sat back and sighed. "It's pretty clear. We've got to figure out a way to get to that chemical plant. Don't know where it is and how we'll get there through the Mexican government. They have lots of people who are protecting Campana."

"Leafy, we can't let anything stop us. We've got to shut down that plant and bring Kane out, alive and kicking. Nonny's life. . . a *thousand* lives depend on it. Kane is the only one who really understands how this GX works. He's the only one who could come up with an antidote."

"Well, we sure as hell aren't going to invade Mexico."

Chapter 21

"**I**s he okay?" asked Lou. Her eyes were moist with tears, as she watched Nonny struggle feebly against the handcuffs that bound him to his hospital bed.

"Not okay, at all," said Abadi. "I give him hot sauce to keep him confused, but he is in bad way. A nurse feed him, but very carefully, so he does not overeat and get sick. I do not know whether he will even survive. Who knows what this drug does to brain?"

"Well, we're stuck for solutions. We've traced the GX to somewhere in Mexico. And since there was a large amount, we have to assume that it's being made in quantity. If the chemical gets into the environment, it will be a global disaster. And the only person who could develop a cure is Kane, whom we assume is there."

"You don't know where factory is?"

"Campana has drug factories all over his territory. We don't know which one."

Abadi clapped his large hands, exclaiming "We can help with that! Remember we are looking at the foods the drug dealers bought. The recipes?"

"I don't know how that—"

"Chef, he figure that some of the foods could be used only to make one recipe. But that recipe lack one ingredient. A very specific, rare truffle oil. Nonny asks his friends in food industry find where some of that rare truffle oil was sent. One place Manzanillo on Mexican coast! So, their boat is there. So, the drug factory must be near."

"Awesome sauce!" exclaimed Lou. "I'm sure Leafy and her pals can figure out which drug plant is the target. But they still can't get at it."

"You can't just go in with military?"

"Leafy says we can't invade another country."

"Can't you ask the Mexicans for help?"

"Chun tells me it would take weeks to go through the red tape to plan a joint operation under the best of circumstances. And it might not ever happen, given that the drug lord who runs the plant is protected." Lou began to stroke Nonny's head, and he stared up at her through hunger-clouded eyes.

"Lou, you're here," he said weakly.

"Yeah, sweetie, I'm here for you."

Abadi took her arm gently and whispered, "I have idea. I think I know how to raid factory, get scientist."

"Daoud, that would be great."

They moved outside Nonny's room, where Abadi said darkly, "Nonny has *friends*."

"Yeah, well, I can't imagine how some other chefs could help."

"Oh, not chefs. Far from chefs. Mercenaries. Guys with lots of guns."

"How the hell would he know mercenaries?"

"You have heard of Gunny Joe's Canteen restaurants?"

"Who hasn't? They've exploded in popularity, pardon the pun. Huge success. They have the military theme and really good food."

"Nonny did the food. He develop their menu, in return for a piece of the company. He keep it quiet because he is gourmet chef."

"So, he knows their cooks. How does he know mercenaries?"

"Well, he make huge money from the restaurants. Millions and still counting. He give it all to military families who lost loved ones. Helped them with homes, education, all their expenses."

"And the mercenaries?"

"All ex-military. He help the families of their buddies killed in action. They tell him they will do anything for him. Now, he need their help. We go see them. They will invade Mexico big time."

"Hell yes!" exclaimed Lou. "What's that marines say? *Hoo-rah!*"

***

"Hell no!" exclaimed Chun. "You are not going into Mexico with a ragtag bunch of wannabe Rambos. I can't even know you're thinking of doing some scatterbrained mission. And quit calling me—"

"Tight-ass, you know that's going to be the only way to get in, get Kane, destroy that chemical plant," said Lou. "And thanks to Nonny, at least we know the area where it is!" She kept her voice down, given that they were in the FBI conference room. "Besides, you feds do off-the-books missions all the time. I've seen it in the movies."

"Yeah, well, that's movies. I've got enough problems here in the US. The Veganites are dying under mysterious circumstances. They could've helped lead us to the source, but not anymore."

"What do you mean?"

Chun consulted her laptop. "Two girls and two men who had vegan tattoos were in a car accident. They went off a cliff."

"Accidents happen."

"Yeah, well these were people our agents linked to hijacking the GX shipment that ended up in San Diego." Chun began to run down a list. "One of the terrorists on trial apparently committed suicide by jumping off a building. Another contracted botulism, looks like from a can of bad beef stew. *Beef stew!* Remember, they were vegans! Another drowned in a swimming pool. Another somehow managed to trip and fall on a kitchen knife. Then, worst of all, for us at least, were what happened to the two leaders."

"What happened?"

Chun laughed ruefully. "They found the leader Baltazar dead in a house in Florida. He had choked on a piece of steak. Again, they're vegans. A vegan dies from choking on meat? Sounds like somebody is trying to taunt us."

"And the other leader?"

"He's called Teo. He went out on a boat and is missing, presumed dead. It's in shark-infested waters, so he was probably a meal for some non-vegan shark."

"But again, at least, we know the area of the Mexican chemical plant, or Kane's lab, or where the drug dealers are," said Lou. "This is now a tragedy for the people suffering. Soon it will be a global tragedy."

Chun stared at Lou for a long moment. She took a deep, resigned breath. "Actually, now we are certain where the factory is. One of the drug dealers' thugs surfaced in New Orleans. A guy named Boudreaux. He told the FBI there everything. But we could not have possibly considered any kind of mission based on his tip. But thanks to Nonny confirming the area, we could. Not that I'll ever tell you."

Chapter 22

"Interesting tats," said the muscular young mercenary with the brush cut. He glanced only briefly at the inked molecules on Lou's back. She was slogging along beside him in a sports bra and shorts, a faint sheen of sweat glistening on her skin in the cool desert morning.

"Yeah, the molecules reflecting different food tastes. That's my profession." She gave him a suspicious sideways look. "Let's see yours."

The mercenary grinned and stripped off his t-shirt, revealing on his shoulder a large, intricate tattoo of a frog skeleton wielding a trident.

"Yours are cool, too."

"Okay, you can see I'm not wearing a wire either. Can we talk now?" He glanced around. There were no other runners out this early, as they jogged along the narrow, dusty running trail outside Las Vegas. The trail wound among the flat landscape of cactus, yucca, and sagebrush. Around them low, tan mountains jutted up from the desert floor.

"Yeah, well, I can manage a conversation," she huffed. "Woulda been more comfortable over coffee somewhere, though."

"This is how I guarantee no surveillance, no recording. You could be a trap, being a fed. And what you're asking would land me and my team in federal prison for decades. Or maybe in a Mexican prison for a much shorter stretch before we were killed."

"You don't want to do it? I can find somebody else."

"You won't find anybody better. Don't get me wrong. I want to do this. So does my team. It's for Nonny. And of course, for all the other poor bastards who got poisoned."

"And because of the money he gave military families."

"Yeah, there's that. And for my baby sister."

"Nonny helped her?"

"Made her cry."

"He does that a lot. For happiness I hope."

"Yeah, a month or so ago, she called up just sobbing. Nonny had made her a sous chef in his restaurant. Her dream."

"So what's the plan?"

"First, tell me where the hell we're supposed to be going."

"Mexico."

The mercenary laughed sarcastically. "Yeah, right, *great* place for an op. Where in Mexico?"

Lou was panting hard now, barely able to get out a full sentence. "The FBI agents I'm working with have found out, but they're not sharing. They're asserting need-to-know. The minute I find out, you'll know. So, what's the plan when you do know?"

Basically, same kind of op we did when me and my team were SEALs. Fly in to the nearest airfield. Take ground transport to target. Destroy target. Fly out."

"And get Kane. Listen. . ." She paused, to catch her breath, waving for the mercenary to stop. Her legs were getting wobbly. ". . . he absolutely *has* to be brought out safely. He's the only one who can save those people, stop this crap from getting out. And about destroying the target. It has to be totally obliterated. By fire. The chemical has to be completely degraded."

"Is it flammable?"

Lou knitted her brow and pursed her lips. "Never thought about that. Yeah, it's an organic compound. So, yeah."

"So, we'll use incendiary grenades. And hope they totally burn the stuff."

"Well, I'll be along to assess whether the stuff is destroyed."

The mercenary shook his head decisively. "No civilians. That would mean we not only have to watch our own sixes, but yours, too."

"Has to be," panted Lou, bending over, her hands on her knees. "I know the science. I'll know what data to gather. I'll be able to persuade Kane. You tough-ass soldiers go in there and scare the shit out of him, he might bolt. And it's my dollar."

"About the money. We'll do our part pro bono. But there are expenses."

"How much."

"A hundred fifty thousand." The man resumed his jog, Lou trundling after.

"Wow!" She was silent for a long minute as they approached the parking area. "Okay, I'll drain my bank account. Take out a loan on the house. I'll do it."

As the parking area came into view, the mercenary exclaimed "What the hell!" The rising sun revealed another SUV parked beside Lou's car and the mercenary's SUV. Leaning against it, her head bowed over a tablet computer was Rochelle Chun dressed in her usual black pants suit, white blouse, and low heels. She looked up and regarded them with a scowl, shaking her head.

"What are you doing here?" demanded Lou, slumping against her car.

"Is she a fibbie?" asked the mercenary. "Is this a bust?"

"Yes, I'm a fibbie," said Chun. "Special Agent Chun, FBI, and no, this isn't a bust."

"How did you find us?" asked Lou.

"Like I said, I'm with the FBI. We know how to find people."

"I'm—" began the mercenary.

"I know who you are. Evan Harwood, Harwood Security."

"Are you going to queer this deal?" asked Lou.

"No. Against my better judgment, I'm going to help with it. I can't let a loose cannon like you go off on a tear without the right backup. I've got a location, satellite imagery, intel."

Lou grinned. "So, now we got a tight-ass on the team."

Chun smiled wryly at the jibe. "You mean a disciplined, experienced tactician."

***

"*¿Cuánto de esta mierda tenemos?*" demanded Eladio Campana, glaring up at the stainless-steel reaction vat. Then, he remembered that Kane didn't speak Spanish. "How much of this shit you make?"

"Three thousand gallons," said Kane.

"Did you see the news from Las Vegas? The crazy people? *Poison! You have made poison!*"

"Well, I wanted to do more testing, but you said—"

Campana slashed the barrel of his pistol against Kane's skull, sending him slamming to the concrete floor, blood streaming from his scalp. "You do not tell me what I said." He turned to the slight, balding chemist. "What do we do now?" he asked in Spanish.

The chemist raised his hands in a placating gesture, replying in Spanish. "We are still okay, I think. Buyers like the samples we sent out. We just tell them it was a problem of dosing, like before. Tell them it means they can dilute the chemical even more. And we tell them the food madness is just temporary, anyway and that the people will recover just fine. As far as we know, they will recover."

"And him?" asked Campana, pointing to the groaning Kane.

"We still need him. He can work on a new compound that does not create the permanent madness, just a temporary hunger. The right amount of hunger that goes away."

"Sell the shit as fast as you can, before customers find out otherwise. Bring in tanker trucks. We got customers in Europe, Asia, so book space on the freighters." He looked down at Kane. "Clean him up, put him back in laboratory."

Two of Campana's men hoisted Kane to his feet. They hauled Kane, his bleeding head lolling, to one of Campana's SUVs.

***

"You ever fired one of these?" Evan Harwood held up a nine-millimeter pistol, staring dubiously at Lou. The armory at Harwood Security held a huge weapons vault crammed with weaponry ranging from pistols to assault rifles to grenades.

"I've seen it done on TV." Lou shrugged.

"Well, then, you're absolutely good. Ready to rock and roll."

Chun laughed at Harwood's sarcasm, taking the pistol from him. She pointed to the barrel. "Okay, LC, this hole is where the bullets come out. You point that where you want to shoot. It's dangerous to point it at people."

"How about the hole where your words come out. That's pretty dangerous."

"Seriously, Lou, I need to take you to their range and give you some shooting practice. You need to develop muscle memory to shoot effectively. Otherwise, if you ever find yourself actually aiming at a human, your muscles will turn into a trembling mass, your guts will revolt, and you won't even be able to see straight."

"Yeah, well, then I won't carry a gun."

Harwood shook his head emphatically. "Nobody goes unarmed on a mission with us."

"Yeah, let's give LC here a Glock," said Chun.

"LC? What's that stand for?" asked Harwood.

"Loose Cannon."

"That's comforting." Harwood gave Lou a Glock pistol, fitted her with a shoulder holster, and gave her a box of ammunition. They walked down the long hall of the sixty-thousand-square-foot, concrete-walled warehouse that was Harwood's Phoenix operations and training center.

"What've we got?" asked Harwood, as they entered the op center. It held a large conference table, rows of computers and three walls covered with large-screen monitors. Two of the monitors showed overhead views of white-roofed buildings set in a flat desert terrain. Harwood's planning strategist—a wiry, sharp-featured man in a crisp khaki uniform—was walking down the row of computers, monitoring the work of their operators.

"Thanks to the FBI. . .," said the strategist, nodding to Chun, ". . . we know that Eladio Campana is the manufacturer. He's partnered with Oskar Dunst and Diana Vodkonen. He's got two key facilities. The lab is apparently in this toy factory, along with his drug distribution center. The chemical they call GX is being made at his chemical factory a couple of miles away. The product is shipped out using his trucks carrying winery tanks."

"So, how do you see the op?" asked Harwood.

"Two teams, two planes," said the strategist. "One team lands and goes for the chemical plant. The other for the toy factory, to get the scientist and destroy their research capability."

"Jeez, I need to be at both places," said Lou, scanning the two monitors. "I need to make sure all the GX is destroyed and take samples to make sure we're not dealing with anything new. But at the same time, I need to see what Kane has been doing in the lab. And he's more likely to go with us if I'm there to explain what we need him to do."

Chun shook her head. "You're needed at the chemical plant. I'll go for Kane."

"Yeah, and you'll go in giving him the 'I'm-with-the-government-and-I'm-here-to help-you' bullshit. That won't fly with Kane. And he'll see that you're with a bunch of guys with big damn guns."

"That's the point. There is much more likelihood of heavy fighting at the factory. You stick with the team at the chemical plant."

"Look—" Lou began, her expression a rising glower, when Chun held up her hand and took out her phone to answer a call. She walked away, with her back to the others. After several minutes of intense conversation, she returned.

"I hope you're ready to pull the trigger on this op," she said to Harwood. "That was the colonel from the Army Chemical Corps. They've been working with the National Reconnaissance Office to do satellite surveillance of the chemical plant. He says that trucks are at the site, loading GX. That means we have to go in immediately."

***

"Idiots," spat Diana. "Do they not know that Kane is a valuable asset?" Curled up on a couch in the skylounge of their yacht, she had just ended a cell phone call with one of their men. He had remained at Campana's factory to keep watch over the GX production and distribution.

"What's happened?" asked Dunst. He rose from his chair to refill his wine glass.

"Eladio beat him and had him imprisoned in the lab."

"Well, that is unacceptable. Does he not realize that the scientist is a key to improving the product?"

"Of course not. He is a drug dealer and a thug."

Dunst tried to brighten her mood. "Well, at least our ladies' subcontractors carried out their assignments well. All the targets were taken out in, I thought, a rather ingenious manner. Lots of accidents." He handed her a paper report that had been hand-delivered that day. The assassins Camilla and Sharon never depended on electronic communications, given that they could be monitored.

Diana scanned the pages. "Except Boudreaux. They have him as a probable."

"Well, I would bet the grenade they shot at him did its job."

Diana rose and paced back and forth, scanning the gently rolling waves glistening under the tropical sun. She removed her sunglasses and turned back to Dunst. "Get some of our people together. We're going for Kane. We've got to protect our investment."

Chapter 23

"How many combatants?" whispered Harwood, as they crouched in the desert scrub brush outside the Mexican chemical plant. Behind them, arrayed in the near-total darkness of a crescent moon, waited the seven-man assault team, along with Lou.

"Six around the perimeter," said the operator of the quadcopter drone. The operator crouched beside Harwood, scrutinizing the screen of the tablet computer showing the overhead video of the chemical plant.

"Weapons?" asked Harwood.

"Assault rifles, handguns," answered the operator. He touched a control stick to send the tiny drone skimming under the high metal roof. The screen showed men dressed in hazmat suits and respirators working among the rows of stainless-steel tanks, lit by banks of fluorescent lights. At one end of the plant sat four large trucks, their back doors open to reveal plastic tanks.

Harwood issued terse orders over his radio for the team to fan out to surround the plant, each member assigned to take out a guard.

"Lights out in ten," he whispered. He instructed the drone operator to continue surveilling the site, as he and another mercenary sprinted to the main electrical circuit-breaker box outside the plant. He carefully opened the metal box's door, whispered a final ten-second countdown, then pulled the main circuit breaker, plunging the plant into darkness.

A chorus of alarmed shouts arose from among the network of pipes and tanks, but Harwood ignored them, waiting for the series of reports from his team members. He flipped down his night vision goggles, scanning the scene. Scattered shots echoed around the perimeter of the plant. Then one by one the attackers reported that they had neutralized the guards. Harwood flipped his goggles back up and shoved the circuit breaker switch to flood the plant with light again. Bellowed commands from the mercenaries in Spanish rose over the workers' shouts.

Lou appeared beside Harwood, wearing a backpack. "Hold the fireworks until I've got my samples," she said, emphasizing her words with a pointed finger.

"Right, right." Harwood nodded and confirmed with the team to hold on demolishing the tanks.

Lou, Harwood, and the drone operator sprinted into the plant to find the plant workers crowded together on their knees, their hands on their heads, surrounded by the assault team. One member was collecting their cell phones, stuffing them into his pack. Shackled to a pipe beside one tank crouched three workers, their respirators removed. Glassy-eyed, they moaned and writhed, struggling to free themselves.

"See them?" said Harwood pointing to the agonized workers. "That's what happens when you get a taste of this crap. Be real damned careful!" At Harwood's command, the other workers were bound with plastic cuffs and marched out of the plant, guarded by two team members.

"Any activity outside?" asked Harwood, and the drone operator consulted his screen, reporting that the area remained clear.

Lou donned rubber gloves and a respirator, and began moving quickly from tank to tank. She stopped at each one to carefully draw off samples from their spigots into small screw-top bottles. She stowed bottle after bottle in her backpack. She reached the last tank and stuffed the last bottle into her pants pocket—a cautionary habit from when she had lost a whole collection of samples on a field mission.

She reached a small office at one end of the plant and ducked inside to find a laptop computer.

"Jackpot!" she whispered to herself, unplugging the computer and tucking it under her arm.

Emerging from the office, she raised her hand and gave Harwood a thumbs-up.

"*Ready!*" shouted Harwood, and his men pulled the gray metal cylinders of incendiary grenades from their packs and clambered up the ladders to the tops of the tanks. They opened the lids on the tanks, and held the grenades over the openings. "*Fire in the hole!*" bellowed Harwood, and in unison, the men yanked the pins on the grenades and dropped them into the tanks.

They slid rapidly down the ladders and sprinted toward the trucks, pitching incendiary grenades into their backs, next to the plastic tanks.

Harwood asked for a head count over the comm and they all answered. They burst from the plant just as a massive fireball enveloped the sprawling complex, sending a blistering wave of heat expanding toward them. They barely managed to outrun the expanding, roiling flames, reaching a parking lot full of old cars and trucks. There waited the two men guarding the plant workers, who shrieked and threw themselves behind the vehicles.

The team members watched the growing inferno, as the flaming tanks exploded, one by one, creating blasts that brought new waves of searing heat enveloping them. Billowing black smoke roiled skyward blocking out the stars.

"*¡Sal de aquí ahora!*" exclaimed Harwood to the plant workers. "Get out of here!" Hands still bound, the men struggled to their feet and staggered away into the darkness.

Lou hurried from vehicle to vehicle, peering inside each one. She stopped at a battered gray pickup, seeing keys in the ignition.

The men pulled out their knives and began to stab holes in two tires on each vehicle. One had just bent down to puncture the tires on the pickup, when Lou exclaimed, "Not this one! This one I need!" She handed Harwood her backpack of samples, then the laptop, saying "Betcha this will have records on where any shipments went. See ya!" She climbed in, turned the key, and its engine roared to life.

"Where the hell are you going?" demanded Harwood. "We've got to exfil!"

"I gotta go see Tight-Ass about a scientist!" she exclaimed, gunning the truck and launching it careening into the night.

***

The guards outside Campana's toy factory shouted curses on hearing the roar of the distant explosions from the chemical plant. They clambered onto the back of a stake-bed truck, which careened away toward the fiery glow on the horizon that marked the plant.

Chun crouched in the darkness beyond the factory's lights preparing for her assault. She secured her pack containing the ten palm-sized explosive charges. She also secured her emotions. She had learned to use to her advantage the fear she always felt on operations. Like when she'd led an FBI assault team into another drug dealer's headquarters the previous year.

Her fear, ironically, steadied her. It was an old, nagging friend, a dread that when she invariably overcame it, rendered her even more effective. For a fleeting moment, she allowed a calming distraction. She wondered whether her husband would finish that painting he'd been working on. But she also used that distraction to bring her focus back onto the mission at hand with even greater clarity. She braced herself to rush the now-unguarded steel door beside the huge building's freight entrance.

Over her earpiece she heard from Harwood's second-in-command, who had accompanied her. He was behind her, hidden in the brush, watching on a tablet computer the overhead scene from a drone. "So far, drone shows nobody in for the last hour," he said. "We got maybe thirty minutes for you to set the charges and bring out the asset."

Chun chambered a round in her carbine and launched herself toward the factory, sprinting across the desert, hauling open the metal door, and ducking inside. She found herself at one end of the empty factory, among shrink-wrapped pallets of boxes with colorful images of toy robots and dolls. She scanned the shipping room to see overhead doors leading to the left. She ducked through to find one of her quarries: a room piled with bricks of white powder and pallets of toy boxes. She would set charges here on her way out. Her main objective was the laboratory, where if she was lucky, she would find Edwin Kane.

Taking a chance that the laboratory was at this end of the factory, she went through a large set of double doors next to the drug room. Success! The room held the same kinds of analytical machines as in the Las Vegas warehouse they had raided, so she knew she had found Kane's lab. But Kane was not there. It was empty, with no activity, save for the blinking lights on the machines.

She realized she needed to set all her charges while she had the chance, so she attached five charges throughout the laboratory, hiding them beneath the machines and among drums of flammable chemicals. As she went, she set the timers to thirty minutes and exited back into the drug depot. She stuck the last five charges among the stacks of bricks of drugs and in the pallets of boxes, where she knew they would spark a destructive blaze.

She had set the last charge and gone back into the main factory to search for Kane, when the crackle of gunfire filtered in from outside the factory.

"Company!" she heard Harwood's man exclaim in her earpiece. "Three vehicles! Get out!"

She sprinted back to the door where she had entered, flinging it open, but leaping back as a fusillade of bullets slammed into the door and exploded into the factory. She crouched and fired back in the direction of the gunfire, retreating into the factory. She ducked behind a pallet of toys, acutely aware that just on the other side of the nearby wall were the charges that would detonate in a few dozen minutes. She would have to find another way out!

She decided the best choice was to make it to the far end of the factory, where there might be an unguarded exit door.

Now the voice of Harwood himself sounded in her earpiece. "We've got wounded! Give us your location. Can you reach the exfil point?"

"Not sure," she replied. "Get your wounded out." She turned to go back into the factory, then stopped short.

Aimed at her chest were two assault rifles held by Campana's guards. Beside them stood Dunst, Diana, Mutante, and Campana himself.

Said Dunst, "Agent Chun, it is not much of a surprise to see you here. . . illegally, as it happens."

"Vacation," deadpanned Chun, placing her own rifle on the concrete floor. She grasped her pistol's grip by thumb and forefinger and extracted it from its holster, also placing it on the floor.

"A working vacation?" asked Dunst.

"A *productive* working vacation," said Chun. "I would suggest that we all move to the far end of the factory."

Campana advanced toward her, scowling. "And why is that?"

"Because this end will go up in smoke."

Punctuating her answer was a series of muffled blasts from the laboratory, where she had set the first of the charges.

Campana's men grabbed Chun by the arms, and dragged her down the assembly lines toward the other end of the factory. They had just reached the far wall when a rapid-fire series of blasts blew jagged holes in the metal wall between the factory and the drug depot.

As smoke billowed from the holes, Campana bellowed "YOU GODDAMNED BITCH!"

Diana, her voice a cold monotone, said, "Mr. Mutante, would you please impress on Agent Chun the consequences of the damage she has caused."

At first, Mutante wrinkled his thick brow in puzzlement, then grasped Diana's instruction. He advanced toward Chun, his large hands curled into fists.

Chun struggled in the grasp of Campana's men, but her struggle was strategic. She wanted them to clutch her tightly enough so they could serve as supports. As Mutante came within striking distance, she used that support to lash out with her right foot, embedding the toe of her boot deep into Mutante's crotch.

The huge man doubled over, gasping, collapsing to his knees. Chun threw both her feet up, planting them on Mutante's chest. Using Mutante's bulk as a solid launch point, she propelled herself backward, carrying Campana's men with her, performing a back flip, loosening their grip and landing upright, with the men slamming to the floor on either side of her.

Bringing up her right foot, she slammed her boot down onto the throat of the man to her right. The man gagged and clutched his collapsed larynx, fighting for breath. Then, she brought up her left foot, she did the same to the other man.

"*MALDITA PUTA!*" cursed Campana, yanking a gold pistol from its holster and firing a bullet into Chun's chest.

Chapter 24

"**O**h, dear God," breathed Lou, as she crept toward the huge building that was Eladio Campana's factory. Under the spotlights illuminating the windowless structure, she could see Campana's men dragging bodies to a pickup truck and hefting them into the back.

She triggered her radio, telling Harwood, "Some bad shit went on here! There are people dead!"

"We know," replied Harwood. "We had three men wounded, one badly. They had to retreat. We've got to exfil."

"*You're leaving? What the hell!*"

"No choice. There are incoming hostiles. Unless we move out now, we'll be cut off from the airport."

"Is agent Chun with them?"

"Negative. She's MIA. During the firefight, she entered the building through a back entrance."

"Are you going to try to rescue her?"

"Not with casualties. We'll have to regroup, develop an alternative plan."

Lou took a deep breath to prevent herself from suggesting where the mercenary could stuff his alternative plan. Instead, she said, "You get the fu—. . . you get back here as soon as you can."

She flattened herself against the desert earth still warm from the hot day and clenched her jaw, trying to figure out a plan of attack. But the only plan she could come up with to get into the building, was one that could get her killed. She decided that more important than her safety was finding Chun and Kane. She had gotten Chun into this mess. And Kane was the key to saving Nonny and all the other zombies in the grip of GX. She could not get out of her head the image of the sweet, wonderful Nonny shackled to that hospital bed. She drew a deep breath and let it out slowly, her determination crystallizing. She pulled out her pistol and pitched it away.

"HEY Y'ALL!" she bellowed raising her arms, but pulling herself to a sitting position. "I GIVE UP! I'VE GOT NO GUN! I HAVE IMPORTANT INFORMATION FOR YOUR BOSS CAMPANA!"

A confusion of shouts arose from the men, along with the metallic clink of weapons being brought up. A searchlight swerved back and forth, finally landing on her. Squinting against the glare, she stood slowly up.

"Campana! Campana!" she repeated over and over, hoping the use of the drug lord's name would keep them from shooting her.

Rushing at her out of the glare came four burly figures, assault rifles aimed at her. One grabbed her by the hair and yanked her to her feet, shoving her toward the factory. She kept her hands high as she stumbled forward.

One of the men swung open a bullet-riddled metal door, and she was shoved in to find herself in the cavernous space that was the toy factory. The acrid smell of smoke assaulted her nostrils, and a swirl of smoke wafted out of a door at the rear of the huge space.

Standing beside an assembly line were Eladio Campana, Oskar Dunst, and Diana Vodkonen. One of the men who had captured Lou approached Campana and said something to him in a low voice.

Campana had a large, gold pistol in his hand, standing over a person lying still at his feet. He was holding the pistol to the person's head. Lou didn't recognize the figure at first, she was so bloody, the face so swollen.

It was Rochelle Chun!

"*What did you bastards do to her?*" demanded Lou, struggling to reach Chun.

"Who the hell are you?" asked Campana.

"Mary Louette Baumgartner, US Food and Drug Administration. I'm the one who has been tracking Edwin Kane's research. Where is he?"

Campana gestured over his shoulder at the end of the building. "An apartment. He did not need to see this." He waved his pistol at Chun, who did not move. "She blew up my shipping center. She blew up the laboratory. And she did that." He waved to men slumped against the wall. One of them Lou recognized from photos as the massive thug Mutante. Two of the men were choking, and Mutante was bent over panting, his hands on his crotch.

"She did all that?"

Chun stirred and croaked through swollen lips. "I did all that."

"Oh, Jesus, you're alive!"

"Took a round in the vest," said Chun. "Then, they had more fun."

"You know she's FBI, right?" asked Lou.

"Yes, so?" asked Campana.

"She is a federale. I am a federale. You kill either one of us, the entire United States government will be on your ass. Do you happen to know a drug dealer known as El Chapo?"

Campana said nothing, but still held the pistol to Chun's head.

Lou continued. "He's now serving life in a supermax prison. Solitary confinement twenty-four hours a day. He got the attention of the US government."

Dunst stepped up, holding both hands in front of him, in a placating gesture. "Eladio, let us solve your problem. You've got your hands full building another chemical plant, putting your shipping center back together. We'll take these two and make sure they are never heard from again, and you will be in the clear. And we'll set Doctor Kane up in a new laboratory, to solve our technical problems."

"A bullet would solve this problem," said Campana, jabbing the gun barrel into Chun's skull.

***

Mutante showed a pronounced limp, as he violently hauled a near-unconscious Rochelle Chun onto the yacht. Her hands were cuffed behind her, as were Lou's, who was dragged onto the deck by another of Dunst's men.

Following them were Dunst, Diana, and Kane, who eyed the two captives with a look of shock. "You can't—" he started to say, then abruptly stopped, bowing his head.

"What will you do with us?" asked Lou.

"We're headed back to the US," said Dunst, a smirk on his face. "We'll drop you off on the way."

"An island perhaps?" asked Lou.

"Oh, within a few dozen miles of one, perhaps. But the currents won't be kind to you." Then, to the men: "Put them in the utilities hold. And we'll have dinner at the usual time."

The men dragged Lou and Chun down a flight of steps into the yacht's interior and down another set at the stern of the ship. They passed the engine room, which resonated with the low thrum of diesel engines idling. Finally, they were hauled through a hatchway into a room filled with large tanks connected to a profusion of pipes. One unit was labeled "potable water treatment" and another labeled "wastewater treatment."

The men slammed Lou and Chun to the deck, uncuffing them and re-cuffing their hands in front of them to heavy metal stanchions that secured the equipment.

After they left, Lou leaned over to Chun. "How bad are you hurt?"

Chun winced, taking several breaths before replying. "Cracked ribs from the bullet, maybe fractured eye socket."

"What happened?"

"The mercs were outside the factory when I went in. I found the drug shipping room, then the lab. I planted my charges. Couldn't find Kane." She paused and winced, then recovered. "Then more of

Campana's men showed up, and engaged the mercs. Campana captured me just as the charges went off. They weren't real happy. I got some licks in, but Campana shot me. He probably didn't realize I was wearing a vest. Then, they decided to do a number on me. I knew they wouldn't kill me because they knew I was FBI. By the way, what the hell do you think you were doing, just coming in?" She glared at Lou with the eye that wasn't swollen shut.

"I couldn't let you have all the fun."

"LC, hope you're a good swimmer."

Chapter 25

Chun groaned and shifted painfully on the floor, her hands bound to the metal stanchion, saying, "I figure the best strategy is we get out of these cuffs, make it to the deck, and slip over the side."

"Yeah, well, we'd have to wait until dark." Lou's answer was all but drowned out by the roar of the yacht's diesel engines coming to life. The steady rocking of the boat and the slap of waves against the hull told them it was pulling away from the dock.

"Too late. Probably won't have time after dark," shouted Chun. "They get maybe a few dozen miles out to sea, and they put us over the side. That way, they avoid the unpleasant chore of actually murdering us."

"Well, we can't do anything unless we get out of the cuffs," said Lou. "They took the key."

"They took *a* key. I carry two since I lost my cuff key in training at Quantico and caught holy hell for it. Check my boot." Grunting in pain, Chun swung her right leg around and bent it so that Lou could reach her foot.

Lou managed to dig her fingers into the boot, discovering a pocket that held a key. Clutching it in her fingers, she managed to unlock her cuffs. But rather than unlocking Chun's she sat back against the bulkhead, her brow furrowed.

"Get me loose!" commanded Chun. But the directive was not as forceful as it might have been, given that her words were slurred.

"And what will you do?"

"As much damage as I can before they take me out."

"Listen, I got an idea."

"My idea is you get me loose."

"Just in case you won't cooperate with my idea, I'm gonna leave you cuffed. And you're in no shape to do any fighting, anyway."

"Goddammit—" began Chun, but Lou had already hauled herself up and moved away down the narrow aisle between the yacht's water tanks. She was gone for almost a quarter of an hour before returning, an odd smile on her face.

"Got a pen?" she asked.

"Get me loose!" commanded Chun again.

Rather than comply, Lou checked Chun's jacket pockets before finding a pen. She proceeded to inscribe something on her palm. She replaced the pen and re-cuffed herself to the steel stanchion, settling back into the position she had been in before.

"What the hell are you doing?" growled Chun. "Are you crazy? Give me the damned key."

"I think I'll just hold onto it for safekeeping. I figured a way for us all to get out of here."

"What way?"

"Just stay cool. You'll see."

Just then, the engines stopped, likely signaling that the site of their drowning had been reached. An hour passed before Mutante appeared with the other thug who had dragged them down into the hold. They uncuffed Chun and Lou from the stanchion, re-cuffed them, and hauled them up to the main deck.

Sitting on the fantail at a table laid out with silver and China for dinner, they found Dunst, Diana, and Kane, who sat stiffly at the table, his food untouched. Dunst and Diana were engaged in conversation as they dined, at first ignoring the prisoners. Chun and Lou were shoved down onto a couch across from the table. Lou shifted her position until she had a clear sight line to Kane, such that Dunst and Diana could not see the hand she held up in greeting.

"Edwin, I hope you're okay," she said, holding her palm toward the scientist in a gesture that she sustained for nearly half a minute.

Kane at first avoided looking at the handcuffed pair, but abruptly fixed his gaze on Lou's upraised palm.

"Okay, you good?" asked Lou pointedly of Kane.

After a long moment, Kane nodded, gazing steadily at Lou, who settled back onto the couch.

"What the hell was that about?" whispered Chun.

"Just a little warning from one chemist to another." Lou showed her palm, on which she had inscribed "H-:O:-H" with a slash through the inscription, as well as a complex chemical structure. She proceeded to lick her palm and rub it on her pants, smearing the message.

Dunst took the last bite of his dinner and settled back. "I thought we'd just drop you off now, but Diana insisted we give you the pleasure of our company until after nightfall."

"Our pleasure will be when you're both in prison. . . . If you make it to prison," said Lou.

"Also, I thought we'd just attach weights to you, but Diana insisted it would be amusing to watch you struggle in the water while handcuffed."

"As would any sociopath," said Chun. "We know your history."

Diana poured herself a glass of sparkling water, saying "Your own history will end shortly. And the process will make our trip tax deductible as a business expense."

Dunst laughed. "Good joke, Diana."

"What joke?" she asked sipping her water.

"Has the crew had their dinner?" asked Lou.

Dunst hmphed, a puzzled expression on his face. "Odd question. Why do you care?"

"Oh, I just like to know people are being taken care of, especially that they are well hydrated in this warm climate." Lou smiled oddly, as Chun gave her a brow-wrinkled puzzled look. The puzzled look continued when Lou whispered, "Get ready. I'm gonna uncuff you."

"About damned time," Chun whispered back.

A white-coated steward appeared, starting to remove their plates. But rather than smoothly whisking the plates away, he stood staring at the table with a blank expression.

Diana looked up at him, dabbing her lips with the linen napkin. "Philippe, will you please clear?" she asked. When the steward did not move, she repeated, more emphatically. *"Please clear and leave. We will not be needing your services this evening."*

The steward picked up Kane's full plate, but instead of carrying it away buried his face in it, snuffling as he devoured its contents.

Dunst bolted upright. *"What the hell are you doing?"*

The steward finished off the plate, pitched it aside, and grabbed the basket of bread, cramming the bread into his mouth.

Mutante appeared from below, his expression also blank.

"What's happening?" demanded Dunst, but the huge man did not respond.

"Now!" exclaimed Lou, uncuffing Chun, then uncuffing herself. She lunged for the inert Mutante, yanking his pistol from his holster and leveling it at Dunst and Diana. "I hoped you two would be affected. But I figure you just drank bottled water, so I guess you get to stay normal."

"What did you do?" asked Dunst.

"Yeah, what *did* you do?" echoed Chun, rising from the couch, wincing in pain.

"See, I'm a careful field scientist," said Lou, relishing the chance to lecture the drug dealers on her field tactics. "When I take samples, I never trust that I won't somehow lose my sample case, especially in the middle of a raid on a drug factory. So, I stuck a sample of GX in my pocket. And that very same sample ended up in y'all's water system. About now, your whole crew is gobbling up your food stores. But Edwin here. . ." She gestured to Kane, who sat wide-eyed staring at her ". . . knew not to drink water because I showed him a water molecule on my hand with a warning slash through it. And I also drew a pretty good diagram of his GX molecule."

"And you're going to shoot us?" asked Diana smoothly. "Really?"

"Yeah, if you don't do what I say." Lou's emphatic reply was undermined by a trembling of her pistol hand.

"I suspect you don't have a lot of experience with weapons, or with shooting people," said Diana, moving slowly toward Lou. She stepped to the side of the table, giving her a clear shot to tackle Lou. At the same time, Dunst moved to the opposite side, causing Lou to shift the pistol back and forth between them.

"I got enough experience," said Lou.

"You're sure the safety is off?" asked Diana, moving closer. "You ever seen anybody shot? It's gruesome."

"Steady," whispered Chun. "Steady, Lou."

Lou took a deep breath, her trembling increasing.

Diana bent her legs slightly, bracing her hand on the table to give her a better base for a leap.

Four blasts erupted from the pistol, two narrowly missing Diana, two blowing holes in the table near Dunst. Both thrust their hands up in surrender. Mutante merely looked dully on the action, licking his lips.

"Damn," said Lou. "Guess the safety *was* off. Okay, you *froggers*, get the *flack* down on the *flickin'* deck!"

"Creative vocabulary," said Chun, managing a pained smile, as she hobbled over to cuff Dunst's and Diana's hands in front of them.

"Put some thought into that speech," answered Lou. She turned to Kane, who was rising up after having cowered on the deck beneath the table. "Edwin, here's the deal. You stay with us and help figure out an antidote for GX, we'll put in a good word with the prosecutors. It could go a long way to helping you out of this horrible mess you started. I'm pretty sure you're smart enough to realize that if you stayed with these two, or with Campana, your life would be pretty short."

Kane nodded slowly, glaring at Dunst and Diana. "I don't have any illusions about what would have happened to me after they decided I wasn't useful. And I can't express enough how much I regret my recklessness. Yeah, I'll cooperate."

"Okay, then. You and me, we're gonna take these two down to the galley. They're gonna fetch all the canned goods we can carry. Then, we're gonna come back up and have some fun." She gave Chun a smirk, and Chun smiled back.

"Shall I get the boat?" asked Chun.

"Get the boat," replied Lou. She herded Dunst and Diana down the yacht's stairs and into the depths of the yacht.

Chun moved to the stern, where she threw the switch operating the lift to lower the yacht's large shore boat into the gently rolling water. She scanned the horizon, seeing no sign of land or other ships.

After fifteen minutes, Dunst, Diana, and Kane appeared from the hold onto the stern deck, hauling large duffel bags.

"We managed to avoid the zombies," reported Lou. "We got into the food locker, while they were still fighting over what was left of the food in the kitchen." Then to Dunst and Diana: "Get into the boat and take the food with you."

"Look, we can make it well worth your while—" began Dunst, but Chun interrupted.

"It'll be well worth my while to see you the hell off the boat."

With Dunst scowling and Diana's expression a grim mask, the pair stumbled into the rocking boat with the duffel bags, and Kane pitched his in as well.

Lou used a can opener to open four cans of tuna and threw them, along with two can openers into the boat. Grinning, she went to the stairwell and bellowed down, "LUNCH IS SERVED!"

From the depths of the yacht came a chorus of growls. Appearing from below stumbled the white-shirted stewards, the engineer, the bosun, the captain, and finally a battered chef, his white smock spattered with blood. All bore the wild-eyed starved expressions that Lou and Chun had seen before.

In a chorus, Lou and Chun exclaimed *"Food!"* pointing to the boat. The crew clambered into the boat, followed by Mutante, who had abruptly come to life at the mention of food. They fought over the cans of tuna, the winners cramming the cans to their faces, gobbling the contents.

As Dunst and Diana cowered in the shore boat's stern, Lou said, "If you want to keep these folks happy, you should probably start opening cans."

Chun freed the boat's mooring lines, and it began to drift away from the yacht.

"We'll die out here!" exclaimed Dunst. "Why don't you just take us in?"

"Because we're in Mexican waters, and your buddy Campana owns the *federales*," said Lou. "And as for dying, we'll send your coordinates to Harwood. They'll be appreciative. They'll fetch you and turn you over to the US feds. Given that you had a hand in wounding their comrades, I'm not exactly sure what shape you'll be in, though."

"Um, LC, you've got one more task," said Chun, moving to the yacht's stern and sitting down heavily in a chair. "Think you can shoot out the engine?"

"Probably. Not sure what else I'd hit, though." As Dunst and Diana leaped away from the shore boat's stern, she raised the pistol and fired five rounds into the boat's engine. They struck with loud metallic thunks. "That oughta do it."

"And, LC, you think you can get this yacht back to US waters?"

Lou began to climb the steps to the bridge, calling back, "I think I'm okay." She reached the bridge and took on a dubious expression, as she scanned the control panel with its profusion of levers, buttons, and screens. "Um. . . but I'm not exactly sure how we'll do once we reach port, though. I used to run Daddy's big damn boat in Savannah. Until I rammed the restaurant by the dock."

Chapter 26

"Is he okay?" asked Chun, leaning against the doorway of the hospital room. Her arm was bandaged, and her eye was still partially swollen shut, the bruise a purplish brown.

Lou didn't answer. She sat, head bowed, beside a feebly struggling Nonny, bound to the hospital bed by padded cuffs. An intravenous tube ran to the back of his hand.

"Sorry," said Chun. "That was a dumb question."

"No, it's a relevant question," said Lou, her voice thick with emotion. "That GX crap in his brain is doing God-knows-what. Oh, my poor, dear Nonny. The docs have given it a name, as if that will help them fight it. They're calling it *gluttonous maximus*. Kind of dark humor." Her smile was wan, as she placed her hand on Nonny's arm.

Nonny was awake, but his eyes were glassy, unseeing, wild with the agonizing hunger. He occasionally moaned, but was otherwise mute.

"Want an update?" asked Chun.

"Yeah, sure." Lou did not take her eyes from Nonny.

"Harwood's guys found the drug dealers and the crew in the boat and turned them over to the DEA. But Dunst and Vodkonen weren't in the best of shape at the turnover. They seemed to have met with some accidents during their time with the mercs."

"Yeah, I can imagine."

"We checked the samples you took at the factory. It's the same stuff as before. And the laptop you gave us also let us trace where GX samples were sent. Interpol has been coordinating raids in Europe and Asia. We're pretty sure we got all the samples."

"'Pretty sure' is still scary. If any of that stuff is out there, some clever chemist could figure out how to duplicate it."

"I know this is a tough thing to ask, but we need you to help us interrogate McAndrews. We're bringing him in to the Vegas office."

"You're sure you need me? I should monitor Nonny's condition. And I need to work with Kane on an antidote."

"You want McAndrews to skate on the charges?"

"Oh, hell no!"

"Then let's double-team him."

***

"I am innocent," declared Gabriel McAndrews, sitting stiffly at the steel table in the FBI interview room. His hands manacled to the table, he regarded Chun and Lou with a clenched-jaw disdain. "I have done nothing illegal. Get these cuffs off me!"

He was flanked by two lawyers, like him dressed in expensive suits with silk ties. Like him, they had trim haircuts, tanned faces, and confident expressions.

Said the lawyer to his left. "I think we can dispense with the handcuffs. Mr. McAndrews is not likely to turn violent."

Chun sat uncomfortably in a chair opposite him, occasionally wincing at the pain from her cracked ribs, "Well, I think it's a good idea to keep him in cuffs. He should get used to the feel," she said. "He'll spend a lot of time in cuffs from now on."

Said the lawyer to his right, "What are you charging our client with?"

Said Lou, "For now, violation of the Federal Food, Drug, and Cosmetic Act. Egregious violation."

The lawyer laughed derisively. "That is a misdemeanor, for God's sake. He'd receive not more than a year in jail and a fine of a couple hundred thousand dollars. That's—"

"Ah, but we're charging him with a couple of thousand counts," interrupted Lou. "One for each person he poisoned."

Said Chun, "And, the Clark County DA's office is preparing a similar number of assault and battery charges."

"Trumped up charges," declared the lawyer.

"Look," declared McAndrews, leaning over the table. "I was led to believe that the chemical that I came into possession of was nothing more than a flavorant. Like sugar. . . a more effective version of sugar. I'm not a chemist. I couldn't have known what it was. And I was perfectly within my legal right to test-market a flavorant. GloboChem and other companies do it all the time."

"We have proof that you bought the chemical from known drug dealers," said Chun.

"Joseph is your proof?" asked McAndrews. "It's his word against mine about what I knew."

Chun shrugged. "Well, we have Oskar Dunst and Diana Vodkonen in custody. When they recover from the arrest, we're sure they'll have something to say about you."

McAndrews paused, shifting uneasily in his chair, before declaring, "Again, their word against mine. I mean, they're *drug dealers* for God's sake!"

Lou's cell phone buzzed, and she stepped out of the room to answer the call.

McAndrews' lawyers launched into a tag-team recitation of their defense against the charges, declaring that McAndrews' arraignment would no doubt result in release on bail. As they talked, Lou returned to the interview room, her expression grave.

"I doubt that bail will be given. That was a call from the field hospital where victims are being cared for. Five have died."

Said Chun, "So, the charges will be involuntary manslaughter."

***

"I can't do it," said Kane, shaking his head. Dressed in a faded t-shirt, rumpled pants, and worn sneakers, he stood and stared at the

269

row of analytical instruments and the laboratory benches holding a clutter of beakers, retorts, and other equipment. Standing beside the benches in the FBI laboratory were white-coated chemists, waiting.

"Can't or won't?" asked Lou.

"Both. Look, I made a terrible mistake, a tragic mistake, when I let my ego get the better of me and went to work for those drug dealers. I have to face the fact that I caused a horrible tragedy. I'm going to jail, and I deserve it. I've turned over all my work, but that's it. I won't compound my crimes."

"You won't be. You'll be atoning by finding a cure for the victims."

"The minute I do, you'll use it to treat them, right?"

"Yeah, we have to."

"No animal testing. No clinical testing."

"Okay, you can do rat testing. But there's no time for human trials. There's what's called a compassionate use protocol when people are dying."

"People died the last time that happened. People were the guinea pigs. And they were killed. All that is on me. No more."

"C'mon, I'm gonna show you something," said Lou turning to leave the laboratory. Kane followed her out of the laboratory building, and after a twenty-minute drive, they came to the Las Vegas Convention Center, entering one of its vast halls.

Stretching away before them lay hundreds of cots, each holding a feebly struggling figure bound to it. The people on the cots had intravenous lines inserted into their hands. Moving among the beds were dozens of masked, gloved, isolation-gowned nurses and doctors. They were taking vital signs, and in many cases, fitting oxygen masks over the victims' faces. A quiet chorus of moaning filled the vast hall, which was permeated with the organic stench of incontinence.

"These are your fault," said Lou, gesturing at the people. "These are the victims of GX. And, Ed, they have begun to *die*." She motioned to one of the doctors, who finished examining a victim and came over to join them. Lou introduced her as the physician in charge.

"You know who this is?" Lou asked the doctor.

"I know," she answered tersely.

"Tell him what we know."

"We've lost eight. We still don't know exactly why. We're doing autopsies, but they won't be finished before we lose more. As best we can figure, the compound not only attaches itself to brain receptors governing appetite. It appears to attach to other brain cells, killing them, essentially rotting the brain. At least that's what it appears to be from the symptoms. The patients lose control of autonomic functions like breathing. They suffocate." She glared at Kane, as she said, "We will lose more. We will ultimately lose them all."

"Ed, these people will die without your help." Lou's voice choked with emotion as she said, "And someone I love will die." Lou let the sentence hang in the air.

Kane let his gaze linger on the victims. He took a deep breath. "I think I have an idea," he said quietly.

Chapter 27

Kane shifted his baleful gaze from one plastic bin to the other. The bins holding the two sets of rats portrayed very different results of the tests of the GX antidote that had emerged from round-the-clock chemical synthesis and animal experiments.

In one bin, the rats moved about normally, sipping water and nibbling on the rat chow in the feeder.

In the other bin, the rats were dead.

"We don't see any rhyme or reason for the differences," said the lab technician standing behind him. He held a tablet computer, swiping it to scan the results. Five other technicians stood behind him, peering somberly at Kane.

"No dose effect?" asked Kane. "No timing effect, like when the antidote was administered after GX was given?"

"We'll go re-analyze the results. Treat some more animals. But no rhyme or reason," repeated the tech.

Again, Kane shifted his gaze back and forth between the two bins, the effect being one of shaking his head slowly in puzzlement.

Kane took a deep breath, as if it would summon both courage and energy. "Okay, let's synthesize some analogs of the antidote. Like we discussed, vary the molecular side chains and the other chemical groups."

The technicians turned back to their work, dispersing to their benches.

Sitting down at a desk before four large computer monitors, Kane constructed a panoply of three-dimensional molecular models, rotating and tinkering with their structures, and transmitting likely candidates to technicians to synthesize.

After an hour of intense work, he heard a familiar urgent voice behind him. It was Lou.

"Do you have it yet? I just came from the hospital. Nonny is on oxygen. You've got to have something, for God's sake!"

"We have analogs that compete with GX to knock it off the receptor in the brain. . . to restore normal function. And, we have created a targeted enzyme that degrades GX in the bloodstream. It'll also detoxify the bulk GX. But. . ." Kane stopped, turning to look Lou in the eye. ". . . the results with the rats are, well, mixed."

"What the hell does 'mixed' mean?"

"Some are cured, some die. We don't know why."

"What is the ratio?"

"Fifty-fifty."

"And what are you doing to improve it?"

"We're making slightly altered versions of the antidote. Trying to get better survival."

"Screw 'better survival,' Kane! You need to figure out why they're dying. You need to get to *total* survival!"

***

Nonny gasped for breath, his chest spasmodically rising and falling. His face was covered with an oxygen mask, and his arms lay at his sides, even his feeble struggle against the leather straps having ceased.

Lou placed her hand on his bare arm, tears welling in her eyes. "What should we do?" she asked. "What would he want us to do?"

"Chef is a courageous man," said Abadi, standing at the foot of the bed. "You know he would demand to be one of the first to test the antidote."

Nonny's physician shook his head, his brow knitted. "Sorry, but he cannot give consent. He is not conscious. And he has no medical power of attorney. We can't assume what he would want."

"He could die," pleaded Lou. "He *will* die. Forty people have died and more will soon. Have you been to the convention center? Seen the body bags?"

The doctor said nothing, but his impassive expression showed that he had not been swayed.

Kane stood by the door, holding a vial of clear, yellowish liquid and a hypodermic syringe. "We've gone as far as we can with the animal studies. We know the rats survive, but we can't tell whether the antidote restores cognitive function. Only a human trial will allow that."

After several minutes, Lou wiped her eyes and turned away from Nonny, moving to the doctor's side. "Could we talk?" she asked, her voice thick with emotion. She cleared her throat and declared more strongly, "Um. . . I need to tell you about some FDA policies that might be relevant to the case."

The doctor nodded, and as they left the room, Lou gave Abadi a long, significant look. Abadi bowed his head and nodded slightly. Lou transferred her intent gaze to Kane who, after a long pause, nodded.

Once Lou and the doctor had left, peering out the door, Abadi gestured to Kane, who filled the syringe from the vial and moved to Nonny's bedside.

Abadi planted his thick body in front of the door, as Kane injected the liquid into the IV catheter inserted in the back of Nonny's hand. "How long before we know anything?" he asked.

Kane stood back from the bed, staring at Nonny. "Well, with the rats, we know—"

He was interrupted by Nonny's sudden, violent convulsions, his muscles jerking as he strained against the bonds. He grunted repeatedly as his body arched off the bed, only to slam back down, shaking its frame. The heart monitor showed the jagged trace of an irregular heartbeat. It emitted a loud beeping alarm that brought the doctor and Lou bursting into the room past Abadi, followed by three nurses.

"*What the hell did you do?*" asked the doctor, bending over the writhing body of his patient.

"What he would have wanted!" declared Abadi.

***

"He's comatose," said Lou, not turning from Nonny's bedside. It had been an hour since Nonny had received the injection. "But at least his vital signs are stable."

Chun had just arrived, asking "So, you don't know whether his brain—"

"Is still functioning?" interrupted Lou. "No. There is activity on the EEG. But it's been four hours and no change."

"What does Kane have to say about his status? Any insights from the animal studies?"

"Well, we can't goddamned well find out," said Lou bitterly. "They've arrested him and Daoud for assault and battery."

"Maybe I can fix that." Chun took out her cell phone and called her field office. She issued instructions that the FBI take over their cases, claiming that it was part of an ongoing FBI investigation. She ended the call, telling Lou. "As soon as our agent gets them released, they'll be here."

For the next hour, the two sat talking quietly, their attention constantly on the inert form on the bed, seeking any sign of improvement.

Kane and Abadi appeared, taking their places in the room.

Lou asked, "Ed, is this what you expected? After the treatment?"

Kane's wrinkled-brow expression indicated he was deep in thought. He held up a hand to indicate he was pondering an idea. He turned and left the room, taking out his cell phone as he left.

He was gone for half an hour, returning with Nonny's physician.

"Talked to my lab techs," he said. "They're still running tests on the animals. Some of them had convulsions like he did. And they lost consciousness. The problem was that the antidote acts as a central

275

nervous system depressant. So. . ." He turned to the doctor ". . . we're going to try a dose of epinephrine to bring him around."

The physician stepped to Nonny's bedside and injected a clear liquid into Nonny's catheter. He turned to scrutinize the display showing Nonny's vital signs. He slowly nodded his head.

"His eyes are open!" exclaimed Lou. *"Sweetie, can you hear me? Are you okay? We're here for you!"* She removed his oxygen mask.

Nonny blinked at the light and took a deep breath, slowly turning his head left and right to look around the room. He saw Lou, and a faint smile rose on his lips. He saw Abadi, whose round face bore the haggard expression of fear and fatigue.

"Is the restaurant all right?" Nonny asked hoarsely.

***

"You know you shouldn't be here," scolded Lou, but Nonny stood silently beside her, not budging, wearing a black t-shirt and his chef's pants.

They looked out over a scene of recovery in the sprawling convention's center hall. Some victims of GX were slowly shuffling about, gaining their balance with the help of nurses. Other were rising to sitting positions on their cots, with doctors examining them.

And some were quietly lining up at the huge buffet that Nonny had ordered brought in from the Gourffet. Their calm demeanor was a vast change from the maddened attack on the food that they would have mounted only a week before.

"Are they being fed properly?" asked Nonny.

Answered Abadi, who stood on his other side, dressed in his culinary whites, "Yes, sir. The dietitians gave us instructions on how to restore their normal, healthy diets."

"Will they need further treatments?"

Lou answered, "No, almost certainly not. Kane said that the animals recovered fully. And the enzyme has scrubbed the chemical from their bodies."

With that news, Abadi left to help the recovering victims, leaving Lou and Nonny standing alone.

"What happens to Kane, the monster?"

"You won't like it. He agreed to help take down Campana and prosecute GloboChem and its executives. And he agreed to help further develop his computer model and drugs. So, they've put him in witness protection. Leafy is escorting him to his new location. Next time we hear from him will be on a witness stand."

"You're right," said Nonny. "I don't like it. But at least he did develop the antidote. And what happens to the poison?"

"Well, the detoxifying enzyme will break down the bulk chemical, so it will no longer pose a threat. And as for Kane's research, it'll be classified top secret. No doubt Congress will pass a law against its use, with heavy punishment. But who knows, maybe some version will prove useful to help cancer patients' appetites." Lou put her arm in Nonny's. "Can we maybe talk a minute about a personal matter?"

Nonny nodded, looking over at her, his eyebrows set halfway up. "How personal?"

"Well, I kind of, sort of . . . um . . . that is to say, I love you. You're decidedly a different critter from the guys I've known in the past. But you are totally amazing. So. . . well. . . I decided you weren't gonna take the first step, so I would."

"What step?"

She turned to face Nonny. "Will you marry me? Listen, I'll get down on one knee if you want a traditional proposal."

Nonny was silent, his expression unfathomably blank. He took out his phone and began to tap out a series of messages, his head bowed.

After two minutes of silence, Lou sighed in exasperation. "What the hell? Are you going to answer? I just poured my fu—. . . My *flexin'* heart out!"

Nonny finished sending the texts. He looked up, brows fully raised. "I've closed the restaurant for Sunday a month from now. For the ceremony. I told Jacques we'll need a vegan wedding cake."

Lou laughed and hugged him; and after a brief hesitation, he hugged her back, replacing his cell phone in his pocket.

"Daoud will be best man," said Nonny. "And maybe you'll want Agent Chun to be maid of honor."

"Absolutely, my love. Shall we get out of here? We could use some R&R at your place."

"Yes. We can move on to chapter 19."

"Ah, chapter 19! An awesome-sauce chapter! Like, literally!" She beamed, knowing that her master chef/lover had concocted some very tasty recipes for edible massage oils. She merrily waved goodbye to Abadi, who grinned knowingly.

"Friggin' great!" she exclaimed to him.